Praise for th

Shop

For Whom the Bluebell Tolls

"The characters in this well-tended plot are warm and multidimensional . . . . The floral angle provides a unique scent to this fun and well-paced installment in the series." —*Booklist*

"A great read . . . . The story is a page-turner of excitement that takes readers along for a thrilling ride." —*RT Book Reviews*

"A well written and highly entertaining cozy with a clever plot and more than a few twists and turns." —Criminal Element

Bloom and Doom

"Captivated my attention from the very first page. With the meanings of flowers skillfully woven throughout the story, it was as delightful as a freshly cut bouquet of ranunculus (radiant charm) and tarragon (lasting interest). Beverly Allen writes wonderfully engaging characters in a lovely small-town setting. Audrey Bloom, the heroine, is quick-witted and clever as she unravels the mystery, which was a puzzler right up to the dramatic end. A thoroughly entertaining and engaging mystery! I can't wait for the next one!"

—Jenn McKinlay, *New York Times* bestselling author

"It's an engaging bouquet of mayhem and murder. What a delight for cozy readers!"

—Erika Chase, national bestselling author of the Ashton Corners Book Club Mysteries

"Allen's upbeat series debut reads smoothly and easily with excellent dialog and an immensely likable cast . . . The flower business really stars in this cozy." —*Library Journal*

continued . . .

"[A] highly entertaining, fun, and snappy mystery . . . *Bloom and Doom* has everything to keep you engaged: a compelling murder to be solved, great humor, warm friendship, and the language of flowers. I cannot wait for more books of this series."

—Criminal Element

"Provides readers with a fresh twist on the amateur-sleuth story."

—*Booklist*

"A terrific start to a new series."

—*Suspense Magazine*

"Has all the ingredients that make up a charming cozy mystery—likable characters, good mystery, and a little fun and romance thrown in."

—Fresh Fiction

Berkley Prime Crime titles by Beverly Allen

BLOOM AND DOOM
FOR WHOM THE BLUEBELL TOLLS
FLORAL DEPRAVITY

Floral Depravity

Beverly Allen

BERKLEY PRIME CRIME, NEW YORK

An imprint of Penguin Random House LLC
375 Hudson Street, New York, New York 10014

FLORAL DEPRAVITY

A Berkley Prime Crime Book / published by arrangement with the author.

ISBN: 978-0-425-26499-7

PUBLISHING HISTORY
Berkley Prime Crime mass-market edition / October 2015

PRINTED IN THE UNITED STATES OF AMERICA

10 9 8 7 6 5 4 3 2 1

Cover illustration by Ben Perini and *Pink Rose Heart* © by Titania/Shutterstock.
Cover design by Diana Kolsky.
Interior text design by Tiffany Estreicher.

In memory of my grandmother
who taught me the simple joys of whispered,
early-morning conversation over mugs of instant coffee.

Acknowledgments

First, I'd like to thank the readers who have told me how much they've enjoyed the time spent with Audrey Bloom and her friends at the Rose in Bloom. I know I've cherished every moment I've been able to spend in the flower shop with them, or wandering the streets of Ramble, gathering clues.

I'd like to thank my friends and critique partners, who challenge me to write the best I can, and then make it better. Kathy Hurst, Debra Marvin, Aric Gaughan, Katie Murdock, and Ken Swiatek, thanks for all your input. Especially Lynne Wallace-Lee, who also shared her zany experiences in historical re-creations. Lori Melton, thanks so much for sharing your dove story with me. Fay, I wish you were still here to read the final product.

Thanks to my agent, Kim Lionetti, and my editor, Katherine Pelz, the wonderful cover artists, the copyeditors who make me look better, and all the folks at Berkley that make these books happen.

And to my family, especially Rob Early, thanks for the takeout, patience, and support.

Chapter 1

"Let me guess, Audrey." Liv pointed to my hand. "He loves you not?"

I glanced down. I'd only intended to remove the guard petals of the rose I was working on. Instead, I'd accumulated a pile of rose petals and one decimated stem. "Sorry. Distracted, I guess." I set the remnants aside on my worktable—little in the floral business was ever wasted—then picked up another gorgeous red rose. Good thing we kept our cooler well stocked.

My cousin, Liv Meyer, came over and pushed a sprig of boxwood into a bare spot in the funeral flowers I was preparing for a feisty local woman. She'd passed away at the ripe old age of 103, and the red roses were ordered by her 79-year-old husband. (Did that make her a cougar?) He claimed they were her favorites and he wanted to give them to her one last time.

Although arranging funeral flowers tended to cast a pall

over the shop, I still smiled when I incorporated a few unopened rosebuds. Not only would the arrangement continue to grow lovelier as they opened, but the meaning of the red rosebud, *You are young and beautiful*, was almost delightfully ironic. This arrangement, as it aged, would play out a slideshow of their lives together. As the roses barely began to bloom, they would represent *timid love*. Then as they opened, a *vibrant love*. I closed my eyes and swallowed the lump in my throat.

"There's still time to get out of this, you know," Liv said. "You don't have to go through with it."

"What, this condolence arrangement? I've made hundreds like it." Although I much preferred wedding bouquets. Even though I specialized in wedding flowers at the Rose in Bloom, the shop Liv and I co-owned, we all pitched in where needed, so I'd done my fair share of funeral arrangements.

"You know what I mean."

"Uh-oh," Amber Lee said. "If it's time for *that* discussion, I'm going up front to check the self-service cooler." Amber Lee, a retired schoolteacher, had come to us with little floral experience but loads of enthusiasm after she discovered that retirement didn't suit her. She was technically my assistant and helped with all the wedding arrangements, but had proved herself capable in almost every area of the shop. She was indispensable. More than that, she was becoming family.

"I just did that an hour ago," Liv said.

"Then . . . well, I'll figure out something else to do," Amber Lee said.

As she hustled out of earshot, I sighed. "We've been through this."

"I know." Liv set down her tools and stretched her back. "And I don't want to tell you how to run your life. It's just such a big commitment."

"And what exactly is wrong with big commitments?" My words came out sounding a bit defensive, so I forced a more casual tone into my voice. "You've made a few of your own, if I'm not mistaken. A husband, a house of your own"—I pointed at her burgeoning belly—"a baby due in about fifteen minutes."

She waved off my concern. "I've got weeks left, and then some. The doctor suspects the baby will be late. But don't change the subject."

"I'm not changing the subject. We're talking about responsibility. I'm twenty-nine years old. Why is it that you can run full-speed into adulthood, but when I take on one responsibility—"

"It's not just . . ." Liv rubbed the top of her stomach and breathed out, a pained expression on her face.

"What is it? A contraction?" My irritation melted into concern. Liv and I squabbled on only the rarest of occasions, and I found staying angry with my cousin and best friend about as possible as man-powered flight, perpetual motion, or a box of chocolates remaining untouched in the shop all day.

"No, I'm fine. And you're right." She put her arm around me. "I don't know why I'm such a mother hen at times. I'll try to support you, even when I don't agree with your decisions."

"Of all people, Liv, you should understand what that cottage means to me." Liv and I had spent many happy childhood summers there with our Grandma Mae. It was she who inspired our love for flowers.

"I do. I have fond memories there, too, remember? But we're not talking about making a scrapbook. Some decisions you have to make with your head, not just your heart. Can't you treasure Grandma Mae's memory without buying her old cottage? You heard what the inspectors said."

"That last one was more positive. The bank approved the loan."

"He also said the sewer line to the road needs to be replaced."

"Well, of course I know the place is going to need some work." All of a sudden, my stomach went a little queasy. "Are sewer lines expensive?" Most of my money would be tied up in the down payment. I'd hoped to be able to do repairs and make improvements little by little.

"Eric said there is no sewer line to the road. The cottage has a septic system in the back. What if the only reason you got the loan was because they somehow inspected the wrong house?"

"What are the odds of that?"

"Better than you think. Eric and I figured out what that scrawl on page three said. Something about the bidet on the second floor leaking."

The cottage didn't have a bidet. Come to think of it, it didn't have a second floor, either. "But maybe it's Providence. Maybe I'm meant to have that house."

"Kiddo, the good Lord would never saddle you with that place . . . unless you've been a lot more wicked than you've been letting on. Besides," Liv said, laying a gentle hand on my forearm, "if you're all that confident, why do you keep stripping our roses?"

I looked down at the second bare stem in my hand and tossed it onto the worktable.

"Would you like to leave early?" Liv asked. "What time do you sign the papers?"

"Not until five," I said. "You just don't want me ruining all the stock."

Liv snapped her fingers. "You saw right through me."

I shook my head. "I have a bridal appointment in a few minutes anyway."

"Oh, new wedding? Who's coming in?"

"Who do you think?" I rolled my eyes.

"Again?"

Amber Lee peeked her head in the back door. "Is it safe?"

"All better," I said.

"Good." She lugged in a large wrapped box and placed it in front of me. "This came for you a few minutes ago."

"For me?" I looked at Liv and she shrugged. But a twinkle in her eye and the half smile tickling her lips told me she knew something about it. I pulled off the bow and ripped open the paper. Inside the box were a tool kit and a cordless drill. "I can't say anyone has ever given me hardware before."

"Consider them a housewarming gift from all of us at the shop. From what Eric told me about the place, you're going to need them."

"I suggested we add a good man to help you with the repairs," Amber Lee said, "but we couldn't quite fit him in the box."

Liv sent her a look, which saved me the trouble. My love life was a bit complicated, since it involved friendly dates with Nick Maxwell, the local baker—who was unwilling to commit. And long phone conversations and regular texts with Brad Simmons, my ex-almost-fiancé—who seemed determined to erase the "ex" part.

"Oh," Amber Lee said, "Kathleen Randolph and her daughter are here for their bridal consultation, take three."

"Four," I said, "but who's counting?"

I propped a smile on my face as I mounted the steps to the wrought iron gazebo we used as our consulting nook. Kathleen Randolph, owner of the Ashbury Inn and prominent—but often long-winded—local historian, had called to say she was bringing a few reference books along to this appointment to help finalize the flowers for her daughter Andrea's wedding. Since the wedding, planned to be held at a local medieval encampment, was now just two weeks away, I hoped they didn't have anything too exotic in mind. But it looked like they'd brought half their library. About fifty moldering tomes were piled in front of them.

I'd like to think my smile didn't dim, but I'm not sure I'm that good.

"We brought more reference books," Kathleen said brightly. "Found some great stuff on the Tudors."

"Nice," I said. I refrained from telling her the only thing I know about the Tudors had to do with stucco and fake wood beams.

The next two hours were steeped in history, leaving me feeling much like a cold, wet teabag. But I managed to sketch out some workable flower suggestions amid their rapt discussion of the Middle Ages.

"And you *must* come to the ceremony," Andrea said.

It wasn't unusual for brides to invite me to their weddings. Ramble, Virginia, was such a small town that I likely knew the bride anyway. And it seemed to reassure them that their flowers would be there, look lovely, and if anything happened at the last minute, I could fix it.

Kathleen pulled out a sheet of folded parchment and smoothed it on the table. "I drew you a map to the encampment."

I looked at the page. It resembled a pirate's map. It only lacked the skull and crossbones, a sea monster, and a big X. I take that back. It had an X in a clearing surrounded by woods. "I can't use my GPS?"

Kathleen and Andrea shared a snicker or two at my

expense, before Andrea took pity and explained. "The encampment is not accessible by roads. Having a parking lot right next to a medieval encampment would make it look too much like a . . . a Renaissance fair." I swore they both shuddered at the words.

Did I dare ask? I dared. "What's the difference?"

"Renaissance fairs are for the . . ." Kathleen trailed off, leaving me to wonder if she was going to say "unwashed masses."

"For people who want to play with swords and speak in dreadfully awful cockney accents," Andrea finished.

"Worse than Dick Van Dyke in *Mary Poppins*." This time there was no mistaking it. They both shuddered.

I happened to adore Dick Van Dyke, so it took great effort to hold my tongue.

"And eat turkey legs!" they both said in unison, with distasteful grimaces on their faces.

I quirked an eyebrow.

"Turkey is a New World bird," Andrea said. "They wouldn't have had it in the Middle Ages."

"The Guardians of Chivalry Encampment is for serious-minded historians who want an authentic experience," Kathleen said. "We camp a mile from the nearest road. No electricity. No running water. Authentic dress is required. We don't just play at the Middle Ages. We live like we are in the Middle Ages."

"We hunt and gather, butcher our own animals, learn the old crafts," Andrea said.

"We have a sizable village constructed," Kathleen said. "We first started, oh, maybe thirty years ago, with nothing more than a caravan of tents. We try to put up a new structure every year. But now we're working on a castle, so it's going to take longer."

"I see," I said.

I'd heard of the encampment, of course, and had seen the visitors on their annual autumn pilgrimages, stopping at the local restaurants on the way in and, a couple of weeks later, much grubbier looking and more foul smelling, on the way out.

"We've decided to go with the hand-fasting," Andrea said. "Although the ceremony was most usually an engagement, many historians say that if the marriage was consummated at that point, the couple were considered legally wed by the church."

"Hand-fasting?"

"We tie our hands together while we give our consent to marry," Andrea said. "No clergy needed. Of course, to make it legal in Virginia, we'll have an officiant. We have someone licensed coming as a friar this year."

"A licensed friar?" I asked.

"No, not really a friar," she said, "any more than the knights have been dubbed by a queen. But he's licensed by the state and will be using the persona of a friar. It couldn't be better."

"So you can bring the flowers the day of the wedding," Kathleen said. "And stay for the grand feast. Of course, it will be too dark to go back, so you'll have to stay the night. And I suppose you might need help carrying everything."

"I . . . I guess I will. We've never made a delivery to the middle of the woods before."

"And you'll need to come in costume." Andrea gnawed at her cuticle. "I don't suppose you have a medieval dress in the back of your closet."

"She'll just have to rent something," Kathleen said. "I mean, it won't be truly authentic, but it'll do the job for someone coming for the first time."

"Most of the regulars own their own medieval wardrobe?" I asked.

"Most of the regulars *make* their own wardrobe," Kathleen said. "Stitched by hand. Some even spin their own fibers and weave and dye their own cloth."

"That must take—"

"Some old-timers work on their clothing all year long," Andrea said. "A few even sew extra to sell—a truly authentic garment can go for thousands. We've been working on the wedding dress for simply ages. Made the pattern based on an oil painting. A lovely blue."

"That's where we get our 'something blue' tradition," Kathleen said. "And you'll bring the bachelor's buttons for the festivities later?"

"They're going to be a riot," Andrea said.

I nodded, but I could feel my cheeks turning peony pink. To the Victorians, the flower known as the bachelor's button often symbolized *celibacy* or the *blessing of being single.* Apparently in medieval times, "blessings" took on a whole new meaning as young women would hide the flowers in their clothing, and the bachelors would be tasked with finding them.

Although, despite the research involved, Andrea's order ended up being small—just her bouquet, a wreath for her hair, and the extra bachelor's buttons—I decided this might just prove to be the most memorable wedding yet.

"There's a nice costume shop that has some decent stuff," Kathleen said. "But they sell out early."

"Of course, you can add the rental charge to our bill," Andrea said.

"Andrea," Kathleen said, "I'm sure Audrey wouldn't mind renting her own. After all, we just invited her to the wedding."

Andrea shot her a look. "It's only right, Mother. It's part of the expense of getting the flowers to the venue. We can always bill it to good old Dad." She turned to me. "It seems he can't make it to the wedding, even to walk his own daughter down the aisle."

I barely squelched a sigh. Fathers weren't usually that interested in flowers, but it was nice to know they'd be involved with the wedding and in their daughters' lives. My sigh came anyway. After all, perhaps someday I'd be faced with the same reality: walking down the aisle alone or choosing some arbitrary male substitute.

She jotted down the name of a costume shop onto a sheet of scrap paper and handed it to me. "Just remember, they sell out fast."

I arrived at Grandma Mae's cottage with only my suitcase and a smile. Okay, I also had a sleeping bag, food in a cooler, an old Coleman lantern, and a couple of flashlights, since the power wouldn't be turned on until the morning. And carpel tunnel from signing all those documents.

Eric, as property manager for the Rawlings—the most recent owners and neglectors of my new home—had been by earlier to build some impromptu porch steps, since the old ones had been torn off to ensure anyone foolish enough to try to climb them wouldn't fall through, hurt themselves, and sue the Rawlings. Not that even the Jehovah's Witnesses or the most ardent Avon lady had the dedication to climb those rickety stairs.

Just getting to the stairs through the jungle of a front yard was difficult in the twilight. But I didn't stop for the burrs that were clinging to the hem of my jeans as if I were dressed in Velcro. I'd waited so long. I pulled the key from my pocket. I didn't want to put it on my ring with my ordinary keys, at least not yet.

The lock turned hard. I worried that the key would break, but finally it yielded. Just another thing to have oiled. Eventually. Just like the hinges on the squeaky door that announced my arrival.

Home.

The walls seemed to squeal it. I closed my eyes—probably a good idea, because the place was truly a shambles; even my enthusiasm for the cottage couldn't hide that fact. But I paused to breathe in the memories. Grandma Mae bustling at the old electric stove. Liv and I sitting at the table on a rainy day with a fresh box of sixty-four Crayolas between us. I could almost still smell them. We'd giggled until one of us had the hiccups and we slid from our chairs to the floor. Grandma chided us, but we could see she didn't really mean it. The twinkle in her eye gave her away, and her shoulders shook in quiet laughter when she turned back to the stove.

The old stove was still there, and I had a sudden craving for a cup of instant coffee, only that wasn't going to happen. Not until there was electricity. Along with water. Eric had promised to help with all of that. But not until the morning.

I lit the old lantern while I still had enough light to do so and cleared a spot in the middle of the living room floor for my sleeping bag. The floorboards squeaked and groaned with every motion.

The air felt stale and foul, so despite the coolness of the evening, I pushed open the only window that wasn't stuck or broken and boarded up.

So, with too much energy to sleep but too little light to do anything productive, I climbed into the sleeping bag and planned what I would do with the little cottage. I'd give the outside a new coat of white paint, and maybe an archway in the front dripping with wisteria: *Welcome, fair stranger.* Of course, it would take me weeks just to weed the old garden.

Almost easier to start new. But preserving any of Grandma Mae's plantings was well worth the extra effort.

Nick and a few others had promised to help me move in. I'd bring my cat over last, since I wouldn't want Chester to run away from strange surroundings when the doors were open.

He hadn't been out of that apartment much since I brought him home from the SPCA, except for an occasional excursion to hide under my neighbor's truck—and the dreaded trip to the vet's office. He'd whine the whole drive, then hop on the scale and refuse to budge. Yes, he was a bit pudgy. Maybe living in the country would be good for him—all those birds and rabbits to watch from the window.

I was still thinking about Chester, so when I heard the plaintive little meow, I thought I'd imagined it. Old houses have strange noises—I knew that ahead of time—but when I heard it again, I could tell this was definitely an animal sound. I scooted out of the sleeping bag and grabbed the flashlight.

The little cry sounded again, followed by what cat owners recognize instantly as the sound of claws in the screen.

I swung the flashlight beam to the open window, and there, crawling halfway up the battered screen, was a tiny jet-black kitten. It mewed again.

"Where's your mama?" I asked.

It answered me with the most pitiful series of mews, as if it were pouring out a tale of woe and sadness. My heart melted for the thing.

"I'd let you in, but you need your mother." The kitten was so tiny and bright-eyed, but fur matted in spots, that I doubted if it had been fully weaned. Still, I searched in my cooler for an appropriate bit of food and decided to try a smidgen of turkey salad from my sandwich. I grabbed two foam plates and a bottle of water and went outside, half expecting it to run away. But it didn't.

I poured water into one plate and put the turkey on another, setting both on the little temporary porch, then peeled the kitty away from the screen. I winced as the wires popped.

She trembled in my arms but didn't fight me. I put her by the food and she sniffed it. Then a little pink tongue came out and tried the turkey. She licked it to death, leaving most of it on the plate and then sniffed at the water, but wasn't even lapping it effectively.

"You're not even weaned yet, are you?"

I scanned the flashlight across the yard, looking for the reflection of eyes, hoping to find a mama cat for this little thing. Meanwhile, the kitten started weaving around my legs and purring. I picked her up and cradled her against my shoulder, and she let out a contented sigh.

"All right, kitty. If no one in the neighborhood claims you, you can stay here with me." I mentally added buying a bottle and kitty formula to my burgeoning to-do list.

"I just hope Chester doesn't have you for breakfast."

Chapter 2

"Audrey, please tell me it's not much farther." Amber Lee set down her box of flowers and dislodged her full-length skirt from a thorny weed. "I never would have agreed to this if I'd known the wedding was taking place in the middle of the woods. The costume shop is never going to give me my deposit back if this dress is torn."

I swatted a mosquito that had braved the fog of DEET I'd misted all over my body, then pulled the map out of the bodice of my dress. "At least you got to wear a decent outfit."

Amber Lee looked every bit the medieval matron, but all the costume shop had left by the time I remembered to get there was a serving wench's outfit that exposed a little more cleavage than I was willing to show. At least they also had rented me a decent cloak which I could use as a cover-up, despite the fact that it was mustard yellow. But I'd converted that to a makeshift backpack of sorts—to carry more of our floral supplies—until we got a little closer.

"I don't understand why they hold this thing in the middle of the woods," she said.

"From what Kathleen and Andrea told me, they figured if people have to carry their own supplies, they're much less likely to bring in anything that is historically inaccurate."

"I doubt they need to worry about anybody lugging a generator and a mini-fridge through this jungle. If I have to go much farther, they're not getting any of these flowers, either. How close are we?"

I studied the hand-drawn page. "According to the map," I said, "we're either almost there or hopelessly lost."

"Such fair maidens could never be lost." Nick Maxwell stepped out of the brush and dipped into a courtly bow.

I couldn't help a chuckle. Okay, maybe it sounded more like a guffaw, but I was used to seeing Nick in his white baker's clothes. Instead, he'd donned tights and a belted sleeveless (but thankfully long) tunic over a blousy work shirt.

As he rose from his bow, he stopped briefly at chest level, then his face colored. "Audrey, that getup. Are you sure you want to wear—"

I tugged up the bodice as high as it would go. "All they had. What about you? I thought you said you had your very own set of armor." When I mentioned I would be providing the flowers for a medieval wedding, Nick had boasted that he was quite involved in the re-creations in college.

"Ah, but in these fair woods, milady, knights are in abundance, and we have lords and ladies aplenty. Even a jester or two, but today they were more in need of a humble baker. Who else can prepare the trenchers or the sweet cakes for the great feast afterward?"

"Cake?" Amber Lee asked. "Oh, this just got better."

"Don't get your hopes up," he said. "They're more of a sweet roll, and not very sweet at that, by today's standards.

Traditionally, guests stack them up in a pile to see if the bride and groom can kiss over the top of it."

"Sounds more romantic than smooshing cake in each other's faces," I said.

"I always thought that was a horrible waste of cake," Amber Lee said.

"Here, let me take that." Nick relieved Amber Lee of her box of bachelor's buttons. "It's not much farther. I was just out collecting kindling."

"Kindling?" she asked. "If we're not getting a proper cake, please tell me we're having a campfire. I haven't had a decent s'more in ages, and I know all the words to 'Kumbaya.'"

"Don't let the anachronism police hear you say that," Nick said. "Europeans didn't know about chocolate in the Middle Ages, so you shouldn't find any in the camp."

"That must be where the evil comes from," she said.

Nick raised his brows. "Evil?"

"In mid-evil. No society can be truly good without the influence of chocolate. I think that's in the Bible."

"Preach it, sister," I said, and high-fived her.

Nick frowned at us. "I don't know if anybody explained this, but you might want to limit conversation like that to when you're alone. Some of the more serious participants are hypersensitive about modern language and behavior seeping into the encampment."

"Sorry," Amber Lee said.

"At least a bonfire will be fun," I said. "Maybe it will drive away some of these insects."

"The kindling is for the oven, I'm afraid," he said. "All period correct. They had to hire me, since I'm the only one who knows how to regulate the temperature without using a thermometer."

"You never fail to amaze me," I said.

He winked and then led us along what seemed a much more traveled path, which opened up into another time and place. If I were an expert, I probably could have told you the date and location, but the best I could narrow it down to was Europe sometime in the Middle Ages. We'd wandered into a medieval marketplace bustling with period correctness.

All except for the man in modern clothing and carrying a video camera.

"Brad?"

He turned around.

"What are you doing here?" I said.

"Surprise!" He looked me up and down. "I was just telling Nick here that I hoped to see more of you, and I guess I got my wish."

I tugged up the bodice of the dress again.

Brad, here? No, that's not how it was supposed to be. Nick was the one who was here, the one who took me out for pizza and occasionally beat me in Scrabble. Brad was the one who flirted with me on the phone, long-distance, from wherever his crew was filming their latest reality show. That was the problem with compartmentalizing. Life had a nasty way of breaking down those perilous walls, like when someone tips your takeout container and the pickle juice leaks into your chocolate cake.

He chuckled. "Seriously, I got the funding I needed to shoot the pilot I told you about."

"Your documentary on the re-creationists? What was it? *Mid-Evil*?"

"Nah, they canned that title. Copy department wanted something with knights in the title. The leading candidate is now *Steamy Knights*." He rolled his eyes. "Whatever it takes to sell it. But it's not a documentary. It's a reality show, so I'm looking for plenty of fireworks between the serious historians and the weekend hobbyists. Hope to get some good footage of the festivities tonight, if my crew ever arrives."

"They're letting in a film crew?" I said. "I would have thought that violated their strict rules."

"Normally, it would have," Nick said, eyeing Brad's modern clothes. "But the powers-that-be have decided a documentary is good for the encampment."

"Audrey, there you are!" Andrea, now a proper medieval bride, picked up her skirts and rushed toward me. "I can't wait to see the flowers!" In her long pale blue gown, she looked like she'd stepped out of a painting from one of their dusty history books.

Kathleen Randolph had described the dress details to me ad nauseum, assuring me it bore no hint of historical anachronism. All I recalled was that blue represented *purity* in medieval times, making it a popular choice for a wedding.

Designing a bouquet that pleased both mother and daughter, however, took considerable research. We'd finally compromised on white roses. These were not the roses found in modern bouquets, however, but an older variety. *Rosa alba*, and boy, did Liv have fun getting her hands on these.

Of course, Kathleen zeroed in on the fact that this particular white rose was the symbol of the House of York. She then went on, in great detail, to highlight the Wars of the Roses, but I think I might have phased out for that part. But these were luscious, fully open double roses with a golden center. They were gorgeous, but I was still a bit torn. The white rose generally represented *innocence*, and in one of Kathleen's old books, she'd found a reference to Dante that claimed the white petals of these roses represented *paradise* and the golden center, *God's glory*. But I found a later reference to the "York rose," which I'm assuming these were, that said the flower had come to symbolize *war.*

But that was the Victorian meaning, and these were the Middle Ages, right?

Before I could debate the matter further, Kathleen bustled up, also in a lavish period gown. She waved a finger at Brad. "It appears I can't tell you not to film the wedding, since you already have approval of the camp." Kathleen glared at him, looking less than pleased at this development. "But can you be discreet? Stay out of sight?"

Brad nodded. "Yes, ma'am."

She turned to me. "Yegads, Audrey! What are you wearing?"

"The dregs of the costume shop, I'm afraid." I self-consciously pulled up the bodice, which had crept down again. Grandma Mae would be rolling in her grave. Actually, I wasn't sure she'd be rolling as much as she'd be plotting her escape so she could drag me home by the ear and give me a good talking-to about modesty and dressing like a lady. "I do have a cloak, though." I unfolded my makeshift backpack and pulled on the yellow cloak.

A titter of laughter went up among the nearby bystanders, and Kathleen rubbed her forehead, as if she were trying to scrub away a sudden migraine. "I knew this was a bad idea."

Andrea laughed. "I was so happy to get my flowers, I didn't even notice. It's just like the book, isn't it? At least it's period-correct."

"Oh dear," Nick said. "Audrey, you can't wear that cloak."

I pulled it closer to me, almost like a blanket. The air seemed chilly in the shady woods. "What do you mean? First you say it's period-correct, but then you tell me I can't wear it?"

Kathleen looked at Andrea, who glanced at Nick, who

blushed and looked back at Kathleen. But before anyone could speak, shouts of greeting came from just across the market. Shelby and Darnell, our two regular part-time employees, ran to greet us. I knew they'd be here, of course. They'd asked for time off to attend the re-creation, since their attendance gave them points in a popular history elective they were taking at nearby Nathaniel Bacon University (good old Bacon U). They were joined by Melanie and Opie, two of our occasional interns. The floral design students helped out when we were swamped with work.

Shelby and Darnell were dressed not too differently from Nick, in tights and tunics, although they also wore scabbards that held swords. Melanie had dressed in an outfit a little like mine—but with a much more modest neckline. I suspected she was portraying some sort of servant or peasant.

Opie (short for Opal), our resident goth, looked splendid in an elaborate black and purple corseted dress that somehow managed to cover most of her anachronistic tattoos. The girls were joined by another young lady I didn't recognize, who, like Melanie, wore the plainer clothing of a servant.

"Wicked togs!" Opie said. "Love the cloak."

"Oh, my," Melanie said. "It's like the picture in the history book. Audrey, you can't wear that."

Opie rolled her eyes. "They don't like mine, either."

"But that's because you were supposed to be dressed as a servant," Melanie said, studying my outfit.

"Okay, I've had enough. This was the only thing the costume shop had. I've already been told it's period-correct." I turned to Melanie. "You said it's just like a picture in the history book. So what gives? Why can't I wear it?"

Again, the little crowd around me grew silent, until Opie nudged the one young woman I didn't know. "Let's let the history major explain it. Carol?"

Carol cleared her throat. "The neckline is a little too low for a servant," she said hesitantly. "So one might conclude that you're a tavern wench."

Not exactly the look I was going for, but not exactly scandalous, either. "So? Weren't there tavern wenches back then?"

"Oh, yes," Kathleen said. "That's why it's period-authentic. Only the tavern wenches often . . . moonlighted."

"Moonlighted?" I repeated.

"In an older occupation," Andrea said.

"Often referred to as the *oldest* occupation," Carol added. "If you get my meaning."

I pulled the cloak closer to me instinctively.

"But I'm afraid the cloak cinches it," Carol added. "In many areas prostitutes were required to wear yellow."

I shrugged the cloak off and it fell to the ground.

Andrea picked it up and shook the dust from it. "This is, however, a very good cloak. Look"—she pointed to a seam—"hand-stitched. Maybe hand-dyed and woven, too."

"Let me see," Kathleen said. She leaned forward and sniffed at the fabric.

"What's she doing?" I asked Carol. She seemed knowledgeable, and so far she'd given me the most answers.

"Authentically dyed yellow cloth," she said. "Well, in the Middle Ages, most yellow dye was made from . . . well . . . urine."

Now I began to itch all over. The whole "no running water" thing suddenly became a big deal. "You mean like cow urine and sheep urine."

"Actually, they collected men's urine," Kathleen said, now apparently in her element (history, not urine). "Not sure why, but some specifically thought that stale human male urine made the best dye. Of course, others insisted the urine had to come from prepubescent boys. A few years ago we set up pots to collect it, but they never really caught on." She sniffed the garment again. "But maybe they got enough to do this one." She handed it back to me. Or rather, she tried to offer it back to me.

"I can't wear that," I said, rubbing my arms against the cold.

"Maybe I have something," Nick said. "You'd have to dress as a man, but you might be more comfortable than . . ."

As he trailed off, I nodded and followed him to what turned out to be a colorfully striped tent. It was tall enough to stand in and remarkably spacious, despite the wooden crates of baking equipment scattered around.

When I got inside, he lowered the tent flaps and drew me into his arms.

"It was an unfortunate costume," I said, "not an advertisement."

He kissed me heartily. Normally he smelled like his bakery, of vanilla and almond. Now, he smelled of woodsmoke and the open woods. And maybe a few pheromones thrown in, because I suddenly didn't want to let go. Instead, I deepened the kiss.

When he finally broke the kiss, he held me for a moment longer. In the dimness of the tent, the shadows added a new ruggedness to his face.

"I suppose we should get you out of those clothes," he said. Then he winced. "I did *not* just say that. I didn't mean . . ."

I laughed and pulled away from him. "I know you didn't." My relationship with Nick Maxwell had always been suitably chaste, by mutual consent. Grandma Mae would have adored Nick's traditional values. "You said you might have something for me to wear?"

"Yes." He led me to a wooden trunk. "I wasn't going to

bring all of it this year, but now I'm glad I did." He rummaged inside and handed me what looked like a pair of skinny jeans. "Basic hosen," he said, then rummaged around some more before pulling out a long black shirt with elaborate embroidery. "A nice tunic."

I fingered the shirt, recalling what was said about participants making their own clothes. "Did you make this?"

"A lifetime ago," he said. Then he reached into the trunk again and pulled out a neatly folded bundle. "And you might as well wear this, since it's cold tonight and I'm going as a baker."

"What is it?" I asked, unfolding the lovely blue fabric.

"A surcoat. Part of a knight's attire."

"I can't—"

"No, please. You'll freeze to death without it, and I'd be happy to see you wearing my colors. I'll, uh . . . wait outside while you change."

Changing into Nick's handmade clothing in Nick's tent with only Nick standing guard outside felt a little uncomfortable—a level of intimacy we hadn't shared before. Still, I couldn't help appreciating the care and attention he must have put into each of these hand-stitched garments. And fortunately, none of them were yellow.

I didn't have a mirror to check the final result, but I was glad to leave the harlot's attire behind, even if I probably now looked more like Joan of Arc.

Let's just hope there were no stakes in my future.

Amber Lee pointed to an area in the clearing, walled in by a three-foot stone fence, but away from the thronging marketplace. "I guess the wedding is going to be held over there."

A few rickety-looking chairs and benches were set up, and those were mostly full. I pointed to the stone fence, and we hoisted ourselves up onto it. Melanie and Opie and their new friend Carol soon joined us.

"Good thing this fence is here," I said.

"Actually, this is as far as we've gotten on the castle walls," Carol explained. "The mortar should be set on this section, so I think we're okay."

"Carol knows the Middle Ages inside and out," Melanie said.

Carol blushed. "Well, I'm sure I don't know everything, but enough to get by teaching it."

"You're a professor?" I said.

"Oh, no, no!" she said. "Just a TA. The time period is a favorite of mine, though. But I'm in that awkward stage of studying what I love, and of course it's something that's not marketable in the least. But for this place? If they ever decide they need a paid historian, I'd be here in a heartbeat."

I nodded politely. For me the idea of studying history for the rest of my life was right up there with waterboarding and flossing. Still, I glanced around. With a little imagination, I could almost see a castle growing up from these stones. And as more guests arrived dressed in their medieval togs, I began to understand the fascination with this time period. It truly was like stepping back in time. Unfortunately, it smelled like it, too. As if to substantiate my thought, a horse tied up just outside the enclosure made a very uncivilized mess on the worn pathway.

I shuddered. Of course there'd be horses here. I took a deep breath and tried to calm myself. There was no shame in being afraid. Everyone has their fears: snakes, spiders, heights, even clowns. Mine was horses. Nothing wrong with that. After all, this was more of a result of that unfortunate merry-go-round incident. Could happen to anyone.

Two men, one older and one younger and dressed in almost regal attire, walked into the enclosure. Someone with a history degree, or even a fondness for the subject, could have detailed their outfits and their entourage. Let's just say they looked pretty snazzy and leave it at that.

"That's the groom," Melanie said. "And his father."

"Megabucks?" Amber Lee asked.

"At least around here," Opie said. "Barry Brooks—that's the father—owns some kind of pharmaceutical company. Apparently he's been coming to this thing for years. He brings the horses and a lot of the livestock from his own stables."

"Audrey!" Brad ran up just behind us. "Oh, shoot!" He looked down before wiping the side of his athletic shoe in the grass. "Stupid horses. Someone should follow them around with a pooper scooper. Hey, can I borrow your girls?"

"My girls?"

He pointed to Melanie and Opie. "They work for you, right?"

"Not at the moment. They're here for school."

"Oh, good. You girls want to earn a little extra cash?"

Melanie and Opie looked at each other, then at Carol.

"We're supposed to be observing for class," Melanie said.

Carol shook her head. "Oh, go ahead."

"Doing what?" Melanie asked Brad, but Opie had already hopped off the wall.

"My crew's still not here yet. Something about a roadblock on the other side of the county. And I'd hate to miss shooting the wedding. Do you think you guys could handle some basic camera equipment?"

"We can try," Melanie said. And soon the girls were

following Brad over to his anachronistic tent. I recognized it right off from the time when we were dating and he tried to get me to go camping with him—not going to happen.

Yet here I was, practically committed to doing just that. Only dressed a little fancier. Melanie and Opie had said there'd be room for Amber Lee and me in their rented cottage—one of the more permanent buildings in the encampment. Maybe it wouldn't be so bad. But I still dreaded that first call of nature. I'd already checked out the alternatives, which included using one of the public and foul-smelling garderobes, which appeared to be basically medieval porta-potties, or a lone trek into the woods.

That thought was interrupted by a buzz from my hidden cell phone. I tapped Amber Lee on the arm. "Save my place. I'm going . . ." And I pointed into the woods.

After walking a safe distance, I pulled out my cell, which had just started buzzing again.

"Audrey," Liv said, "I can't find that little black kitten. You don't think it could have gotten out?" Liv had promised to check on the cats for me.

"She just likes to hide. Especially when Chester is around."

"Chester is acting weird, too. I put his food out, but he's not eating. He just keeps staring at that old hutch in the kitchen."

"Then I think you've found the little black kitten. Look underneath it."

"Oh, Audrey. I'm not getting on my hands and knees and crawling around on that old floor."

"Is Eric there?"

"He's patching a couple of shingles on your roof. They're saying we might get some rain soon."

"About time." The whole county was under a severe

drought. We hadn't had more than a few drops since spring. "When he's done with that, ask if he could put Chester in my room. His litter box is already in there. I thought they were starting to get along, but—"

"Oh, there it goes!" Liv cried. Then I heard nothing but a few screams and some crashing sounds. One of which I think was Liv's phone hitting the floor. More yelling followed and then more crashing. I sure hoped Liv's manner with cats didn't translate into how she'd parent her children.

A few minutes later, Liv came back, breathless. "Okay, Chester is now eating the food in the kitchen, and the little one is in your room. Will that work?"

"It's going to have to. I'll be back tomorrow anyway." I refrained from explaining about cats, territories, and litter boxes. If they didn't adjust to the litter box switch, at least all the flooring needed to be replaced anyway.

"Oh, good." Liv sounded relieved. I pictured her sitting at my table in Grandma Mae's old kitchen. "You're going to have to come up with a name for that kitten. I don't know what you're waiting for."

I swallowed. My vet hadn't been all that keen on the little thing when I took her in. He seemed a bit pessimistic, not only about her survival—since she had lost her mother before she was weaned—but also her ability to adjust to being a house cat, let alone learning to socialize with another cat. Especially Chester. When he cautioned me about what kind of behavior I might find from taking in a feral cat, I had second thoughts about keeping her. Until she curled up and put her paws on my hand as I gave her the bottle of kitty formula. Then I knew I could never let her go.

But naming her was another story. Giving a cat a name is like giving them a piece of your heart. What if she didn't make it? Or if I couldn't make it work with the two cats?

"I'll come up with something," I said.

"Hey, how's the camp?"

I quickly filled her in on the experience so far, leaving out the dress and cloak fiasco. She homed in on the fact that Brad was here.

"I thought you were back to being steady with Nick."

"Well, dating Nick exclusively. But I've been talking and texting with Brad."

Silence.

"Liv?"

"What would Grandma Mae say about all this sneaking around?"

"I'm not sneaking around," I said, then lowered my voice. "If you recall, Nick was the one who suggested I see other people. And Brad knows I go out with Nick."

"I don't understand how you're all okay with that."

"Easy. Apparently none of us are ready to make a commitment. Nick, because he wants his business to be more secure first. Brad, because he's pursuing his dream career."

"And Audrey because . . . ?"

The blast of a trumpeted fanfare sounded from the clearing.

"Look, I have to get back. I think they're starting the ceremony. Thanks for checking on the cats. See you tomorrow."

As I made my way back to the castle-in-progress, I wondered what I'd tell Liv when she asked the question again. Because she would. Did I tell her that I didn't think I was ready for a life-long commitment, either? That I feared getting in too deep? After all, Liv had grown up with both mother and father. They'd recently celebrated their thirty-fifth wedding anniversary and are still going strong. Maybe even a little bit frisky for a couple their age. It was all right for Liv to believe in happily-ever-afters. She'd grown up thinking that was normal.

But that was not always the case, and as if to illustrate my point, as I entered the clearing, Andrea was walking down the aisle with her mother.

And my parents . . . my father had taken off without warning when I was nine. Just went to work one day and never came home. Granted, my mother wasn't the easiest person to live with, but what kind of coward takes off like that? Sure, a divorce would have been rough on me, too, but nothing like not knowing. Or feeling like I didn't matter to him. Like I didn't matter at all . . .

And here I was, practically getting ready to shed tears long dry, and on the happy occasion of Andrea's wedding. I swallowed hard, trying to clear the emotion out of my throat and plastered on a smile before reentering the now full clearing.

I regained my seat on the stone wall, just as the hire-a-friar began explaining the symbolism of the hand-fasting.

That voice . . .

I tried to convince myself that my imagination was running wild. I had just been thinking about my father, so surely the power of suggestion caused me to notice the similarities. But as I squinted at the older man in the simple brown robes, there was no mistaking it. He now had a circle of gray hair surrounding a mostly bald head, and more than a few crow's feet at the corners of his eyes, but the man now officiating the wedding was Jeffrey Bloom.

My father was back.

Chapter 3

The light was beginning to fade, sending shad-ows from the forest across the wedding guests. Goose bumps erupted on my arms, but my face flamed hot as I glared at the man I'd once called Daddy. What was he doing? Did he know I was here?

He had little to do with the ceremony but smile some silly beatific smile and nod pleasantly. The parents gave their consent, as did the bride and the groom as they wrapped a decorative cord around their wrists to join them forever in wedded bliss. At least, I thought, if my record held. No bride who'd ever carried one of my bouquets down the aisle had ever split up.

I breathed in the cool evening air. I would not let my sour attitude toward my father ruin Andrea's big day.

But I couldn't take my eyes off the man officiating the wedding.

Once he looked up at the crowd. When his eyes passed in

my direction, his smile faltered and his skin blanched. Yes, he'd recognized me. No, apparently he hadn't known I would be here. He managed to refocus his smile on the happy couple.

My brain played my options:

I could act dumb. Pretend I didn't recognize him. I wasn't sure how to explain the glaring. Maybe that unfortunate past incident with a friar?

Or I could leave. Now. While he was busy and before darkness fully settled, trapping me overnight in the encampment.

Or I could confront him. Demand an answer to those questions I've had throughout the years. But did I really want answers? Or just the chance to ask the questions.

Or I could . . .

Before I could plan another response, the wedding ended with a kiss and a shout. The bride and groom picked up the handles of a large covered basket, and opened the lid. Two white doves took off flapping.

One headed straight for the bride's hair. Andrea screamed and ducked, then tried to swat it away and stepped back. Too far. Her arms windmilled as she tried to catch her balance. She failed to recover and instead tumbled off the makeshift platform.

The other dove swooped in a wide, low circle over the rest of the crowd, who squealed and shouted, and more than one hit the dirt. Then the bird gained altitude and fluttered off into the sky.

A few people applauded, then the shadow of a large hawk zoomed over the guests. I was afraid to look. An "oooh" came from the crowd, then a collective gasp, and people winced and turned away.

But then friends and family gathered to congratulate the happy couple . . . after they helped Andrea out of the dirt.

The friar turned on his heels and strode quickly into the woods.

Without another thought, I hopped off the wall and ran after him, grateful I didn't have to worry about that long dress catching in the brush.

He, however, wore long clerical robes, and I caught up to him while he leaned against a tree, out of breath, trying to dislodge his vestments from a prickly bush.

As an angry teenager, I had penned long speeches of what I would say to my father if I ever saw him again. The gist of all these missives was that I'd been getting along fine without him and didn't need him now. Not that that was entirely true, I later considered, or I'd never have written them.

But none of those words were coming, so I stared at him, both of us out of breath from the exertion.

"Audrey?" he finally managed.

I nodded and brushed an unwelcomed tear from the corner of my eye.

"I must say, you've grown into a lovely young woman."

I crossed my arms and looked away into the woods to avoid his gaze. Everything from my throat down to my chest felt heavy, like my lungs were suddenly recast in lead.

"I'm sorry." He closed the distance between us. "It must be a shock to see me like this. If I knew you were going to be here, I wouldn't have come."

"Is that supposed to make me feel better?" I snapped, looking back into his face in the darkening woods. "Not sorry you walked out of my life. Just sorry you came back."

"I never meant to walk out of your life. Things just got . . . complicated. And I still haven't come back. You must understand, I can't come back. Please, Audrey, I can't explain it right now, but you need to trust me. Dangerous things are happening here, things I can't explain. I'm going to have to ask that you pretend you don't know me."

"I *don't* know you."

He took a step back. Even I was surprised at the venom my words contained.

"Fair enough," he said.

"I didn't mean . . ." I started. But maybe I did mean those words.

He opened his mouth to respond, but just then a scream sounded, coming from the encampment.

"Help, oh, help!" someone cried. "I think he's dead!"

No one was dead by the time I arrived, but a man lay on the ground in the middle of a convulsion while people dressed in medieval attire stood in a wide circle around him, some of them holding torches.

"Is there a doctor?" I asked, rushing into the circle. The man writhing in the dust was Barry Brooks, father of the groom.

"No, just an herbalist," someone said.

"Oh, and we have leeches," another added. Fat lot of good that was going to do.

Andrea and her groom dropped to their knees next to him. "Dad?" he said.

I crouched on the ground next to the ailing man and managed to get a pulse. It was irregular and racing out of control. His skin felt cool to the touch, but sweat beaded on his forehead. He was conscious only long enough to vomit onto the dusty path.

"When did this start?" I asked.

"Just before the wedding," Andrea said. "He said he felt a little dizzy."

"He has high blood pressure," the younger Brooks said, "if that makes a difference."

"Did he have anything to eat or drink just before?" I asked.

Andrea shrugged and shook her head.

"He ate some of the stew I made for the wedding feast," Nick said, leaning in to my ear. "You don't think it could be tainted, do you? I tried to keep all the ingredients cool. It tasted fine. I ate some myself, and I'm okay."

"Just . . ." I had a bad feeling about what was happening. "If I were you, I'd keep everyone else away from the stew. Could you do that?"

"Gotcha." He took off.

"This man needs medical attention immediately." I pulled out my cell phone, ignoring the tsks and gasps of the encampment, and dialed 911. Within minutes I was talking with a doctor and the dispatcher, describing the symptoms, the limitations of my nursing background, and the remoteness of the location. They were sending a medical rescue helicopter to the nearest road, and the county sheriff was on his way.

I turned to the crowd. "We need to get this man to the road. Any volunteers? I could use a few strong men to carry him and something to put him on."

The crowd managed to round up a rough-hewn cot and some rope. Then a few of the burly college students, including Darnell, tied Barry Brooks to the makeshift gurney.

"The helicopter will meet you at the road," I said. "Now hurry."

They lifted the unconscious Brooks up like pallbearers hoisting a coffin. Hopefully that's where the analogy would end. But I didn't like the looks of him.

With one young man holding a torch in front of them, they started trotting off into the woods.

I turned to follow them.

Amber Lee stood in my path. "Where are you going?"

"I should go with them."

"And do what?" she said. "At that rate, they'll have him at the road in minutes, and I'm not sure you can keep up with them, especially in the dark. You'll end up getting lost."

I looked up, and already the men were out of sight. "You're right."

When I turned back to face the crowd, they applauded.

"Great job, Audrey," Brad called, his video camera hoisted on his shoulder. "I got it all. Just fantastic."

I could feel the color rush to my face. I turned and paced toward the woods.

I had jumped in out of instinct and need, but now the familiar doubts roiled in my stomach. What if I did something wrong? What if I failed to do something I could have? What if Barry Brooks dies and I could have done something to prevent it? This was why I became a florist and not an RN.

I shivered and crossed my arms against my chest at the advancing cold and darkness, as a thousand and one different courses of action ran through my brain.

Amber Lee laid a hand on my shoulder. "You did a great job. Don't second-guess yourself."

I let her pull me into a hug.

Soon Shelby, Melanie, Opie, and Carol made their way over to join us.

"What was it?" Melanie asked. "Some kind of seizure?"

I gathered them into a tight circle. None of what I would say needed to spread around the camp.

"Was it the food?" Amber Lee asked in a hushed whisper.

"Please tell me it didn't turn. That could mean lawsuits for Nick. He's catering this whole shindig, you know. I saw the stew. It was in a caldron-type thingy, and he stirred it with a big old paddle, like a witch making a potion."

"I don't think it's food poisoning," I said. "The symptoms are wrong and way too quick." I paused as the rotors of the helicopter zoomed over us, rushing Barry Brooks for further medical attention. I let my gaze follow the copter until its lights were no longer visible over the tree line.

"But I heard you tell Nick not to let anyone near the stew," Amber Lee said.

I scanned the faces, now barely visible in the distant torchlight.

"I think Mr. Brooks was poisoned," I said.

Most of the encampment had quieted and huddled around a central bonfire—sans marshmallows and "Kumbaya"—when a bit of a hubbub occurred. Two men in contemporary uniforms emerged into the clearing. And I'd have recognized that sneeze anywhere.

Kane Bixby, Ramble's chief of police, pulled out a handkerchief. I'd imagine he was as uncomfortable with the allergens in the middle of the woods as he was with the flowers from our shop. While he scrubbed the area under his nose raw, the beam from his high-powered flashlight bobbed over the faces in the crowd. Bixby was joined by Ken Lafferty, the town's rookie. Recent rumor had it that Ken was moving quickly up in the ranks the old-fashioned way. Nepotism. He was dating Bixby's only daughter.

Finally Bixby's flashlight beam found my face. "Audrey Bloom. I should have known."

"What are you doing here?" I asked. "I thought the

sheriff was coming." The encampment was outside of Ramble proper, and therefore out of Bixby's territory. A fact I'd ascertained from Brad, who, in his younger and wilder days, had a few altercations with both jurisdictions.

"He's coming," Bixby said. "A bit tied up with the wildfires on the other side of the county." Bixby glared at our bonfire. "Be careful with that. There's a burn restriction."

"We have an exemption," one of the men said. "In writing. Should I go get it?"

"Foley will want to see it," Bixby said. "And whatever you do, be careful. With the drought, these woods will go up like a pile of kindling. So, who can tell me what happened here?"

I swear every head in the encampment swung in my direction.

"I should have guessed." Bixby rolled his eyes and drew me aside. "So what do we got?"

"Shouldn't we wait for the sheriff? If this isn't your jurisdiction . . ."

"We have reciprocity in emergency situations. Since I was closer, he asked if I'd come check it out, just to secure the crime scene, if we have one. Do we have one?" Bixby was a man of several different temperaments. He could be the no-monkey-business cop sometimes, with a grim expression and those gunmetal gray eyes. At other times, he could be the lead runner in a Mr. Rogers look-alike contest. This is when he was most dangerous, since he could get people to tell him—or do—almost anything. Just to be his neighbor.

"You tell me," I said. "All I know is that Barry Brooks is pretty sick. Vomiting, irregular heartbeat, chills, convulsions."

"Is he the only one sick?"

I hazarded a glance around the encampment. What would we do if an epidemic arose? They'd have to call in the National Guard to get all these people out of this remote location. I had to bet the people who programmed this little shindig hadn't been counting on reproducing the plague for the enjoyment of their guests. Talk about authenticity.

"Thankfully, yes. At least so far." Although I grew queasier by the moment. "The thought did cross my mind that he might have been poisoned."

I winced. I truly hated bringing this up, especially without any real evidence. My theory, if Bixby took me seriously, would have ramifications. Nick had prepared the food. I explained about Brooks sampling the stew before the ceremony. "Nick is making sure nobody else has any," I said.

"I'll check it out. Before I do, any ideas—if Mr. Brooks was poisoned—who might have had reason to?"

I shrugged. "Not a clue. I just met the man this afternoon. Although I did get the impression that he was not universally liked in the community."

Bixby's phone beeped, and he pulled it out to read a text. He shook his head.

"Well, if you're right, then we might just have a murderer on our hands. Brooks was pronounced dead when he arrived at the hospital."

Chapter 4

Bixby stood, practically agape, staring at the large cast iron cauldron. He shook his head. "I don't envy the sheriff at all. That's going to be hard to log into evidence."

"There's more." Nick pulled a flaming torch from a pole and held it over a wet mark in the dust.

"What happened there?" I asked.

"Mr. Brooks didn't like the stew, apparently. He threw it on the ground and marched off." Nick winced. "While threatening to stop payment on the check." He sighed. "And telling me that I'd never work one of these gigs again."

"And the stew came directly from the pot?" I asked.

"Before the wedding. He came here demanding to try it. I dished it out for him and handed it to him myself."

"But you said you had some and are feeling okay? No dizziness?" I pressed my hands against his cheeks, and then his forehead. His skin felt normal, not the sweats or chills that Barry Brooks had experienced.

"No, I feel fine," he said. "But I'm wondering . . . could something he'd eaten before the stew have affected his taste buds? 'Cause it tasted normal to me. Thrilled, in fact, with how it turned out."

"What's in it?" I asked. "Beef? What else?"

"Venison, actually. Let me think. Onions, carrots, cabbage. The old recipe I found called for parsley roots, but I could only find parsnips. Then there's pears and currants, things they would have had in the Middle Ages. And honey for sweetness."

"Did you bring all the ingredients in with you?"

"All except the venison. That I . . . locally sourced. And the spices and herbs I got from the camp herbalist. And the water from the main supply." Nick looked around his work area, as if trying to make sure he had listed all the ingredients.

I gave his hand what I hoped was a reassuring squeeze.

Ken Lafferty leaned over the pot. "It smells good, that's for sure."

"Get away from that," Bixby said. "Until we know what we're dealing with."

"Oh, right," Ken said. "Something could be in the air." He then forcibly exhaled until his eyes were about to pop.

Bixby rolled his eyes.

"Halloo there," a boisterous voice called as a high-powered lantern swept our location.

Even in the torchlight, I could see Bixby's posture straightening. Town gossip had it that Bixby didn't have a high regard for Sheriff Foley.

I'm not sure I disagreed with Bixby. Reports of Foley's arbitrary appointments and law enforcement policies had circulated all over the county. Justice for all, but not always for his supporters, at least if they were at fault. That went double in an election year. Rumor had it that he'd never pulled over a car with his own bumper sticker on the back.

As for his appearance, the man's face was almost a perfect square with big ears jutting out from under his mop of silver hair. His head was mounted directly, sans neck, onto a bulbous body trying to bulge out of its too-small uniform. Still, he walked with a purposeful stride and his ever-present whistle, which combined could be attributed to either confidence or arrogance.

"What's up?" Foley said. "And why all these fires?"

"Apparently, they have an exemption from the burn ban," Bixby said, pulling out the paper that a member of the encampment had provided him earlier.

"Half the county is up in smoke," Foley said. I couldn't tell if his face was turning red or just reflecting the glow from the torches. "What fool would issue an exemption?"

"Let's see . . ." Bixby focused the beam of his flashlight on the paper. "I can't quite make it out. Oh, yes. I think it says Ronald Foley."

Sheriff Foley ripped the paper from Bixby's hands and studied it. He missed the half smile that streaked across Bixby's face, then disappeared. No doubt these two men did not get along.

"Yeah, well." Foley shoved the paper into his pocket. "What do we got?"

"Possible homicide, actually," Bixby said. "Suspected poisoning, unless they discover natural causes. Victim died en route to the hospital. The last thing he ate was that." He pointed to the caldron.

Foley walked to the pot and took a big sniff. Bixby didn't correct him, even when Lafferty opened his mouth to say something.

"And there"—Bixby pointed to the ground—"is where he threw what he was eating. Apparently he didn't like it."

"Smells good. Anyone else sick?" Foley asked.

"No," Bixby said.

Foley spun to look around the group. "Anyone else eat any of the stew?"

"I did." Nick stepped forward.

"And you're not sick?"

"No, sir."

Foley turned back to Bixby "And you think it's poisoning . . . why?"

Bixby gestured to me. "Miss Bloom supplied some basic first aid to the victim. It was her assessment that he might have been poisoned."

"Are you a doctor?" he asked.

"No, but—"

"A nurse?" He loomed about a foot from my face now.

I could smell the smoke from those wood fires on his hair and clothing. "I had some nursing training, but I never finished—"

Foley turned back to Bixby. "Has the hospital determined cause of death?"

"You know toxicology won't come back for weeks."

"So"—now he was in Bixby's face—"based on the guess of a nursing school washout, you're going with poison?"

"Miss Bloom was on the scene and did her best to aid the victim. And she's proved . . . helpful . . . in a couple of previous investigations in Ramble." Bixby's hands went to his hips. "But *I'm* not going with anything. My job was to secure the scene. The scene is secured. Have a nice day."

He started to walk off.

"Wait a minute," Foley said. "Don't go getting all uppity with me. I've been up for days dealing with that dad-blamed fire. If you say it's a possible homicide, I'll say let's run with that."

Bixby turned around. "*Let's* run? Oh, no. You're not saying—"

"Yup." Foley grinned. "I'll clear it with my good friend, your mayor, at whose pleasure you serve, but Kane Bixby, I hereby deputize you and put you in charge of this investigation."

Bixby said nothing, but clenched his jaw so hard he was in danger of snapping a molar.

Foley just grinned and started his signature whistle. He'd taken two steps back toward the path to the road before he whipped around. "Oh, yeah. You know what? You're going to need manpower, and I can't spare any of my people." He pointed to Lafferty. "How about this man?" Then he looked in my direction and smiled. Or perhaps he smirked. Hard to tell in the torchlight. "And since she's been so helpful, as you say . . ." He pointed to me. "What's your name again, sweetheart?"

"Audrey Bloom."

"Well, Audrey Bloom, consider yourself deputized, too." He turned to Kane Bixby. "See? I'm even giving you help."

"Over there, son."

Bixby had commandeered Brad and his still camera to take crime scene shots. Maybe he was grateful he didn't have to walk two miles in the dark to retrieve his own camera, but given their past skirmishes, "son" was probably overdoing it.

Brad took a few more shots of the stew lying on the ground, the flash lighting the area in brief bursts. Bixby had already decided that the dust was too disturbed by people tramping all over it to get a decent footprint, but he had wanted to document the scene.

"What should I be doing?" I asked.

"Stay out of the way?" Bixby said. "Look, thanks for jumping in and trying to get the victim to the hospital. I only wish it had turned out better. But as far as the investigation goes, let the police handle this."

"If you haven't noticed, I kinda am the police, too. I've been deputized. I should be helping."

Bixby turned to face me. Even the darkness couldn't hide the sneer on his face. "You know he only did that to irritate me, right? The next time I have a conversation with his good friend the mayor, I plan to tell him how irresponsible it was to put you in possible danger. You're not trained in evidence collection or experienced in police procedure. Or armed, for that matter." He lowered his voice. "And if it is murder . . ." He flicked his head toward the crowd still behind the makeshift police barrier. No yellow tape here, just a string of colorful flags.

"You *did* tell him I was helpful," I said.

"I could see he was leaning toward assuming some natural cause of death. Key evidence would be lost if—"

"But you believed me."

"As the closest thing to a medical professional on the scene. You know, it's still possible that the medical examiner will discover he died of natural causes."

I glared at him.

"I just don't want anyone further contaminating this crime scene."

I crossed my arms and waited. Grandma Mae always said that women had no greater weapon than well-timed silence.

He threw up his hands. "Fine. Tell you what, Miss Poisons

Expert. How about that as a job? It's going to take quite a bit of time to get toxicology results back. Go and see if you can find the murder weapon."

I paced up and down on the dirt floor of the "cottage" we shared with the girls. It turned out to be more of a low-ceilinged hut with a thatched roof. The one small room was jammed with sleeping mats on the floor, so only about three feet of pacing room was available. One tiny lone window faced the stocks in the courtyard, gleaming in the moonlight, empty but foreboding.

"Will you try to get some sleep?" Amber Lee said. "Some of us older folks need our beauty rest."

"I can't." My brain was spinning. My father was here. And then the murder. My argument with Bixby. "Find the murder weapon." I sighed.

Opie hoisted herself up to sitting and crossed her legs. In the privacy of the cottage, she had changed into modern sweatpants. "Maybe you should do it."

"Find the murder weapon? You know he just said that to get rid of me."

"That might be true." Amber Lee yawned and rolled over to face the rest of us. "But I have every confidence you can do what he said."

"How am I supposed to find a murder weapon when we don't even know if a murder has been committed?"

"Well, what do we know?" Melanie slapped a card onto the hand of solitaire she was playing in the light of her cell phone. Why she wasn't just playing on her cell, I have no idea.

I stopped pacing and ticked the one thing I knew off on my finger. "Barry Brooks is dead."

"What else?" Opie asked.

"There is nothing else," I said.

"You got a good look at him before they carried him away," she said. "What were the symptoms?"

"Okay." I sat down on the mat and raked my brain. "Chills. Vomiting. Racing, erratic heart rate. Probably a fever before the chills, because he was all sweaty. Convulsions." I rubbed my forehead, as if that would fire up the old neurons. "Headache." Maybe it worked.

"You have a headache or he had a headache?" Amber Lee asked.

"Yes," I said.

Carol tossed me a bottle of Tylenol.

"Thanks." I shook out two and washed them down with a bit of water before tossing the bottle back to her. "I would have thought you'd suggest blood-letting or something. After all, you're a history major."

She drew up her knees to her chin. "Just not as hard-core as some of the folks here."

"She's the best TA," Opie said.

"Which only means I let you get away with too much," Carol said, but with a smile.

I nodded, but my brain still cycled through the symptoms. "Maybe . . ." I pulled out my cell phone, then let out a disgusted sigh. "Low battery."

"We can fix that." Opie dug around in a dusty backpack and pulled out a small device with a hand crank. "It's a generator. It has a light, a weather radio—and a USB charging port. Not quite all the comforts of home, but not even a pound of extra weight to carry."

"Brilliant," I said. "You come prepared."

"Well, it's mostly because of my Candy Crush addiction," she said. "But you're welcome."

"Do I have to crank it?"

"It should be fully charged. Just plug it in."

As my phone connected, the low-battery message disappeared, and soon I was sitting on a straw mat in a medieval village while surfing the Internet.

"You have an idea?" Amber Lee said.

"Just wondering if I could narrow down the type of poison by entering the symptoms."

The room hushed while I typed the various symptoms in, with the keyword "poison," and then looked for a reputable source. Or maybe they kept talking and I just didn't hear them because of my concentration. I had no idea how much time passed before I came across the National Institutes of Health report that best fit the bill.

"You got it?" Opie asked.

I looked up to see they'd all been staring at me.

"Aconite poisoning. I think."

"So what now?" Melanie asked. "We search the camp for a bottle marked aconite?"

"We?" Carol asked. "Are you all into this stuff?"

Opie laughed. "We might have helped a little bit. Audrey here is a certified A-1 amateur sleuth."

When Carol looked confused, Melanie explained. "Not that anyone certifies amateur sleuths. But she's solved a couple of murders already."

Carol's head whipped back to me. I guess I didn't look like the detecting kind.

"Only this time she's not an amateur," Amber Lee added, "since she's been duly deputized. Hey, does that make us deputy deputies?"

"I'll settle for minions," Melanie said. "I always wanted to be a minion."

"Not if it's going to put you in danger," I said.

"See," Opie said, "she's talking like Chief Bixby already."

I flipped on the LED light on the generator. It wasn't a spotlight by any stretch of the imagination, but it produced a nice steady glow. Hopefully enough for what I needed it for. "May I use this?"

"Sure," Opie said. "Just crank it if it starts to get dim. Are you going somewhere?"

I pulled on the surcoat Nick had loaned me. "Yes, looking for the murder weapon."

"The aconite?" Amber Lee said. "You know where to find it?"

"I think I might."

"Then, wait. I'm coming with you," Amber Lee said.

"Me, too," Opie added.

"Ditto," said Melanie.

Carol looked rather stunned as she scanned our faces. She shrugged then pushed herself off the mat. "Count me in."

I looked at the small group, and for the first time got just a little glimpse into why Bixby was irritated with me poking my nose into one of his investigations. I didn't want anything happening to Amber Lee or any of these young women. I resolved to try to be a bit nicer to the man. As I shoved the murder weapon in his face. Well, not actually in his face. With his allergies . . . "Should we try to find the boys?" I asked. "I'm sure Darnell must be back by now." He'd gone with the group that took Brooks to the helicopter.

Melanie shook her head. "Trust me. They're useless. As soon as they strapped on swords, it was like their brains got sucked out."

"She's right," Opie said. "Hopeless. You'll see. But you got us. What's the plan?"

"Aconite comes from plants," I said, as the ladies gathered their wraps. "Specifically monkshood."

"And you think someone brought one of these plants in?" Amber Lee said. "Please tell me there wasn't any in our flower arrangements."

I shook my head. "We just brought roses and bachelor's buttons, so it didn't come from us. And I don't think the killer had to bring it with him, either. It was already here. I half remember spotting some growing wild in the woods on my way in."

"So basically, we're looking for the plant." Melanie said.

I described the plant to them, with blue flowers shaped like the hood of a monk. And coincidentally not too much different from the hood on the back of the friar's cloak, the one worn by my father. My father, who didn't want me to reveal his identity and who warned me that dangerous things were happening here. After I delivered the murder weapon into Bixby's hands, I needed to have a talk with that man.

"Every part of the monkshood plant is poisonous," I said, relating what I'd learned from the NIH article, "but to cause that much of a reaction, I'd think the victim had to ingest the root."

"So somebody dug it up," Opie said.

"Or pulled it up," Amber Lee said.

"We could have all been killed, then," Melanie said. "Oh, Audrey! If we'd eaten the stew . . . Is that what someone tried to do? Kill everybody here?"

"Any way it could have been an accident?" Carol said.

I shrugged. "All good questions. Keep them coming. In the meantime, let's look for answers. Don't go out of sight of the camp."

"And we have our buddies and fresh tissues," Opie teased.

I shook my head. "I don't want to lose anybody in the dark. We want to find the flowers. Then look around the base, to see if some of the plants might have been dug up. Call if you find any monkshood. But don't touch it."

"You want the glory?" Amber Lee teased.

"No, just don't want any of us getting a nasty rash—or worse—from touching the leaves or flowers. Every part of this plant is bad news."

We split up into two groups. I took Melanie and Opie and used the light from the mini-generator. Carol went with Amber Lee, using a contraband flashlight that one of the girls dug out of her sleeping bag. That way we could cover more ground.

"You should have changed out of your mundanes," Melanie told Opie, who was still dressed warmly in her sweats.

Opie shook her head. "And freeze? No one's going to see me in the dark anyway."

"Mundanes?" I asked as I shined the flashlight over the plants just outside the clearing. It was probably a snipe hunt in the dark, but I doubted sleep would come tonight, and I would enjoy dropping the murder weapon at Bixby's feet.

"Yeah, the modern clothes," Melanie said. "Only the hardliners here look down their noses at you when they say it. *Mundanes.*" Melanie pursed her lips like she'd just bit off half of a lemon and pretended to shiver. Or maybe she really shivered. The air seemed to grow colder as we spoke. "They really didn't want any of us wearing street clothes."

"So I've been told," I said, shivering either at the cold of the night or the memory of the serving wench outfit.

"What can they do to me?" Opie asked.

"Send you home, that's what," Melanie said as she swatted at a mosquito on her arm. "And then you'd still have to write that paper."

"At least I'll still have blood left," Opie said.

"Ah, is that what this is about?" I asked. "Either attend the re-creation or write a paper?" I had wondered why the event was so popular among the college students.

"You bet," Melanie said. "Thirty pages on some aspect of the Middle Ages."

"Here's one," I said, shining the light on the blue flowers of a tall monkshood plant, then redirecting the beam to the ground around it. The flashlight beam was alive with moths and other insects attracted to the light.

"Any sign of digging?" Opie asked.

The ground showed no signs of disturbance. "No, but now you know what we're looking for." I shined the light on the plant so the girls could get a closer look.

"Those flowers are really pretty," Melanie said. "I can see the little hood shapes. I can't believe the plant is deadly."

"Very," I said. "They called it monkshood for the shape, but it had other names, too. Wolfsbane. I've also heard it called devil's helmet."

"Does it have meanings, too? In your language of flowers?" Opie asked.

"I suppose so, but I'd have to look it up. It's not one I'm all that familiar with. We obviously wouldn't use it in a bouquet. Just touching it could make you very sick."

"I saw a movie once," Melanie said, "where they used wolfsbane to protect a baby from vampires. Put it all around her neck. Scary to think of what might happen if someone tried that in real life." She slapped at a mosquito on her neck. "But I might try it if I thought it would work against these little bloodsuckers."

"I think I'd rather take my chances with the vampires," Opie said. "Here's another one."

"A vampire?" Melanie asked.

"No, a monkshood, you . . ." Opie pointed to another tall plant, but the ground around it showed no disturbance, either.

"Hey, over here!" Amber Lee called. "Quick!"

We followed her into the woods. When she stopped, she

shined her flashlight on Carol. The beam reflected the tear tracks on the young woman's cheeks.

"I'm sorry," she said. "I'm sorry. I got so excited I wasn't thinking."

"What happened?" I asked.

"She touched it," Amber Lee said.

"It itches," Carol said.

"Come on back to camp," I said. "They may not have running water, but we're going to have to wash that somehow."

"Look!" Opie said. "She really did find it. Someone's been digging here." She pointed her flashlight down at the recently overturned dirt.

Chapter 5

"I am so stupid," Carol whined as I poured more water over her hand. "You warned us not to touch it. And what do I go and do?"

A few of the reenactors were giving me the stink-eye, probably because I was depleting their precious water supply at a fantastic rate. I'd probably get mad, too, if I had to carry all my water over a mile to the camp. But it couldn't be helped.

The rash on Carol's hand looked ugly, but she didn't know—because I didn't want to alarm her—that I was secretly taking her pulse while I poured water over those hands. Her heart rate was mildly elevated, but not erratic. That and the rash and the self-loathing seemed to be the limits of her reaction.

I also experienced a measure of self-loathing. This girl was barely past her teen years. And within hours of meeting me, she was running around in the dark trying to find a poisonous plant just because I'd asked her to.

Opie put her hand on my shoulder. "You didn't make any of us go."

"Did I say that out loud?"

Opie smiled. "No, but I know you by now."

The advancing sun washed over the encampment with milky whiteness. A rooster crowed.

Bixby and Amber Lee stepped back into the clearing. Bixby held a cluster of monkhood plants, with their turnip-like roots, in one gloved hand, while he tried to suppress a sneeze with the other. Amber Lee gave me a thumbs-up.

Bixby blinked hard against the approaching sneeze, then relaxed and sniffed. "Is she all right?"

I nodded.

"Look," he said, "when I told you to find the murder weapon . . ."

Welcome to the self-loathing party. Instead of saying this, I sent him a reassuring smile. "She's all right. We're all okay, and now you likely have the murder weapon."

He returned the smile, but our touching Kodak moment was interrupted by trumpets.

Bixby jumped a foot. I might have bested him by three inches.

Soon the crowd which had gathered around parted and a regal figure appeared. By regal figure, I mean he wore a literal crown and a lavish medieval outfit in jewel-tone satin and gold. Several reenactors bowed low to the ground as he approached.

"You'd better bow," Carol said. "It's King Arthur."

I did my requisite bow, then whispered, "He's playing King Arthur? The whole round-table bit?"

"Well, he's king this year, and his name is literally Arthur. So he's King Arthur. I think his last name is Schwartz. Dr. Schwartz. He's a dentist."

I bit back a remark about him being used to pricy crowns.

Dr. Arthur Schwartz stopped when he reached Bixby and gave him a look up and down in that regal "I am not amused" manner.

Bixby didn't bow, didn't flinch, didn't look like he had any inclination to. "May I help you?" he said instead.

King Arthur's face flushed (would that be a royal flush?) and his jowly jaws tightened. I half expected him to yell, "Off with his head!"

Instead, he turned to one of the men with him. "I don't want to see any more mundanes in camp. We allowed the cameras, that's enough. Anyone who wants to remain will need to dress in a manner which respects the kingdom." He waved his hand with a flourish, as if he were signing his decree into law.

Then he turned to me. "I hear you've been using all of our fresh water."

"It was an emergency . . . sire. I . . ." I stumbled to recall anything I might have learned from old movies. Robin Hood maybe. "I beg . . . clemency, your highness." And I ended that with a curtsy. Yes, Grandma Mae had taught both Liv and me to curtsy. I had never found it of any use until now.

"If you dress like a man, bow like a man. But we appreciate the effort. You may stay. But you must replace the water you have used."

"Yes, sire," I said, wondering how I was going to do that. And wondering if there was anything he could do if I left and never followed through on my promise. I'd be carting water through the woods all week.

He gave a curt nod, then turned and left. His entourage remained behind.

One of the men went immediately to Brad, and the two of them headed off to have an animated discussion. Another took Bixby by the arm.

"I have to what?" Bixby shouted, shaking him off.

Yet another headed to Opie, still in her sweats from our midnight romp in the woods. I couldn't tell what they were saying, but after a few moments Opie rushed away, brushing a tear from her cheek.

I followed her. "What happened?"

She shook her head. "I have to leave. Second strike, I guess. They weren't happy with my dress choice. Now I have to go back. It's going to be a research paper for me."

I pulled her into a hug. With a possible murderer running around the camp, maybe she was safer back in town. Maybe we all were.

That's when we heard the gunfire.

I was well behind Bixby—jogging has never really been my thing—headed in the direction from which the shot came. Chickens fluttered, half running and half flying down the pathway.

The path, probably an old deer run, ended abruptly at a decrepit fence. Bixby got there first. "What are you doing?" he shouted.

When I came out of the woods, I saw Larry, our main local flower supplier and dear family friend, standing next to the fence and holding a shotgun.

"Trying to keep those dad-blamed chickens out of my fall bulbs. They're rooting up everything."

"You can't go shooting them," Bixby said.

"I wasn't shooting them," Larry said. "If I was shooting them, they'd be dead. I was shooting near them, to drive them back onto the other side of the fence. This is a zoned agricultural area. I have every right." He turned to look at me. "Audrey? What are you doing here? And in that getup?" He snickered. "You look like Joan of Arc."

"Long story, Larry. What are you doing out here?" Before he could answer, I looked past the fence to where the forest gave way to neatly planted farm rows. Behind them, I could just make out a greenhouse. "Wait, is this the back of your second location? The one you rent from the Rawlings?"

Larry had kept the greenhouse private while he worked on cultivating a blue rose that he'd named after our Grandma Mae. He sends us all we can sell, and we ship them around the country.

Larry smiled his signature Kewpie doll smile. "One and the same. I just started clearing the fields for spring bulbs." His smile dimmed and his grasp on the shotgun grew tighter. "Only the livestock from that stupid camp keep breaking down the fences."

"Wait. Do you mean to tell me the road's right through there?" Bixby asked.

Larry nodded. "Private property, though."

Bixby sent him an incredulous sneer. "Would have helped to know that last night," he muttered.

"What?" Larry asked.

"There was an emergency here last night," I said. "They had to carry a man a mile to the nearest road. Didn't you hear the helicopter?"

"I did," Larry said. "But I thought it might have been something about the fires. Wow, I would have let an emergency crew through. I just want to keep the goats and chickens and things out. I hope he's all right."

I shook my head. "But may I cut through your property? I promise to avoid your plantings."

"Sure, Audrey. Anytime you want."

Bixby cleared his throat. "And may I?"

Larry squinted at him for a second. I half expected him to say no. It seems Bixby's allergies had put him on strained terms with anyone connected to the floral industry. Larry grunted. "I guess it would be all right. Just avoid any freshly turned dirt. And the flowers."

"No problem," Bixby said.

"Oh, and Larry?" I eyed his hose. "How far does that hose stretch? And any chance I could bum some water from you?"

"I would have liked to have seen Chief Bixby's face when the sheriff deputized you, too," Liv said Monday morning when we were going over the orders for the week. The one small wedding on our calendar for Saturday wouldn't require much effort—at least until Thursday or Friday.

I yawned and leaned on the workbench. It had taken most of Sunday to recover from a sleepless Saturday night, and my internal clock was off by more than a few hours.

"It was priceless," Amber Lee said. "I thought he was going to have a cow, especially when Foley got to the part about his buddy the mayor"—she bulged her cheeks and put on her best Sheriff Foley impression—"at whose pleasure you serve." She picked up a completed arrangement for our self-service cooler and walked it to the front of the shop.

Liv wiped away a tear. "Sorry I missed it. So when are you going back?"

"Nah . . . I did my bit. Bixby wanted the murder weapon. He has it." I hadn't mentioned to Liv or Amber Lee my other reason for not wanting to go back. My father had managed to avoid me for about twenty years. I hoped to honor the family tradition and avoid him for another twenty.

"You're just going to sit this one out?" she asked.

"Yup. Bixby might work at the pleasure of the mayor, but I'm a florist. No law says I have to protect and serve. I looked it up on the computer before you came in." I'd also looked up aconite poisoning, but as it would weaken my argument for not wanting to be involved in the case, I didn't mention my research to Liv.

"Well, maybe you don't have to go back. What did you say the victim's name was?"

"I don't recall mentioning it."

Liv put her hands on her hips and glared at me. It might look menacing if she weren't five-three and cute as a proverbial button. Or as a bachelor's button, which, thankfully, were forgotten and probably rotting in the box back at the encampment. I caved anyway. "Brooks. Barry Brooks."

She marched to the computer, hit three keys, and smiled. "You are such a liar."

"What?"

"I type in three keys, and 'Barry Brooks' pops up. You've been searching already."

Amber Lee came back and tossed some floral foam into the sink.

"I may have Googled him," I admitted, "just out of idle curiosity."

"And yet you're telling me you have no intention of getting involved in this case," Liv said. "Why?"

"Look, I don't have to be involved." I drained my coffee cup while I planned my argument. "I'm sure Bixby doesn't want me involved—"

Amber Lee cleared her throat. "Think again."

"What?" I said.

"Either he had a doozy of a blowout with Mrs. Bixby and he's thinking about buying her flowers . . ."

"Never gonna happen," Liv said. Kane Bixby's allergies were legendary.

"Or he wants to talk with one of us," Amber Lee continued. "He's passed the shop at least three times."

"You're kidding." I went to the doorway and peeked through the shop. Sure enough, Kane Bixby, a bulging folder tucked under his arm, stood uncomfortably in front of the bay window. Then he tented his eyes and peered inside. I waved at him.

He waved back.

"This just got weird," I said.

"Better go talk to him," Liv said.

I hung my apron on the hook and walked through the shop. He was still out front when I pulled open the door and joined him on the sidewalk.

"Miss Bloom," he said.

"Something I can do for you?" I asked.

"I'd like to talk with you." He gestured down the street, where the sidewalk tables from the Brew-Ha-Ha were getting the morning sun. "Coffee?"

He didn't wait for me to answer, just started walking down the street in long strides that made me half jog to keep up.

"I'm not sure I have anything to add to the statement I already gave you."

He opened the door. No sunny table for me today. The air-conditioning and the aroma of coffee were pleasant enough, though. We ordered at the counter, where the display of scones and other baked goods fresh from Nick Maxwell's bakery tempted my eyes. But I was good. (I only ordered one.) We carried our drinks to a large table near the window before he spoke.

"I didn't actually ask you here to go over your statement."

He pushed his coffee cup to the side of the table and opened the folder. "I have the statements here from the other witnesses at that compound. I wondered if you'd be . . . well, I'd like if you'd look over them with me."

I practically choked on my scone. "Like, work with you?"

"As my receptionist has pointed out to me on more than one occasion, just this morning, in fact, sometimes a fresh set of eyes on a problem helps put everything in perspective. Foley can't or won't offer me more men to work on this. I can't pull mine from Ramble to work on something outside their jurisdiction. So I wondered . . ."

"What about Lafferty?"

"His day off. And he and my daughter are off making wedding plans. She'd kill me if I called him in to work." Bixby sipped his coffee. "He, on the other hand, might thank me."

"Congratulations. I didn't know they were engaged." I smiled. "But yes, grooms are usually less excited about the details."

"I hope you're not offended if we don't get flowers from you. My daughter was all for it. She saw that thing in the paper about you and the language of flowers and all that. But with my allergies, we've been trying to talk her into silk."

"We do silk flower arrangements, too. But if you'd rather someone else . . ."

"No, I wasn't aware. She'd like that. I'll let her know."

And I'd probably kick myself later, but I pulled the folder closer to me. There were five paper-clipped bundles at the front.

"I put the most likely suspects first."

"Why are these the most likely, again?"

Bixby's face went blank as if he were trying his best to hide a scowl. I'd bet money on it. He took a sip of his coffee. "They best knew the victim. Friends. Relatives. Co-workers.

Of course, we can't eliminate the possibility that Barry Brooks was not the intended victim. For all we know, someone wanted to wipe out the whole camp. But these still seemed a good place to start."

"Of course." As I skimmed through the top pages, I almost spewed my coffee across the table. "Kathleen Randolph is a suspect?"

"Keep. It. Down," Bixby said with a forced smile, then nodded to a patron across the restaurant before leaning in closer. "Did you know that Kathleen Randolph was once married to Barry Brooks?"

"No, she hadn't thought to mention that in any of her four consultations. You're saying her daughter married the son of her ex-husband? Is that even legal?"

"Not blood relatives. The kids never even lived in the same house. Granted, it's going to make family reunions a little tricky."

The next file was Andrea's. "Why would she kill her father-in-law?"

Bixby flipped to the next file, which showed a picture of the young groom. He placed them side by side. "The happy couple will inherit. Megabucks. Not to mention the senior Brooks was reportedly not all that happy about the marriage. Insisted the bride sign a prenup. Implied that if she were anything like her mother . . ."

"Which opens the old wounds with Kathleen." I sighed and studied the pictures of the three of them. Kathleen's bitterness over her ex-husbands, all three of them, was no secret, but I doubted she'd kill any of them. "She was all over the encampment that day, which is understandable since she was the mother of the bride."

"How'd she seem?"

"Busy."

Bixby's face froze into an unreadable expression. Apparently that wasn't the response he was looking for. "I meant," he went on, "did you detect any tension or anything odd about the way Kathleen was acting?"

"Chief, you have a daughter, right? How do you think *you're* going to hold up on the day of her wedding? Yes, I guess you could call Kathleen tense, but probably no more than anyone else would be, given the circumstances."

"Including what might have been an unpleasant reunion with her ex-husband."

"Sure, that had to make it even harder. But to poison her ex on the day of her daughter's wedding? She once told me that there were easier ways of getting rid of a husband than murder."

Bixby sent me what seemed a patronizing smile and then went back to the counter for a refill.

I flipped to the next bundle. The buxom woman named Raylene Quinn was apparently a longtime employee of Brooks and listed as the Director of Research and Development. She looked every bit the sexy scientist and was one of those women who was probably older than she first appeared. Her platinum blonde hair betrayed her at the roots.

As Bixby slid into his seat, I said, "And she traveled with him regularly?"

"You're wondering if they had some kind of romantic relationship besides the business one."

"Thought crossed my mind."

He shrugged. "Not one that she was forthcoming about."

"She wouldn't be."

The small nod I got back from him belied the impression that I was getting closer. I hadn't come up with any new revelations, but at least we were on the same track.

"Was there a Mrs. Brooks?" I asked.

"On her way from Richmond as we speak. That's where Brooks Pharmaceuticals is headquartered."

"She didn't come to the wedding of her own son?"

"Apparently the current Mrs. Brooks isn't the mother of the groom, either, and she's more into society parties than 'running around in the woods' as she told me over the phone."

The final entry in the most-likely-suspects category was a Chandler Hines. "Another co-worker?"

"Not exactly. He's the only one of our initial persons of interest who didn't know Brooks outside of the encampment. But his name came up three times when I asked people if they knew anyone who might have wanted to kill Brooks. And after interviewing him, I could see why."

"He must have made quite an impression. They've only been at the site, what, three or four days?"

"Ah, but both Hines and the victim were regulars, with apparently a lot of bad blood between them. Hines claims to be one of the founders of the group. Really rigid."

"Just the type of fanatic who might want to poison a whole camp full of people?"

Bixby shrugged. "He is, I discovered, the one who put that King Arthur character up to the restriction that everyone has to be in medieval dress. So if you go back there—and you shouldn't go alone—you will need to be in costume, otherwise they pretend like they can't see or hear you."

"You tried?"

He nodded.

Underneath those first five bundles was a single page with two columns of names.

"The minor players," he said. "There's a few more of Brooks's employees in there, too."

"But they didn't make the most-likely-to-murder-your-boss list?"

"None of their names came up when we asked people who they thought might have killed Brooks. Doesn't mean they couldn't have. Just that nobody thought to throw them under the bus."

Yet Brooks had made enough enemies in his life to make naming the most likely suspects easy. The list of witnesses and secondary suspects was alphabetized. I saw my own name under "Bloom," but no "Bloom, Jeffrey." My scone caught in my throat, and I washed it down with coffee.

"Did you get a statement from everybody at the encampment?" I asked.

"Yes, all there."

Had my father left? And if he had, was he avoiding me or involved somehow in the poisoning?

"Something you noticed?" Bixby glanced at me, and then down at the page I was looking at.

That man was too perceptive for my own good. I tried for a conversational tone, even though my heart beat out a tango. "Did you . . . uh . . . talk to the friar who was doing the wedding? I wonder if he might have seen something. He would have been facing the wedding party." Lame reason, but Bixby might buy it.

"Yes, yes we did." He pulled the file toward him and shuffled through it. He pushed a single page onto the table in front of me.

"Richard Wilson?" I said, reading the name at the top of the page. "The friar's name is Richard Wilson?"

Okay, Dad. Why are you back? And why are you using a fake name?

Chapter 6

I begged off work early, claiming the lack of sleep was catching up on me. I'm not sure Liv bought it. I could feel her gaze trying to break into my skull. It's her superpower. I needed to either get out of the shop or seriously invest in a tinfoil hat.

I wasn't ready to talk about my father with anyone.

It felt weird even thinking about him as "my father." Even weirder was me putting air quotes around the phrase while talking to myself as I drove home in the CR-V that I shared with the shop.

When I parked in my overgrown driveway, Eric Meyer—Liv's husband and my contractor—was on my roof.

"Another patch?" I called.

"Audrey, this roof has more patches than a pirate convention. I'm not sure it's going to last the winter for you. I'd offer to reroof, but I have a feeling it won't just be a matter of tearing off these shingles and putting on new. I don't like the way she feels. Squishy."

"Is that a builder's term?" *Squishy Patches* sounded like the title of a bad memoir. I wasn't ready for more bad news about the cottage, either.

"If you're lucky, all you need is new sheathing under the shingles. How lucky are you?"

I let out a disgusted sigh. "You don't want to know." I was going through a few squishy patches myself.

When I opened the door, Chester was nowhere to be seen. Probably hiding under the bed, afraid of the pounding. The little black kitten yet to be named, however, stared at me impudently from the kitchen counter, the one place in the house that I'd declared forbidden.

"Get down," I said.

She stood up, blinked, stretched her back, then lay back down, resting her head on her front paws. I was a failure as a cat trainer.

I scooped her up into my arms. But she wriggled out of my grasp, dug her claws into my shoulder, then step by excruciating step, climbed up until she was resting around my neck like some fox stole with her tail slapping my cheek.

Leaving the cat balanced on my shoulders, I headed to my laptop, still on the kitchen table. I brushed off a layer of drywall dust that seemed to have fallen from a new crack in the ceiling and powered it up. Mrs. June was a dear and suggested I use her Wi-Fi until I could get my own. She never mentioned a cutoff date, and I hesitated to bring it up. Not with my newly emptied bank account and a cottage that bled money.

The first name I typed into the search engine was "Richard Wilson."

I paged past several screens of illustrious men named

Richard Wilson. Executives. Philanthropists. A ball player and then a teenager with a racy Instagram page.

None of the faces matched. Up on my shoulder, my feline fashion accessory sighed.

I almost missed the listing for the bail bondsman. "AA-1 Bond Service." Give me a break.

There was no picture. Not quite sure a bail bondsman would want his picture up on the site, since most people perusing the page would be criminals. Or rather alleged criminals. But a Richard Wilson was listed as the proprietor and the physical address of the bond agency was in the same zip code as the address my father had given Bixby.

A sudden barrage of drywall dust fell on the table. I closed my eyes for a moment and concentrated on the contented purr from the kitten on my shoulders.

A click of claws on the floor announced Chester's arrival. When I glanced down at him, he meowed at me. I've never been good at cat-speak, but he was either demanding more food or protesting the new kitten's prime real estate.

"You jealous, bud?" I scruffed his neck and he hopped up on my lap. I was feeling the love, but then Chester's real motive appeared. He took a swat at the kitten's swinging tail.

The kitten hissed then launched off my shoulders, digging her rear claws deep into my skin. She landed on the counter, then zoomed into the living room.

Chester launched next (also digging his claws deep into my thighs). He skidded on the old linoleum as he chased after the kitten. The sound of drumming paws raced through the small house. At least Chester was now getting more exercise.

After blinking away a few reactionary tears, examining the new hole in my best work pants, and idly threatening to drive both cats to the SPCA, I stared at the computer screen and paged through the AA-1 Bond Service site. It listed no personal information about the proprietor, and considering the type of business, that was probably a wise choice. But a page entitled "Other Services" touted that Richard Wilson sidelined as a bounty hunter. Other than that tidbit, I could find no more reference to him anywhere online.

My fingers hesitated over the keys. Then I typed in the name I had typed and deleted and typed and deleted over the years. Wanting to know. Fearing to know. I typed in "Jeffrey Bloom."

And then the roof caved in, and no, I'm not being metaphorical. Large chunks of drywall, splinters of wood, and pink fiberglass insulation showered the table. When I gathered the courage to look up, Eric's work boot dangled through the hole overhead.

"Sorry, Audrey," was his muffled response through the ceiling.

"Are you okay?" I called.

"Yeah, I . . ." The work boot swiveled and then pulled back up through the gap. After another brief drywall dust shower, Eric's scruffy face appeared in the hole. "Sorry about that. The patch obviously is no longer an option, but I'll make sure I cover the roof until we can figure out what to do."

I dumped the debris off the laptop and moved my computer to the relatively unscathed counter while Eric thumped and bumped on my roof.

When the sound of tapping knuckles hit the glass window of the back door, I flipped down the screen.

Eric peeked his head in. "Audrey, sorry again about the roof. I don't have a tarp large enough in the truck, but I'll get something on there before that rain they keep talking about."

"Thanks, Eric."

"You okay?"

"Fine. Just a little tired." I pulled a bit of drywall out of my hair.

He pointed to the computer. "Working on that murder out at the encampment, are you?"

"Not really."

He came in and pushed the door closed behind him. That last inch or two takes quite some force. "I'll have to remember to plane that door down for you sometime. Add it to the list." He pulled out a chair at the table and sat. "Audrey, I need to ask you a favor."

"You asking *me* a favor? That's new." I felt awkward imposing on his skills and materials gratis, even though he swore to me he only used material left over from other jobs. "Anything up to and including a pound of flesh. In that case, take more. I would gladly spare you five, or even ten . . ."

"I know you're getting involved with this whole murder investigation thing. It's all over town how Foley deputized you and everything. I'm not sure it's such a good idea—"

"I agree with you. In fact, I'm sure it's a very bad idea. There's nothing I'd like more than to stay out of it."

"But . . ."

I inhaled deeply. And then had to stifle a sneeze because of all the dust in the air. I so wished the old cottage had retained some of Grandma Mae's scent. "But there's something I can't tell you about, something that's drawing me back in." I didn't know that my father was involved with the murder—and I didn't know that he wasn't. But I realized when I typed in his name that I had to know the truth.

He nodded. "Here's the favor I want. Keep Liv out of it. I don't care if you have to lock her up, lie to her, or pitch a fight. I don't want her in danger. Not ever, but especially not now."

"I don't want that, either. You know I'd do anything for her."

"And she'd do anything for you. And that's the problem. Promise me?"

I considered what the promise would entail. Lying to Liv was almost impossible. And she was such a naturally gifted snoop that keeping anything from her required superhuman cunning. But then I flashed back to that point, early in Liv's pregnancy, when she'd tackled a murderer who had come at me with a knife, claiming it was okay, since she led with her shoulders.

"I promise to do my best."

The computer yielded no clues to Jeffrey Bloom. It was like he fell off the map. Which one might expect, since apparently at some point he became Richard Wilson.

How did that happen? If my life were a movie, I'd say he entered witness protection, or joined the CIA. But those were probably the wishes of a little girl who wanted her father to be some kind of hero. The truth was probably darker and less palatable.

When tires rumbled on the stone driveway next door, I decided a visit with Mrs. June might be in order. I doubted she'd have any more news on the official investigation, since it was outside of Ramble proper. And if Bixby didn't feel comfortable tying up town resources for county business, Mrs. June ranked high on that list of town resources. Then again, even if I came up empty in terms of information, at least there'd be cake.

"I wish I had something for you," she said as the knife hit the bottom of the glass cake plate that I'd never seen her table without—or empty of its orange chocolate cake. "I copied that file for him, volunteered as a personal favor. Even did it on my lunch hour. But then he took all the fun out of it by giving you the information himself. Sorry about the ketchup on page forty-seven."

"He didn't say anything else?"

"Only some choice words about Sheriff Foley, but I won't repeat them." Mrs. June licked a glob of frosting from her thumb. "They might peel the paint off the walls. And I'm awful partial to this color."

"That bad? I thought they were all in the same political party."

"It gets more complicated than that. Mind you, I only know this because my daddy was chief of police for a lot of years. And I tell you, it's a hard job to keep. My father was an exception to that rule, as is Bixby. Foley really stuck it to him."

I washed down a bite of cake with a sip of lemonade. "Sheriff Foley must have confidence in Chief Bixby to entrust him with the investigation."

"See, that's how most people think. And that's how Bixby still thinks, even after all these years, or else he'd find some loophole to wriggle out of. But he's determined he's going to figure out who the murderer is and bring him to justice."

"Well, that's his job, right?" I dug my fork into the last bit of moist chocolate, saving the frosting for last.

"That's Foley's job. Only right now he's too busy giving sound bites to reporters on the other side of the county. All he's basically doing there is drinking coffee and manning the roadblocks, trying to pretend like he's some hero, stopping, dropping, and rolling to prevent the spread of the flames to those expensive homes owned by some of his most ardent"—she rubbed her fingers together in the universal symbol of megabucks—"supporters."

"Sending a killer to justice is heroic." I even found myself defending Bixby.

"Ah, but there's the rub. The chief will be branded a failure if he doesn't. And then the mayor replaces him. Bixby can come out all right if he succeeds, then the mayor holds a press conference and pats him on the back. That is as long as the investigation doesn't step on the toes of too many supporters."

"Surely people want to see the killer in jail." And here I thought Bixby's job was more about fighting crime and less about politics.

"Sure, but in the meantime, they don't want to be detained, questioned, or otherwise inconvenienced while he does the job. And heaven forbid the investigation has an impact on the local economy. You might not believe it, but that silly camp brings in a lot of local revenue. And then if Bixby does succeed in catching the killer while not ruffling any other feathers, folks better not like the person he arrests."

"So much for protect and serve."

Mrs. June shrugged. "What can you do?"

"Well, I guess I can help him."

"That-a-girl."

"Just, if you happen to talk to Liv, tell her I'm *not* working on it."

My fingers tapped the table inches from where my phone rested. Just how badly did I want to learn about my father?

My mother liked to live with the idea that he fell off the face of the earth. Grandma Mae had explained to me that he was gone. She'd let me cry on her shoulder. Mother never mentioned his name again. She removed every trace of him from the house. Disposed of every family picture that he was in. It was like we'd stepped into some *Twilight Zone* alternate reality where he had never existed. I certainly wasn't going to tell her that he'd just resurfaced, and in the middle of a murder investigation. Not that I had mentioned to my mother anything about what Liv called my recent sleuthing experiences. And Liv had promised not to tell her mother. Apparently, as identical twins, our mothers lived completely different lifestyles yet were still unable to keep secrets from each other.

But my mother also was the only person who would know the full circumstances of my father's disappearance. Maybe there was more to this story, something I was never told because it was too painful or I was too young.

Finally, with my gut twisted into a knot, I called her.

"Audrey? Is something wrong?" Okay, it had been a while since I had called her.

"No, Mom. Everything's fine. Well, almost. I . . . well, I just started seeing a new doctor." Which was true. My old one had retired.

"Seeing as in dating? Or seeing as in paper gowns and stethoscopes?"

"As a patient."

"I knew it. I told myself that Audrey doesn't call at dinnertime for no reason. I knew there had to be something wrong."

"I interrupted your dinner. I'm sorry."

"Nonsense. If you can't call your mother during dinner, who can you call? Maybe the chef can reheat the plate for me if it gets cold."

"Chef? You're in a restaurant. Now's not a good time. I'll call back."

"I'm not in a restaurant, and don't you dare hang up. What was this about a doctor?"

"Just that . . . I was filling out the forms for some tests

he wants to do . . ." I didn't mention it was just my cholesterol screening. "I'm sure it's nothing."

"Always best to get these things checked out, I always say."

"Yes, well, the chart asks for medical information for both biological parents. I have all the information from your side of the family, but the father's side is completely blank."

Dead silence. Time for plan B. Too bad I didn't have a plan B. Plan A was simply to get the subject around to my father and hopefully let her normal talkative nature fill in the details. That wasn't working.

"Fine," she said. "What do you need to know?"

"Heart problems?"

"Oh heavens! You have heart problems?"

"No, just a generic question."

I could hear her soft sigh of relief. "Well, I think his father passed away of a heart problem. But he was well into his seventies at the time."

"Family history of stroke?"

"Not that I'm aware of."

"High blood pressure?" I sure hoped she'd cave before I got to gout and halitosis.

"I don't know. He might have, but it was so long ago. He might have developed something after he left."

Was that enough of a crack? "Mom, this is hard to ask, but is there any way you know of that I could get this information from him?"

Dead silence again. I'd pushed too hard.

"I don't know where he went," she started, her voice soft and tentative. "I'd say to check with his doctor. He might have asked to have his medical records forwarded. Or maybe his former employer. His last paycheck must have gone somewhere. I sure didn't see it. Then again, they might not have given it to him under the circumstances."

"What circumstances? Who was his employer?"

"Well, I didn't want to tell you this when you were younger. I know you adored your father."

I worked hard to control my breathing. Did I want her to go on?

"But there was some problem at the company where your father worked."

"Problem?"

"Some silly accounting thing, most likely. I can't say I paid all that much attention." I could imagine her waving it off. "I'm not sure it had anything to do with him leaving when he did. You must have known we were having problems."

Yeah, the screaming was a huge hint. Not that you can see that in her personality now. She'd become a queen-of-ice society maven.

"Still," I said, "maybe they kept some records. Health records, I mean. Or forwarding information."

"I suppose it's possible. But do me this one favor. If you find your father . . . don't tell me."

"Gotcha."

"Well, Audrey, I hope your tests go well. Let me know what they find out. But now I really must dash back to my dinner. Can't keep the governor waiting."

"The governor?"

"Yes. Didn't I tell you? We're having dinner at the governor's mansion."

I briefly recollected her saying she wasn't at a restaurant. "I'll let you get back then. Oh, wait! His former employer. What was the name?"

"Brooks Pharmaceuticals."

Chapter 7

I added just a bit of wax flower to a get-well arrangement I was making for a retired teacher recovering from a recent stroke. This one flower stymied me when it came to meanings. The wax plant carried the meaning of *susceptibility*, which is not one that I'd want to give to someone already infirmed, however true that might be. But I wasn't quite sure the modern wax flower came from what Victorian gardeners called the wax plant. I think the flower was actually called a wax myrtle, which carried the meaning of *discipline* and *instruction*. Not what I would put in a get-well bouquet either, although you could stretch it to consider that perhaps the sender had received instruction from the recipient and was grateful. Now, myrtle would have signified *love in absence*, which made more sense to me . . .

Then again, this was another arrangement from a picture and someone had probably chosen the flower because of color, texture, and cost. So unromantic. Which was why I was more than happy to leave the bulk of this part of the business to Liv and concentrate on bridal bouquets.

I glanced up at the clock. And then at Liv, hoping she didn't notice me watching the time. I also hoped she hadn't caught on to how quickly I was working through our light workload. That would spoil everything.

But just then the door burst open. Eric didn't even stop to greet his wife. "Audrey, you have to come right away!"

"What is it?"

"It's the cottage. We've run into a bit of a . . . sticky issue with the septic system. We need you right away to figure out what to do about it."

I glanced at Liv. "I hate to leave you with all the work."

She shooed me away. "No, you go ahead. Take care of what you need to. Amber Lee is still here, and Opie wanted to pick up some hours tonight since she got kicked out of that silly camp. And we somehow got ahead of ourselves this morning anyway."

Was that a flash of suspicion that crossed her face? I hung up my apron and grabbed my light jacket. "Thanks, Liv. You're a doll."

"Just go take care of that cottage." She shook her head.

As I rolled away in the passenger seat of Eric's truck, I waited two blocks before speaking. "What in the world is a sticky septic problem? Do you think she bought it?"

"I'd say it's our best bet. She knows that place of yours is a money pit. Sorry, Audrey. But it's true."

My head bumped against the ceiling of his truck's cab when he pulled into my rutted driveway.

"Are you sure you don't want a ride to the encampment?" he said. "I heard it's quite a trek into that place."

The CR-V was still back at the shop, where it could be used for small deliveries. And hopefully help convince Liv that I was back at the cottage with Eric.

"No, it's okay. I found a shortcut through Larry's place. And I can bike there from here." Although the thought of biking to Larry's in medieval garb did give me pause. At least I could wear Nick's loaner clothes and not that serving wench outfit. I had returned that fiasco to the costume shop. All except the medieval yellow urine cape, which had disappeared amid the excitement of Brooks's death. The owner of the shop had raised a fuss and was still figuring out what to charge me. If it were my shop, I wouldn't want it back.

That was yet another reason to return to the encampment. Maybe I'd come across the cape and get away with late fees instead. Then again, that might mean touching it.

Bixby's advice not to go alone flashed briefly into my mind, but I still knew a lot of people there—Nick, Brad, Melanie, Carol, Shelby, and Darnell—so I didn't imagine I'd be alone for long.

As I pushed open Eric's truck door, I stopped for a moment. "Thanks for giving me an excuse to get out of there."

"And thanks for leaving Liv out of it. But mind, you be careful, too. If anything happened to you, I'd never forgive myself. And if Liv found out I was colluding with you, she wouldn't forgive me either, for that matter. So my life and future happiness are in your hands."

"I'll do my best."

He flipped off the ignition.

"You're staying?"

"I hate to tell you this, but you really do have a sticky problem with your septic system."

Larry was hosing out a plant tray when I came huffing and puffing up his driveway. I'd deserted the bike and locked it to a skinny tree at the main road, since access to his place was up a steep incline. It wouldn't be so bad going home.

He did a double take. "Well, so Joan of Arc is back. I take it you're here to sneak through my property and not to see an old friend." He tilted his head. "Coming to play dress-up in the woods or are you working on the murder?"

"The second, but if you see Liv, I wasn't here at all. I'd appreciate it, and Eric might even pay you for your discretion."

"Ah, I can see where that would be a problem. Your cousin doesn't take well to being left out of the thick of things. Sure. She won't hear anything from me. But if you're going on to that camp, could you tell those yahoos that the invitation to cut through my property doesn't extend to all of them?"

"More people are cutting through here?"

"I think so. Found some footprints along with the livestock tracks. Unless they were just here to collect the animals. Looked like there was a pig rooting through here last night, too. If he's not careful, he's going to end up as bacon."

"You wouldn't do that."

A smile tickled the corner of his mouth. "Maybe not. But I heard Bacon U might be looking for a new mascot."

"I'll pass the word. Private property."

"Hey, Joan, if they invite you for lunch, avoid the steaks, eh?" He winked and the corners of his eyes crinkled.

I groaned and saluted and crisscrossed over the muddy puddles Larry's hose had left as I made my way over his fence and along the old deer path to the encampment.

Again, the transition seemed almost magical.

Merchants' tents flapped in the breeze and cooking smells came from several of them, masking the rawer smells that I was sure were there. A few peasants strolled past the vendors, who called out, hawking their wares. My stomach rumbled just a little, but I wasn't sure what they used for money in this place. And with a poisoner on the loose . . .

Was poisoner even a word? Poisonist? Poisonista?

Anyway, it wasn't an appetite stimulant, that's for sure.

"Well, hello, Audrey!" Andrea was the first person I recognized. She was still in her blue dress.

"Andrea, I would have thought you were on your honeymoon by now."

"This is our honeymoon! Nothing we like better." Her face dimmed. "Not that anything has gone exactly as we might have planned."

"I'm so sorry about your father-in-law."

"Sad thing is that you might be one of the few who are." She sighed. "That sounded bad." She took me by the arm as we strolled down the main thoroughfare. "It's not that anyone really wanted him dead. They're just so relieved he's not alive anymore." She stopped in her tracks. "That didn't come out much better."

"I've heard that he could be difficult."

"That's one way of putting it. Do you know he actually tried to buy me off?"

"Buy you off?"

"Pay me not to marry his son. Said he'd make it worth my while. I refused, but I still signed his silly prenup, just to prove to him I wasn't after the Brooks bank account."

"I'm so sorry. Families can be difficult."

"And don't tell Mom about the prenup. She would have had a cow. You know what Mel did? It wasn't fifteen minutes after the ceremony that he tore the thing right in two and threw it into the fire, just to spite his father." She winced. "Oh, that sounds even worse."

"Mel?" I wasn't sure that I'd even heard the groom's first name before.

"Short for Melvin."

"Yikes." Mel Brooks? Like the director? Scenes of old movies started running in my head. Poor kid. What was his father thinking? And why didn't his mother stop him?

"That's what I'm saying. If your father named you Melvin, would you like him, either?"

As we rounded the corner, I swear I saw Peter Pan with a video camera. When I blinked, I realized it was Brad in green breeches, a green tunic, and a green hat. I couldn't help a chuckle.

"Joan of Arc has no right to laugh at Robin," he said.

"Robin?" Andrea asked.

"I must look like Robin Hood, right? I hoped I wouldn't have to film in costume, but this camp has a rep for being strict, so I'm glad I came prepared. But it's giving me some strange desire to hide in the woods lying in wait for crooked lawmen."

"Well, as a duly deputed lawman, I appreciate your restraint. As to the costume, I was thinking Peter Pan actually," I said.

"Ditto," Andrea said. "I mean, verily."

"Thanks, now I have to avoid crooked sheriffs *and* pirates. Good to know." He set the bulky camera on the ground.

"Your crew still not here?" I asked as Andrea rubbernecked a vendor tent.

"Last I was able to check, they were stuck between roadblocks in two different counties. Can't go forward and can't go back. What idiot does that? But I'm out of communication now. Say, Audrey . . ." He leaned closer. "You don't happen to have a cell phone on you, do you? My battery and my backup battery died last night."

"Yeah, but don't tell anyone." I turned around to retrieve the cell from my cleavage, the only place I could think to keep it since Nick's clothes didn't have pockets, then palmed it to Brad.

"Still warm." He sent me a wicked grin that brought the heat to my cheeks as he made his way out to the woods.

Andrea stared off at Brad. "I thought you were seeing that baker guy, Nick."

"It's complicated."

"I guess so."

"And I'd appreciate it if you wouldn't blow me in."

"You mean Nick doesn't know? Or is it Brad that doesn't know about Nick?"

I laughed. "Nick and Brad know about each other. I meant please don't turn me in for the cell phone."

"Gotcha. Oh!" Andrea stumbled forward as she was bumped from behind. She caught her balance and turned around.

I couldn't believe my eyes. Shelby and Darnell, swords drawn, were circling each other.

I took a step back. "Are those sharp?"

"No," Andrea said, "they're dulled so they're safer. Just annoying."

"Oh, come on, man," Darnell said to Shelby. "I don't want to hurt you." Darnell played football for Bacon U, and he cut an imposing figure, even without the sword in his hand.

Shelby was shorter and much slighter, but seemed to be brandishing his weapon with more finesse. "Ah, but while you were carrying the pigskin down the field, I was fulfilling my PE credits with fencing class." Shelby demonstrated a series of complicated moves, ending with removing Darnell's hat. He waved his sword in front of Darnell's face. "I am Inigo Montoya. You killed my father. Prepare to die."

"Oh, I love that movie," I said.

Darnell hadn't given up, however, and did his best to hold

off Shelby's advance while Andrea and I stood watching them. Shelby clearly had the skill advantage, but he was well matched by Darnell's size and athleticism. When no winner was decided after ten minutes, they called it a truce, wiped the sweat from their brows, and headed off for a tankard of something.

"There you are, my love." Melvin Brooks came up behind Andrea and circled his arms around her waist.

Melvin Brooks. Mel Brooks. The guy with a motive from birth. And as he trailed kisses down his bride's neck, he didn't look like he was mourning all that much for dear old Dad. No wonder the happy couple was high on Bixby's suspect list.

"I'm so sorry about your father," I said.

Melvin straightened up, cleared his throat, and tried to look appropriately sober. "Thanks, Audrey. I really appreciate that you tried to help. Everyone else just stood around."

"I'm not sure anything could have been done at that point. Any idea who might have wanted to poison your father?"

Andrea looked at Mel.

Mel looked at Andrea.

Andrea spoke first. "There is that Hines fellow."

"Chandler Hines?" I asked. There was another of Bixby's prime suspects.

"You know him?" Andrea asked.

"His name's come up," I said.

"He and Dad never got along," Mel said. "But it was nothing more than a difference of opinion about how things should be handled here. Ego, mainly, I think. They both wanted to be big shots for different reasons."

"Did they quarrel?" I asked.

"More than quarrel," Andrea said. "There was that threat."

"Threat?" I turned back to Mel. "Hines threatened your father?"

"More like they threatened each other," he said. "Publically. I thought it was more of an act, a staged disagreement. Like that sword fight. They were going to settle it with a joust—not murder. To poison someone like that . . . it really doesn't fit into that whole Guardians of Chivalry ideal.

"Personally," he continued, "I think what happened to Dad must have been just a terrible accident. I saw what that monkshood root looks like, and it probably went into the stew as a turnip. I hope our corporate lawyers aren't too aggressive with that poor Nick Maxwell. Apparently those vultures are already faxing forms to my office for me to sign, seeking punitive damages. But I'm no ambulance chaser. They're just going to have to wait until after the funeral."

"And the honeymoon," Andrea said.

"Suing?" I'd never even considered the idea that legal actions could be taken against Nick, probably since I couldn't fathom Nick being involved—intentionally or unintentionally. I glanced over to his tent, where loaves of bread were piled waiting for customers—who all seemed to be avoiding that space.

But surely they couldn't sue Nick if the real killer were caught. For Nick's sake, I forced my attention back to Mel and Andrea and the one man on our suspect list who had seemed eager to charge at Brooks with a pointy stick. "A joust sounds dangerous. Can't someone be killed?"

"They have special rules to prevent that kind of thing," Mel said. "The lances are designed to break apart before they cause serious injury."

"People still get hurt," Andrea added.

"Mostly from falling off a horse," Mel said. "Which, I

must admit, had a lot to do with the horses that Dad brought in. They tend to be a little high-strung."

"Except for his," Andrea said.

"Ah. So Chandler Hines might not have wanted to settle his dispute on the tournament field if he didn't think the competition was fair."

Mel's countenance fell. "I never thought of it that way. I just assumed he loved the attention of challenging the dark knight. That's what my dad liked to call himself."

"Maybe that's the case." I sent him what I hoped was my most reassuring smile. "If I wanted to have a word with this Hines fellow, where would I find him?"

"Chandler Hines is the blacksmith," Andrea said. "At the edge of the encampment near the tournament fields. You can't miss the sound."

I stopped to listen. Even above the crowd sounds and the buzz of the surrounding forest, the unmistakable clang of metal striking metal chimed out at regular intervals.

"Thanks."

As Mel and Andrea walked off to explore the vendors, Brad came out of the woods and palmed my cell phone back to me, keeping a grip on my hand.

"Uh, Audrey. Now's probably not the best time, but there's something I need to talk with you about. In the next few days."

"Sure." I pulled my hand back and turned toward the woods to replace my cell. I sure hoped he didn't want to talk about "us." I had no idea where I wanted to go with our relationship. "Any news about your crew?"

He shook his head. "Not any good news. They're still trapped between roadblocks, but a farmer took them in, apparently trading food and lodging for help on his farm." He chuckled. "I can't see any of those guys milking a cow.

I hope I can't be held liable if they mess up." His smile dimmed. "And I really hope the farmer doesn't have a daughter. One hears things."

I hit him in the arm. "I'm going to talk to the blacksmith. Want to come?"

"That depends. Are you curious about the ancient art of iron working? Or is this part of your quasi-official investigation?"

"The investigation," I said.

He took my arm as we headed toward the metal sounds. There was something both old and comforting about Brad's touch, but also exciting. He was always spontaneous and a bit adventurous. I could see he loved his new job, despite the lack of a regular income. Our conversations on the phone had revolved around his travel experiences and the interesting people he encountered. A life with Brad wouldn't be predictable.

As we strolled past Nick's stand, I was going to wave to him, but he was busy and facing the other way when we passed. Or was he pretending to be busy? He certainly had no customers to deal with.

The idea that I might have hurt Nick caused me pain. It was different when Brad was long distance and Nick was here. But the two men together in the same place made it obvious to me that I'd have to make a decision between the two. It wasn't fair to pretend a relationship had a future when it didn't. Only which one was I going to let go?

I was so lost in thought that Brad had to steer me around a pile of manure in the pathway in front of the blacksmith's forge.

"Be right with you," the hulky man who I assumed was Chandler Hines said. He made several more strikes of his hammer on the piece of iron he was working on his anvil, sending flakes of red-hot metal flying into the dust near his boots.

I knew what an anvil was from watching Wile E. Coyote as a child.

Hines quenched the metal in a wood trough before tugging off his gloves. He pulled a rag from his pocket, wiped his forehead, and approached the fence that cordoned off his work area, probably to keep curious kids and animals away from the hot metal.

"Well, if it isn't Peter Pan and Joan of Arc." He squinted at Brad's camera. "And I categorically refuse to be filmed. You can't put me in your little video without my consent. And you don't have it."

I may have been wrong about Chandler Hines squinting at Brad's camera. It seems Hines bore a perpetual squint behind what looked like ancient service-issued plastic-framed glasses. He had a sparse head of close-cropped white hair, a mouth void of many of its teeth, and porous, sunburned skin. Or maybe his complexion came from working near the heat wearing a long-sleeved tunic, heavy breeches, a leather apron, and gloves.

"Are you sure?" Brad said. "The series might be good for business."

Hines just continued to squint at him, then turned back to shovel more coal into his forge. Heat rose in waves above it, and as he stared inside, the glow from the fire reflected from his glasses and face.

"Wait!" I said. "That's not why *I'm* here. I have nothing to do with the filming. I just wanted to ask you a few questions about what happened the other night."

"I don't get paid none for talking."

"What if I bought something?" I looked around at the

wares of his shop. Nothing struck me as exceedingly useful. Unless I wanted a horseshoe for good luck. Maybe if I tacked it up over the door of Grandma Mae's cottage, a stiff wind wouldn't blow the whole building down.

Then I saw some narrow farming implements and had an idea.

"Plant stand? Like a shepherd's hook? Can you make me one?"

He looked doubtful. "Not much call for those in the Middle Ages."

"If it helps, you can pretend I'm herding sheep with it."

He rolled his eyes but put the end of a metal rod into the flames. "What do you want to know?"

"I've heard you weren't a fan of Brooks," I started.

"A lot of people here weren't exactly fans."

"Why didn't you like him?"

"Not much there to like, in my opinion. Pompous braggart and cheater."

"Cheater?"

"Some of us work hard at what we do. I travel the circuit, from the serious re-creation camps to those silly Renaissance fairs, working metal year round. I've made more than one suit of armor. Brooks admires mine one day. Asks me if I'd make him a suit. Can't say I was motivated to give him the friends-and-family rate."

"So he went elsewhere."

"Which was fine by me," Hines said. "That was kind of my objective. Only a month later, guess who comes strolling up in a shiny new suit."

"And that's a problem?" Brad asked.

"He didn't get a craftsman to make that for him. It would take months." Hines spat at the ground. "Now, I've heard of a sweatshop in China that uses modern machinery and child labor to make armor for clients at half my going rate. And that's probably with the factory owners taking most of that."

"And you didn't like him showing it off?" I said. Could Brooks have been killed because he wasn't wearing authentic made-in-America armor? "You must have been concerned that if word got around, the Chinese might eat into your profits."

"No, I didn't like him showing it off. But it turns out I didn't have to worry about the Chinese. That fool Brooks pretended that he made it himself."

I quirked an eyebrow.

"Oh, yes, he acted like he'd whipped it off in his workshop over the weekend. I didn't like him strutting around as if that made him a legitimate craftsman. And I didn't like him pretending to be some kind of philanthropist simply because he trucked in his horses and some rented livestock for a week. In short, you could probably say that I didn't like him."

"But he's dead . . ."

"Doesn't make him a stand-up guy now." Hines pulled the glowing rod out of the fire and started forming it into a familiar hook shape.

"Do you have any idea who might have wanted to see him dead?"

"Besides me, you mean?" He looked up. "Because that is what you mean."

I shrugged my most innocent shrug.

He finished shaping the hook then quenched it in a trough of water before speaking. "You know, it seems to me that poison is a sneaky kind of weapon." He crossed two beefy arms across his chest. "I figure you're looking for a sneaky kind of killer."

"What are you getting at?"

"Look, if someone had bashed his skull in . . ."

"Say, with an iron rod," Brad said.

Hines glared at him. "Yes, with an iron rod, then I might be a good suspect. But it seems you've got yourselves a sneaky killer. And that's probably someone sneaky enough to come off as liking the guy."

"And that helps how?" Brad asked.

"Because he wasn't very likable," I said.

Hines squinted and nodded, then handed over my completed shepherd's hook. "That'll be sixty-nine ninety-nine."

"But I can get the same thing at the hardware store for ten bucks," I said.

"Not handcrafted in an authentic medieval forge."

"I can pay you in American currency? I don't have to trade in for doubloons or something?"

"Nope. We've talked about developing our own script, but never did. Regular U.S. money is fine."

I turned to Brad. "Could you pay the man? I'll pay you back."

"You didn't bring any money?"

"I did, but I can't get to it right now." It was stuffed in my unmentionables along with my cell phone. And I wasn't going to pull it out in front of Chandler Hines.

Brad removed a wad of bills from his pocket. "I don't suppose you'll give *me* the friends-and-family discount."

Hines shook his head and pocketed the cash in his apron.

"Oh, one more thing," I said. "You said we should be looking for someone sneaky. Someone who seemed to like Brooks. Can you think of anyone who might fit that bill?"

Hines thought for a moment, and then nodded. "There's this one guy. New to the circuit. Caught him snooping around a time or two, asking a few too many questions. And he did seem rather interested in Brooks."

Now we're talking, I almost said aloud. "And who is this?"

"That guy in that stupid cassock. Richard something."

"Wilson?"

"That's it."

Of course.

Chapter 8

Brad excused himself to film a demonstration on tanning. I assumed he wasn't talking about the tanning that takes place on a beach with a good book and a thermos of lemonade. As he excitedly explained the process, going on about a solution of lime and removing the hair from an animal hide, it threatened to turn my stomach. But apparently not enough to keep me from lunch.

Nick's stand in the medieval bazaar was just as void of customers as it had been when I passed the first time—and the stack of bread just as tall.

"Got any bread to spare for a hardworking lawman?" I said as I slapped the counter. "Wait. What did they call lawmen in the Middle Ages?"

He handed over a whole loaf of crusty brown bread. "For my special customers," he said with that twinkle in his eye, "I might have even saved some butter." He reached below the counter and pulled up a ball of pale gold butter. "They churn it fresh daily. I've never had anything like it."

I tore off a bit of the bread and spread the butter on it with a scary-looking knife he provided.

"And as far as what they called lawmen back in the Middle Ages," he said, "each shire or county would have a reeve—a representative of the king. I guess shire-reeve eventually became—"

"Became *sheriff*. Cool." I took a bite of the bread. "Is that honey?" Then I closed my eyes and enjoyed the blend of sweetness and whole grains with the creamy and salty butter. "Mmmm."

When I opened my eyes, Nick was grinning and several customers had lined up behind me.

"I'll have what she's having," one said.

"You should make this in the shop," I said when Nick finished dealing with the new customers.

"I do. But something about the wood oven and the open air makes it even better."

"Hey"—I picked up my shepherd's hook—"can I leave this with you?"

"Sure." He lifted it over the counter and slid it under the table. "I . . . uh . . . saw you and Brad headed that way this morning. Learn anything?"

"Chandler Hines thinks we need to look for someone who was pretending to like Brooks. Says anyone sneaky enough to poison him would be sneaky enough to avoid looking like he had a motive."

"Ah, the old sneaky killer theory."

"Okay, pretty basic stuff. But you've been part of these encampments. Can you think of anyone who fits that bill?"

"Who liked Brooks? I can't say I've seen too many buddy-

buddy with him. Although he seemed pretty friendly with that co-worker of his that came down. Raylene something."

"More than co-workers, you think?"

"I couldn't prove it," Nick said. "Brooks seemed to like the ladies. Which you probably would have found out if you'd stayed a few minutes longer in that serving wench's getup. I mean, wow."

I could feel the heat rush to my face. Fortunately, that's when another customer came up to the counter for bread.

I composed myself by slathering another bit of bread with butter. Or maybe I finished the loaf.

"Whoa," Nick said when he turned back to me. "Would you like another one?"

"Save me one for the road, will you?" I brushed the crumbs from the counter and leaned toward him. "Another name did come up, though. Someone Chandler Hines said seemed interested in Brooks."

"Who was this?"

I felt my throat go dry and wished for water to wash down the last few crumbs of bread. "Richard Wilson," I managed, but found it impossible to keep eye contact when I said it.

"I don't . . . wait. Is that the friar? We just call him Father Richard."

"He's not a real priest, you know."

"I kind of figured that. Come to think of it, I did see him with Brooks once."

"Chandler Hines also thinks Wilson was sneaking around the camp."

Nick crossed his arms in front of him. "He was asking questions, but they didn't seem out of line for a newcomer."

"He's not been a part of the re-creations before?"

"Nope. First timer. At least to this one. Can't swear that

he hasn't been to others. I don't get to them like I used to. The whole responsible adult thing."

"Can I ask you a hypothetical question?"

"I think you just did."

I slapped his arm.

"Okay, shoot. What's the question?"

I sighed. I needed advice about what to do with Richard Wilson, aka Daddy Dearest, and if I asked Liv, she'd never let me keep it hypothetical.

"Say someone you loved disappeared from your life. Just gone. And then maybe years later reappears. No reasons. Just vague excuses. Would you give that person a chance? Even if that meant you could get hurt again?"

"Was this someone important to you?"

"I said it was hypothetical."

Nick leaned against the counter and reached out his hand. He pointed to a spot of coarse skin on his thumb. "Here. Feel this."

I ran a light finger against it. "What is it?"

"I had a defective oven mitt. I've gotten rid of it since, but before I did, I burned myself more than once. I guess that's nature's way of protecting me from my own foolishness."

"So you're saying I should protect myself."

He shook his head. "I'm saying the opposite. When you ran your finger across that spot, I couldn't feel anything. Not pain. Not pleasure. Nothing. I'm not so sure that's a good thing."

"What are you trying to tell me?"

"Audrey, I'm not sure I'm the best person to be asking this." He took my hands in his. "It's up to you how much of your life you open to someone else. But if the fear of being hurt rules your life, you'll put up guards and barriers and end up feeling nothing. And I'm not sure that feeling nothing isn't the worst pain of all."

I looked down at our clasped hands as he ran his thumbs across my knuckles. Was pain truly better than feeling nothing?

"Audrey," he said, "there's something I'd like to ask you, and not quite as hypothe—"

"Oh, that bread looks marvelous!"

The familiar voice made me whirl around. "Liv! What are you doing here?"

"Apparently interrupting a tender moment. But if I can get one of those loaves of bread, I'll gladly let you two pick up where you left off."

My jaw must have dropped as I scanned her outfit. I should say *my* outfit, because her medieval costume came right out of my closet. She wore one of my longer, elastic-waist skirts, with the waistband hiked up just above her baby belly. Because she's considerably shorter, the hem trailed just above the ground. And a white shirt was loose enough to button just above her baby bump. (Did they have buttons in medieval times, or was it just the Amish who don't wear them?) She'd rolled up the sleeves and looked like a proper peasant woman.

"I'm awfully hungry. It's still quite a hike from Larry's place."

"You walked from his place? Liv, Eric is going to kill me."

Nick placed a loaf of bread on the counter for Liv, brought up the remnant of the butter, and wisely turned to help another customer.

"Not if you don't tell him I was here," she said as she tore off a piece and slathered it with butter. She took a bite and closed her eyes. "How does he make it taste like this? It's just bread, right?"

I shook my head.

"It's not just bread?"

"I can't believe you followed me out here. In your condition."

"I can't believe you conspired with my husband to keep me from coming. If you both hadn't been so all-fired sneaky, I might not have come. As for my condition, I am not an invalid. I am not a child. I don't need anyone's permission to go where I want and do what I want."

"We're going back right now. One man has died here already. It could be dangerous."

Liv gestured toward the crowd. People strolled around the bazaar, all dressed in their finest medieval togs. A group of minstrels tuned their strings, and several children engaged in a game of tag near the edge of the clearing. The atmosphere was sunny and cheerful. "The most dangerous things are those garderobes. I'm not going back until I eat my bread and look around a bit. Besides, I'm not eating anything but Nick's bread."

"That's not the point. Well, that's part of the point. Maybe Brooks died because it took him so long to get help. What would happen if you went into labor right now?"

"We'd go to Larry's. Come on, Audrey. Childbirth isn't like that. Especially for a first baby. It's usually hours and hours of contractions." Her face paled when she said that last part. "And I'm not due for another two weeks."

"I don't want to be responsible for putting you or your baby in danger."

"You're not. I came out here on my own two feet." Liv glared at me with that determined look in her jaw, then tore off a bit of bread and popped it into her mouth.

Still, I wasn't about to tell her that her arrival put a kink in my new resolve to talk with my father, for which I was almost relieved.

"Is it safe?" Nick asked as his latest customer wandered away.

"Stalemate," I said. "But you were going to ask me something."

"It can wait until later." He ran a rag along the wood planks he was using as a countertop.

"Good." Liv turned to me. "So are you going to show me around?" She gobbled her last piece of bread.

I took Liv by the arm. "One stroll through this place and then we go."

I think we'd taken three steps before she stopped to watch a glassblower. He worked on his design, blowing, shaping, and then reheating the glass, while a pudgy woman at the counter sold one of his creations. His glassware was pretty and his methods traditional, but I doubt many people in the Middle Ages would have use for his mostly decorative work. But one tall red vase in the back caught my eye. Liv and I went for the price tag at the same time.

She reached it first. "This would be perfect for our annual Valentine's display. Or even Christmas." She lowered her voice. "But it's three hundred dollars."

"Aren't you supposed to dicker at these places?" I said.

"Can I help you?" The pudgy woman had made her way to us.

"We were admiring this vase," Liv said.

"But it's more than we can pay," I added.

"Sorry to hear that." She started to turn away.

"Wait!" Liv called after her. "But we do own a local flower shop, and I was wondering if maybe we could come to an arrangement."

The glass blower finished his demonstration to the mild applause of the bystanders and made his way over to us. "What's up?"

"These people want a discount on the red vase," the woman said.

"For our shop window," Liv said. "We own the local flower shop. It would be on display several times a year for the whole town to see. And if people admire the vase, we can definitely tell them where we got it."

He stroked his chin. "I could do two hundred."

Liv bit her lip, but I could see the determination grow. "And if we sold it to them and then bought another one? Say on a consignment basis?"

The pudgy woman sent Liv a nasty look then walked away to another customer who was admiring the "medieval" reflecting balls.

"I could do one fifty."

"And if we displayed your card predominately right next to the vase?"

"You're killing me," he said. "One hundred. Final offer."

"Sold!" Liv said.

As Liv counted out her cash, I turned around and caught a quick flash of cassock headed around a corner. Apparently I needn't worry about avoiding my father. He seemed to be avoiding me.

The herbalist shop was closed as we passed, but I stopped to peek at the fresh potted and dried herbs on display. I couldn't wait to revive Grandma Mae's herb garden in the spring. I saw rosemary (*remembrance*), sniffed the fresh thyme (which can mean *activity*, *courage*, or *thriftiness*), and stopped when I saw the basil. While I adore it on pizza, the meanings always confused me. Sweet basil, which I guess was the kind most used in Italian food, carried the meaning of *good wishes*. We'd given a large pot of it to Jenny and her mother at the grand reopening of their restaurant. But basil? I wasn't sure the Victorians were that keen on it, since in the language of flowers, basil translates to *hatred*.

Had the killer hidden his hatred of Brooks under the

guise of good wishes? And why monkshood? If he was cold and calculating, the killer might see poison as a bloodless way of getting the job done. But if someone had truly hated Brooks, he might have chosen monkshood for the suffering it caused. And then watched it happen. I shivered at that thought. Had the killer been one of the bystanders gathered around Brooks as he writhed on the ground?

Which also reminded me that I still needed to look up the meaning of monkshood. Not that the killer would have chosen the plant for its meaning, but it bothered me that I didn't recall it.

But it also occurred to me that an herbalist might have been able to identify monkshood and know of its deadly qualities. And Nick did say he got his herbs from the camp herbalist. Only monkshood root looks more like a vegetable than an herb. Nick wouldn't have made that mistake.

But that would have to wait until next time, because Liv's excited squeals told me she'd found the butter vendor. There'd be no haggling there. The pretty . . . well, I guess I'll have to call her a wench. Or maybe a dairy maid. Either way, the well-endowed brunette in the tight, low-cut bodice knew a sure sale when she had one. It wouldn't surprise me that the price had doubled since Nick bought his. She handed Liv two butter balls crudely wrapped in waxed paper.

"Here." Liv handed me one.

"What am I supposed to do with this?" I asked.

"You like butter."

"I know, but I've got nothing to carry it in. It will melt in my hands by the time I get it back home."

The dairy maid pointed across the aisle. "The woman over there is selling homemade bags. I send a lot of business her way."

"Great!" Liv headed over.

"Thanks," I said to the clerk.

"Anything else I can get for you? I also have some nice cheeses."

I scanned her selection of cheese, which, I must admit, I prefer to see in plastic wrappers or at least behind a glass case. The flies seemed to like them, though.

"Just looking." I aimed for a casual tone. "Some excitement here Saturday night, huh? Did you know the guy who died?"

"Trawling for information?"

"What gave me away?"

"Just about everyone here saw that sheriff deputize you. Word's gotten around that Joan of Arc is on the case."

There'd be no clandestine snooping here. "Thanks anyway."

"Hold on. I didn't say I wouldn't help. Brooks was no saint, but I can't say that I disliked him enough to wish that his killer gets away scot-free."

"Did you know him well?" I asked.

"Only on the circuit. Many of the vendors—we go to a lot of these. Some of the enthusiasts travel, too. Brooks would go to a few of these every year, so you get to know him."

"I heard he likes the ladies."

"Is that why you came to me?"

I could feel the blood rush into my cheeks. "I didn't mean—"

"Of course you did. And don't think it offends me. It's my schtick. How do you think I get most of my business? Couples walking through here. He holds the purse strings. She's all, 'Honey, can we get one of these, one of those?' and he's like, 'But it's so expensive,' and then she's like, "Can we at least get a pound of fresh-churned butter?" and he's about to say no, but then he sees me, and I might lean over a little.

And suddenly it's all, 'Whatever you want, honey.'" She laughed. "Happens every day."

"I—"

"But to answer your question. Yes Brooks liked the ladies. I used to have to fight him off with a stick. Well, not literally . . ."

"Did you ever see him with Richard Wilson?"

"The priest?"

Liv came rushing back with her newly purchased bag.

"Funny you should say that. Once I swore I saw him watching Brooks."

"Who?" Liv asked.

"The priest," the dairy maid said. "Richard Wilson."

"Oh, Audrey. A clue!" Liv practically squealed for the whole bazaar to hear. "Do you think the priest could be our killer?"

"No." I turned to the dairy maid. "Thanks anyway." I spun on my heels and started walking back.

"Audrey?" Liv called.

I didn't stop. Didn't turn. Just kept walking, almost wishing I were a child again so I could stop my ears and stamp my feet. I didn't slow until I heard Liv running behind me.

"Audrey, wait!"

I froze in my tracks until Liv caught up. "Audrey, what is it?"

"We need to go back," I said.

"But we . . ."

I turned to look at her, doing little to hide the tears now streaming down my face.

"There's something I don't know, right?" she said.

I nodded.

"Come on, kiddo. Let's go back." She took my arm and we negotiated the deer path to Larry's. We didn't talk as I helped her climb the short fence. Nor did we talk as we walked down that steep driveway.

Her car was waiting at the bottom. I managed to jockey the bike into her trunk. She drove me home, tapping her fingers in nervous energy on the wheel.

Suddenly I felt like I was seven, being driven home from school when the nurse realized I had the chicken pox. And almost just as itchy. I'd have to tell Liv something.

I swallowed and watched the fence posts passing.

Eric was gone by the time we pulled into the cottage driveway. He must have left before Liv had arrived, to allow her the opportunity to raid my closet and sneak off to the camp. As soon as we were in the back door, Liv put the kettle on the old electric stove and we both sat at the table, silent.

I closed my eyes. "It's my father." Then I opened my eyes quickly to see what Liv's reaction would be.

Only confusion. "Your father?"

"Richard Wilson, the priest, is my father."

"The priest is your father?"

"He's not a real priest."

"But you knew your father. His name wasn't Richard Wilson."

"It is now. At least when he's not known as suspect number one."

Chapter 9

Liv tacked another three-by-five card onto the board we normally used to track arrangements for large events.

"Do we have another job?" I asked.

"No. Slow week. These are suspects," she said. "I thought we could use this as our murder board."

"A murder board? You can't be serious." I looked up at the cards she had placed: Chandler Hines. Andrea and Mel Brooks. Raylene Quinn. Kathleen Randolph. I pulled down one card. "What's an unsub?"

She snatched the card back and tacked it up again. "It stands for 'unknown subject.' Don't you watch any television? Really, Audrey. You should make more of an effort to learn, especially since you're now officially in law enforcement."

I barely resisted the temptation to roll my eyes, but I got

her point. Whoever killed Brooks might not even be on our radar. Then my eyes fell to the card in her hand. "You got another one?"

Liv bit her lip. "I wasn't going to put it up." She hid it behind her back.

But Amber Lee was one step behind her and whisked the card away from her.

"Hey!" Liv cried. "Give it back."

"Highest bidder?" Amber Lee teased, fanning her face with the card. "I'll settle for my own parking space."

But our expressions must have dimmed the mood, because her smile faded and she handed the card back to Liv. "Wow, someone's got the grumpy bug today."

Meanwhile Opie pulled open the back door and returned to her pile of books stretched out on one of our worktables. Although business was too slow to categorize ourselves as shorthanded, Opie had begged some of Darnell's and Shelby's hours while they attended the re-creation. She was working on her paper between deliveries.

I held out my hand and Liv handed me the card. "Richard Wilson." I shrugged and pinned it onto her board, gaining just a little too much satisfaction as the push pin stabbed through the corkboard.

Liv winced. "Sorry, Audrey."

"Who's Richard Wilson?" Amber Lee asked.

"He's the friar, right?" said Opie. "Father Richard?"

I nodded.

"That's one spooky dude," she said. "Oh! And it makes sense! He's the friar, and Mr. Brooks was killed with monkshood. Why, that's diabolically clever. Like a signature."

"I think a truly clever killer would divert suspicion *away* from himself," Amber Lee said.

"Unless by obviously pointing to himself, he becomes

less of a suspect," Opie said. Then she knit her brows. "I don't know if that's clever or just confusing."

"But it reminds me . . ." I reached for my language of flowers guide and thumbed through until I found monkshood.

"What does it mean?" Liv asked.

"Knight-errantry," I said.

"Okay, you have to admit, that's spooky, too," Opie said.

"Spooky?" Liv asked.

"When you said the friar was spooky," I said, "what did you mean?"

Opie put the cap on her highlighter. "Nothing scary. Just very quiet. Always watching. Like he was studying everything and everybody. At first, I thought it went with the persona he was playing, but I don't know. He looked almost nervous, and it didn't seem like he was there because he enjoyed it."

"And that's not typical?" Liv asked.

"Well, a bunch of the college kids are like that, because we had to be there." She looked down at her stack of books. "And now I wish I was there. But Father Richard didn't seem all that thrilled with the place."

"Yet nobody was making him stay," I said.

"Sounds like he's a good suspect then," Amber Lee said, then stared at me. "But you're not happy."

I swallowed hard. I wasn't ready to share the news of my father's return with more people. Especially since he was now a suspect in a murder investigation. I'd felt much relieved to have shared the news with Liv. And she'd promised to discreetly see what she could learn from her mother and the Internet. Liv had a black belt in Google.

But I wasn't ready for everybody to know about my father just yet.

I was rescued from having to answer Amber Lee by the ding of the bell over the door.

"Audrey?"

I rushed to the front room and found Mrs. June hovering over the potted plants.

"You know," she said, "I still have a few of the perennials your grandmother gave me. I'll bet some of them could be grown from cuttings. Feel free to help yourself whenever you want."

"That's great," I said. I'd contemplated asking her. It would add another touch of Grandma Mae back into the old place. "I'll stop over and take a look."

Mrs. June leaned closer. "The plants are only one reason why I've come. I have news on the investigation."

I shook my head as imperceptibly as I could, even though Liv was in the back room. "Eric still wants to keep her out of it, but I don't think I can."

Mrs. June nodded.

"You might as well tell her now," Liv called out. "Because I will find out later." She peeked her head in the doorway. "There's no harm in just listening, right?" Liv smiled her cutest pixy-like smile, perhaps her most effective weapon. Those dimples alone were deadly.

Mrs. June looked to me, then to Liv. "First," she said, "we got some toxicology results back."

"That fast?" I said.

"Yes, it seems Sheriff Foley decided to contribute to the investigation, after all, and called in a few favors. He made a case to the FBI that if someone had tried to poison the whole encampment, we could have a serial killer on our hands, so they tested the stew in the pot, and the remnants that Brooks had apparently thrown on the ground, as well as the, uh . . ."

"Vomit?" I suggested.

"That's the word." She then waited—that flair for the dramatic again.

"And?" I finally said.

"The large pot was clean. But the food he'd thrown on the ground and the . . . other sample did contain some remnants of aconite. So—"

"So whoever put the monkshood in the stew had targeted only Brooks," Liv said. "That's good news, although kind of what we were going with."

"We?" I asked.

"*You*, I mean." She raised her hands in mock surrender.

"Does this mean the FBI has now taken over the case?" I wondered if my deputyship were now obsolete.

"Doesn't work like that," Mrs. June said. "I mean, they might have had more interest had the whole pot been poisoned, but as it stands now, local law enforcement has the case. Which means Foley, who's more than happy to delegate to Bixby. And you. But there's more. Just as I was getting ready to leave, a woman popped into the station and asked where Jans and Son was."

Jans and Son—the son in this case being Joe, whom the locals called Little Joe—were the local morticians.

"They need a bigger sign," Opie said. By this time Opie and Amber Lee had made their way to the front.

"But all the locals know exactly where they are," I said, "so this would have been . . ."

"The not-so-grieving widow," Mrs. June said. "She was mighty anxious to make arrangements, even though the body hasn't been released yet."

"Making arrangements here?" I asked.

"I guess she wants the remains cremated so she can travel with them more easily. That's all I really got from her. She doesn't seem the chatty type."

"That seems cold," Liv said.

"Or just pragmatic," I said. "I suppose I should go talk

with her. Maybe get a feel from her if Brooks thought he was in danger. Or if she knew of anyone who might have wanted to hurt him."

"She's staying over at the Ashbury," Mrs. June offered.

"I'll go with you," Liv volunteered. "Just to pay my respects, of course."

I held up a warning hand. "Just to the Ashbury, and then you come right back. I have to go back to the encampment." I sent Liv a knowing look. "I suppose I need to ask Richard Wilson a few questions."

"Oh!" Opie said. "If you're going back, could you find Carol for me? She has a book I need." She scribbled the title on a piece of paper and handed it to me.

"*Daily Life in the Middle Ages*?" I read. "Isn't that something she's going to need at the camp?"

Opie shook her head. "I think she knows it by heart."

Liv gnawed her cuticle. "Maybe you should take Opie with you."

"I'm not allowed back," Opie said.

"Or Amber Lee," Liv said.

"I already took my costume back to the shop," she said.

"Maybe I could just—" Liv started.

"Come to the Ashbury?" I said. "Sure."

The front desk was empty when we pulled open the restored doors of the historic inn. It took a moment for my eyes to adjust, but there was nobody at all in the lobby. It wasn't until we poked our head into the bar area that we saw an interesting assortment of characters. More than one were in medieval dress, but sitting in a Revolutionary War Era inn complete with up-to-date electric lighting and modernized to meet Virginia code. Apparently one didn't need a blue police box to travel in time. I only hope the merry men who sneaked off to frequent the local tavern didn't all cut through Larry's property and trample his plantings.

We found Kathleen Randolph sitting at a table with a blond woman with big hair and wearing a black pantsuit. A half-empty bottle of some kind of liquor—I'd say scotch, but I'm not an expert in potent potables—stood on the table between them, and based on their slouched postures and loud cackling laughter, I'd say they'd been at it for some time.

Liv leaned closer to me. "They don't seem all that broken up about it, do they?"

Kathleen raised her gaze to meet mine, smiled, and beckoned us over, managing to knock the liquor bottle over in the process, which was met by more raucous laughter. "Audrey, Liv. Come sit down and drink a toast with us. We're toasting the dear departed."

Kathleen tried to rise out of her seat, but lost her balance and fell hard against the old wood chair, which creaked in protest. Not that Kathleen was a large woman, just that the chairs were all exceptionally old.

Liv waved her back down and slowly lowered herself onto the third chair at their table. I pulled another one from an empty table and joined them. No, as Liv pointed out, neither of these women seemed especially distressed by the recent death. But on the other hand, it hardly proved their guilt, either. But maybe while their lips were sufficiently loose . . .

"We need more glasses," Kathleen said.

The big-haired blonde pointed to Liv's belly. "Maybe they want something else," she said in a drawl I suspected was as much booze as it was Texas. Maybe sixty-forty.

"Oh, right. Good idea." Kathleen signaled the waiter, who rushed over. Liv asked for a lemonade and I seconded that.

"See?" Kathleen told the blonde. "That's how they stay

out of trouble. Make a lot fewer mistakes that way." And then she stared morosely into her glass.

Yes, apparently misery loves company, but only if that company is also suitably miserable. Or comparatively toasted. So much for loose lips.

The blonde, whom I had decided must be Mrs. Brooks, seemed to pick up on Kathleen's mood shift. She lifted her glass and stared at the amber liquid. "I wonder how many bad decisions they pack into every bottle." She pushed herself into a straight posture. "I was drunk when Barry Brooks proposed to me. Not that it was one of them romantic proposals. He was drunk, too. Suggested we drive to Vegas and get hitched. Hardly the proposal of a girl's dreams. Apparently I was fool enough to go along with it, even though I was sober by the time the limo pulled into that chapel."

"That doesn't sound like the Barry I married," Kathleen said. "What? No prenup?"

My ears perked up at that. Even though Mrs. Brooks wasn't at the reenactment, she'd have a motive if she was going to inherit part of the estate. She could have hired someone.

"Ah," said the blonde, "apparently I signed that before I sobered up." So if the current Mrs. Brooks, who seemed to be enjoying her new single status, had wanted to divorce Barry Brooks, she would have done so without any of his money. I wondered if his will offered her better parting gifts than his prenuptial agreement. If it had, the victim might have handed his wife a really great motive.

"That's my boy," Kathleen shouted. "Liked his booze. Liked his women. Loved his money."

"Hear, hear!" Mrs. Brooks said, and raised her glass before downing it in one gulp.

The waiter slid two glasses of lemonade onto the table and wisely skedaddled while Kathleen refilled the whiskey glasses, sloshing a good part of the bottle onto the tablecloth in the process.

Liv sipped her lemonade while I cradled my glass in my hands, trying to figure out how to approach this woman. "Mrs. Brooks," I finally said.

"Oh, call me Dottie."

"Dottie, I was wondering . . . Did your husband seem apprehensive at all about coming to the camp this year?"

Dottie squinted at me, or maybe she was trying to look backward into her own skull to find the answer to my question. "I don't think so. He lived for these things. I don't know that he was looking all that forward to the wedding. I'm not sure he trusted his future daughter-in-law." Dottie reached out and patted Kathleen's hand. "No offense. I don't think he trusted anybody." She turned back to me. "But he was happy he didn't have to wear a tux. He hated those things." She snorted then turned back to Kathleen. "I should have him laid out in one. What do you think?"

"Cummerbund and everything?" Kathleen asked.

"With a big loud bow tie," Dottie said.

Kathleen clinked glasses with her. "Do it."

I waited for their cackling laughter to die down. "What about the people that your husband traveled with?" I said. "Could one of them have wanted him . . . you know."

"Dead?" she said.

Again the mood at the table had shifted to the morose. I was such a party pooper.

She sniffed. "Well, the first person who comes to mind would be Raylene, his mistress."

"You knew about his mistress?" Liv asked.

"My husband could hardly be considered discreet."

"Why do you think she might have killed him?" I asked. "Had the relationship gone south?"

"Well, I'm only guessing, but Barry had a short attention span, if you get my drift. He was always playing around. One of them tarts could have done him in, too, but who can keep track of them? But Raylene was more serious. She's a smart woman, smart like a fox, and Barry did ruin her life."

I cocked my head and waited for her to go on.

"Raylene was smart enough to rise in the ranks of Brooks Pharmaceuticals"—at least I think she was aiming for the word "Pharmaceuticals." Excessive scotch and good diction don't mix—"on her own. But Barry, he was the gatekeeper. I'm sure he made it very clear to her what promotion in the company would entail for a pretty woman."

"That's sexual harassment," Liv said.

"Yep. I suppose it is," Dottie said, then snorted. "After all, a glass ceiling is basically a horizontal surface, and Barry was fond of horizontal surfaces. And then there's the men in the company, all who couldn't advance because of . . . Raylene's unique qualifications."

"They might have been jealous and wanted him out of the way so everyone advanced," Liv said. I knew she had more names to add to her murder board.

"And"—Dottie shook her finger at the air near me—"there's everyone who ever did business with the man. He was ruthless."

"Hear!" Kathleen said.

"And devious."

"Hear, hear!"

"And didn't think the rules applied to him."

Kathleen stood up and hoisted her glass. "To Barry!"

"To Barry." Dottie crossed herself.

"To Barry," Liv said, and clinked her lemonade glass with mine.

Chapter 10

I arrived at Larry's just after one of Ramble's three police cars. I pulled in behind it. Other cars, several with out-of-state plates, were parked along the shoulder of the rural road. I suspected some of the reenactors had moved their vehicles from the parking lot to the road to be closer when they sneaked through Larry's property.

The driver's side door of the police car swung open and Bixby climbed out a bit hesitantly. I expected it had to do with his costume. He'd gotten with the program and was attired in what was probably not a very authentic peasant's outfit. He wore what looked like worn work pants that had been purposely tattered on the bottom and an oversized shirt that someone had tea-dyed to look old.

"Chief," I said, "you look—"

"Ridiculous," he growled.

Lafferty climbed out of the passenger seat, looking

almost an exact duplicate. "Oh, hi, Audrey," he said, twirling like a debutante so I could see his new duds. "Aren't they great? Judith made them out of old clothes she got from the thrift store. She can do anything."

At Lafferty's praise of Bixby's daughter, the chief couldn't hide a prideful smile. Bixby squinted at me. "Are you going to the camp? I thought I advised you not to go alone."

"Good thing you're here, then," I said.

I struggled to keep up with them as we climbed the steep driveway that led to Larry's greenhouses. This time there was no sign of him planting, weeding, watering, or fertilizing. I almost mistook him for a scarecrow when I finally spotted Grandma Mae's old friend parked by the fence with his shotgun in his hand.

"You be careful with that thing," Bixby called to him as he climbed the fence.

"Can't you do anything about those trespassers?" Larry said.

"Wish I could," Bixby said. "But you know it's not my jurisdiction. You have to call the sheriff."

"I do, but he just puts me on hold. I guess I'm not a priority."

Bixby shrugged.

"I'll remember that come the next election." Larry lifted his gun and took a warning shot over the heads of a group of chickens that were headed his way. They squawked and fluttered and took off in the other direction.

"Just don't shoot anybody," Bixby said, and he offered an arm to help me climb the fence.

As we made our way down the deer path, running the gauntlet of mosquitoes, which seemed to be out in full force, Bixby struck a casual tone. "So what brings you out this fine afternoon?"

"Thought I'd talk to a few people." I pitched his casual tone right back at him. "And what brings you out?"

Bixby laughed. "A few follow-up questions." He squinted at me. "Who are you planning to talk to?"

Of course he had to ask that. Good thing I had a double-header planned. "I was hoping to meet Raylene Quinn. Dottie Brooks had some interesting things to say about her."

"I'm sure she did," Bixby said. "Wives usually have interesting things to say about their husbands' mistresses."

"But you don't think Raylene could have done it?"

"Oh, I think she could have done it, all right. Brooks would have given her plenty of motive. But she's a smart cookie. PhD in biochemistry. Advanced degrees coming out of her ears and other selected orifices."

Lafferty nudged me. "Isn't it great? She's got a PhD. Get it? That makes her Doctor Quinn. And she's a medicine woman, like on TV."

Bixby sighed through bared teeth. "Anyway, sufficiently motivated, she could have murdered Brooks in any number of ways, in any number of locations, and made it look like Brooks died from natural causes. I did a little research. In the labs at that place, she'd have access from everything from the common cold to anthrax. The thing you have to ask yourself is—"

"Why here?" I said. "Why now? And why with monkshood?"

"Right." He stopped to pull a limp tissue from his pocket and wipe his nose.

"So if it was Raylene," I said, "it wasn't planned way ahead."

"We call that premeditated," Lafferty offered.

"Thanks," I said. He did sound like he was trying to be genuinely helpful and not condescending. Not sure he succeeded.

"So if Raylene was the killer," I went on, "something new must have set her off, and she had to work with what was at hand. I should be asking what pushed her over the edge and made her want to kill him."

Bixby shrugged. "Or you could ask the same of anybody."

"Thanks," I said.

"No problem, Deputy." His tone was teasing on that last word, but I could have sworn he winked at me.

"So, who were you headed to talk to?" I asked. "Excuse me, follow-up with."

"I had Lafferty run some basic backgrounds on the witnesses and he came across a few idiosyncrasies with one of them."

"Oh?"

"Guy appeared out of the blue," Lafferty said. "I think it's suspicious."

"But that was almost twenty years ago," Bixby said, "and he's been clean since, so I'm sure it's just some paperwork glitch."

I nodded. I knew where this was going.

"Unless he's in Witness Protection," Lafferty suggested. "That would be cool. Or a retired spy. That would be even cooler."

Apparently Lafferty had the same hopes for my father that I did.

"Good luck with that," I said after we reached the clearing.

"Um, Deputy?" Bixby grasped my arm, not harshly, but firmly. "Is there something you'd like to tell me?"

I shrugged my shoulders and aimed for my most innocent look. "I barely know the man." Which was true.

He squinted at me. "What man? I never told you who we were talking about."

I inhaled while I tried to frame an answer, then exhaled without speaking. After too long of a beat, I finally said, "That's right. You didn't."

Stupid, stupid, stupid. I wanted to bang my head against a wall, but there were no walls in sight. Just tent after tent, rippling in the light autumn breeze, which was sending just a tinge of the odor of woodsmoke our way from the wildfires on the opposite end of the county.

Bixby had been trawling to discover if I knew anything about the mysterious priest with the lack of a past. And I'd fallen for it. I should have known he wouldn't voluntarily discuss the case with me.

"Stupid."

"Whoa," Melanie said. "Someone's got your hackles raised." Melanie, a little grimier and with a few more dark circles under her eyes than she had the other day, was walking through the bazaar with Carol. I must have looked puzzled because she tried to explain herself. "I don't actually know what that means, though. Hackles, that is. I hope I didn't say something bad."

I shook my head. After all, I wasn't sure what hackles were, either. "No, you're fine. I was just thinking." And while I was thinking . . . "Oh, Carol. I'm glad I ran into you. Opie wanted to know if she could borrow a book. I have the title right . . ." I didn't have to reach into my cleavage to retrieve the title, thanks to the bag that Liv had bought for the butter, into which I'd shoved my money and my cell—and my keys and license. All the modern contraband I shouldn't have in camp at all.

I handed her the paper, and she opened it. "No problem. I can get it right now, if you want. Are you going to be around the bazaar?"

"I was just going to talk to Raylene Quinn. Do you know her?"

"Oh, yeah. I know her." By her sour expression, either Carol wasn't fond of Raylene Quinn or she'd developed an instant case of indigestion.

I raised an eyebrow and she went on.

"My persona this year is a stable hand, so one of my jobs is to help take care of the animals. She stepped on a bit of manure the other day and nearly had a cow." Carol stopped and chuckled to herself. "Well, it was horse manure, really. I mean, what did she expect? Into each stable some poop must fall. It's not like we can follow them all around with pooper scoopers like they do the little dogs in Central Park."

"I was there," Melanie said. "Man, she lost it."

"So you'd say she has a temper?" I asked.

"Yes," Melanie said. "Ooh, is she a suspect? Didn't she work for Mr. Brooks? On the outside, I mean."

I nodded. "Although their relationship might have been a little more involved than that."

"Oh!" said Melanie. "They were having a *thing*!" She turned back to Carol. "Well, that explains why she was so miffed at you then. She saw you talking to her boyfriend."

"That was nothing," Carol said. "He talked that way to all the girls."

"He came on to you?" I asked her.

"No more so than anyone else. It was a little creepy because he's so much older, but it was mostly flirting. I shut him down pretty quick."

"And you said he did this to a lot of women here?" I asked.

"Almost all of them," Melanie said. "I think he tried to pinch me once, but thanks to these full skirts, he didn't get very far."

I paused for a moment to consider unwanted advances as a motive. Might someone have been that angry that they killed Brooks when he tried something? It didn't, however, seem likely. A good slap would suffice. But if Raylene was having a *thing* with him, as Melanie had put it, and she had seen him trying to flirt with someone else—now that seemed more plausible. That could explain why Raylene in a fit of pique would have resorted to whatever weapons were close at hand.

"Any idea where I can find Raylene?" I asked. I was a little averse to honoring her PhD's because then I'd have to call her Dr. Quinn.

"She's probably working her booth," Melanie said.

"She has a booth?" I asked. "I thought she was some high-powered executive in Brooks's company."

"Yes, but that's in the real world," Carol said. "Here, everyone has a job. A persona. And since she apparently didn't want to be cleaning out stables with the rest of us, she applied as an artisan."

"What does she do?"

"Oh," said Melanie. "Oh! I never thought of that."

Carol raised her eyebrows. "I never thought of that, either."

"What is it? What does she do?"

Melanie turned to me. "She's the herbalist."

Raylene Quinn was standing behind the rough plank counter at the herbalist's stall, the same one I'd passed the other day, located between the glass blower, whose assistant gave me a dirty look, probably worried I was there to ask for another discount, and the dairy maid, who again was bent over her wares. Raylene wasn't exactly a young woman, but well maintained. I couldn't tell if it was genetics or cosmetic surgery, but if it were the latter, she had a good surgeon. No unnatural or stiff facial expressions.

And the cool blue eyes she studied me with seemed to radiate depth and intelligence: just the kind of woman you'd expect *not* to be hooked up with a womanizer like a Barry Brooks. And now that I was standing right in front of her, inspecting the herbs, spices, and tonics she had for sale, I had no idea what to ask her.

Instead I absentmindedly fingered the potted rosemary, which stood for *remembrance* but also for *fidelity*. I'd put a few springs into boutonnieres before.

When she cleared her throat, I stammered, "I'll . . . I'll take the rosemary."

I paid her the money, and was getting ready to run off like the chicken I was, when she asked, "Is there something more I can do for you?"

I whirled back around and said, "Yes. Well, it seems I've been deputized to look into the death of your . . . boss. Not that I have a lot of experience in this kind of thing."

She half smiled at me. I wasn't sure if she was relieved or amused by my ineptness. "And you'd like to talk with me?"

"Just to get a better feel for what he was like. You worked with him a long time?"

"Not here," she said as she glanced meaningfully at the nearby vendors. "I'm already the talk of the encampment." She flipped a sign to "CLOSED" and gestured toward the well-trodden path. Only when we were well past the nearby stalls did she begin, and so softly I practically had to shoulder up to her to hear over the hubbub of the marketplace.

"I've worked for the company for seventeen years. When I started, I had just finished my first PhD, had no real-world work experience, and was awash in debt. Still, Brooks

Pharmaceuticals took a chance on me. After only a couple of years I was promoted to head my own lab, thanks to the confidence Barry had in me. I've been head of Research and Development, and pretty much his second in command for six years now."

Sounded like a success story, if it was truly his confidence in her that led to her advancement in the workplace. "Several people I've talked to have spoken highly of your education."

That seemed to please her. "Yes, well . . ."

"And you're also the camp herbalist. I'm surprised I didn't see you there trying to help Barry."

She looked considerably less pleased. "The only thing he told me was that his stomach was upset. I had suggested that he go back to his tent and lie down. He told me to mind my own business. So I did."

"That wouldn't have helped him."

"I assumed he had food poisoning, that it had to run its course." She shook her head. "I'm a research scientist, not a diagnostician or medical doctor."

"How was he to work for?"

Raylene paused, as if to consider her words. "He was old school, maybe a bit autocratic for modern times. But he could run a business well. The company made money. The stockholders were happy. The board of directors was happy."

"That seems a rather dispassionate description."

"Are you suggesting I give you a more passionate one?"

I could feel my cheeks color. "I just meant . . . it would be helpful if I could get a better picture of him as a person. What he was like on a daily basis."

By this point we had passed the last of the food vendors and craftsmen and approached a field. In the distance, a man on horseback had reached a gallop and advanced on a large target with his lance. Shortly after the lance hit the target, however, the rider lost his balance and hit the ground. The horse trotted off. I could have sworn it looked amused.

"Rookie." Raylene rolled her eyes.

Closer to where we stood, smaller targets were attached to hay bales, and a man was charging exorbitant rates for a trial run at a long bow. I guessed they'd gotten that name since the bows were almost as long as Raylene.

"Care to try?" she asked. "Reggie owes me a favor anyway." She smiled at the man who must have been Reggie, who then handed us each a longbow. We made our way over to a spot marked, not with a bright white painted line, but rather worn patches in the rough sod. I set my pot of rosemary on the ground and tried to mimic her actions as she lined up an arrow on the bow and let it fly. It hit the outer rim of her target and lodged there.

I mimicked her actions the best I could and started to pull back the bow.

"No, wait," Raylene said. "You could take off your finger like that." She came up behind me and repositioned my hands on the bow.

I pulled back and let the arrow fly. It went about ten yards and stuck in the weeds. At least I hadn't sliced my finger off. I'm rather fond of all my digits.

She retrieved another arrow from the quiver but paused. "Barry was . . . well, not much to tell, really. He was dedicated to his wife. To his son. To his job."

"In that order?"

She shrugged and regained her shooting stance. "Hard to rise in business when you keep your priorities straight. There's always someone underneath you ready to lay it all on the line to advance. Barry knew that. He was just as savvy as his father in that sense." She let another arrow fly. This one lodged in the hay above the target. She grimaced.

"His father?" I did my best to imitate her stance, then pulled the bow back around my ear, and let fly. The snap of the bow stung my finger a bit, but this time the arrow traveled all the way to the target. Unfortunately it was the wrong target.

"Nice distance," she said, reaching for another arrow. "Yes, Melvin Brooks, senior. He was in declining health when I joined the company, apparently from a series of strokes, but what a man. Brilliant. Two PhDs. Well respected in his field. Barry was so proud of the old man, he named his son after him, but a hard legacy to live up to."

This time her arrow fell just below center.

"Did Barry fall short of his father's ideal?" I asked.

"Oh, my. I didn't mean to imply that. Barry was successful, but he took a different path than his father wanted. He dropped out of an Ivy League school to join the military. But he rose in the ranks." She leaned in and lowered her voice. "He was decorated when he saved three men. Practically carried them out of harm's way. Later . . ." She stopped to help adjust my aim.

I let the arrow fly. This time it hit my own hay bale, inches from the target.

"Better," she said, remaining just behind my shoulder and speaking barely above a whisper. "I don't know if I should be telling you this, but he's gone so I suppose it no longer matters. You might need to know. Barry was a covert operative in the CIA."

I whipped around to face her.

Raylene nodded. "And I'm not talking about the kind that sits in an office and surfs the Internet for chatter or eavesdrops on the cell phone conversations of foreign diplomats.

I'm talking the kind that parachutes into remote jungles and takes meetings with clandestine paramilitary organizations with which we share certain common interests. Barry's been all over the world. Okay, so his degrees are honorary more than academic. I still think he's earned them." Raylene's tone had grown defensive.

And I wasn't about to argue with a woman armed with a longbow, either. "I'm sure he has." Meanwhile my mind was spinning. If Barry was former CIA, didn't that mean there could be a lot more suspects? And dangerous ones? At least if the movies were accurate. I mean, motorcycle chases, bombs, guns. Deadly weapons disguised as normal bowler hats. If there was such a thing as a normal bowler hat.

"Anyway," she went on, "he had great leadership skills. He took the company his father founded from a small pharmaceutical manufacturer to one of the leaders in the business. Quite a legacy."

"Does that mean you'll be in charge now?"

She blushed but managed to send an arrow hurtling right to the center of her target. "Well, that will depend on the board of directors, won't it? Far from a done deal. They might want Melvin to carry on the family legacy. Although he doesn't really know the business."

"But you can't think of anyone who might have wanted to kill Barry? I mean, the CIA ops were a long time ago, right?"

"There were rumors that he still did odd jobs for The Company."

"What company?"

"*The* Company. The CIA," she added, as if I were dense. Maybe that was good, because I didn't get that from "The Company."

"Rumors?" I repeated.

"Of shady dealings. Of calls nobody was allowed to know about. Times where he took off for several days and we weren't supposed to ask why." She nodded sagely.

I returned her sage nod, even though I wondered if those trips for The Company weren't with some blonde. Or brunette. Or redhead. I decided to change the subject.

"So you're the herbalist. Do you ever do anything with the native plants? The ones already growing in the woods?"

"Quite a few of them," she said. "Better than carrying them all in."

"What about monkshood?"

"Of course . . ." She lowered her bow and stared into the trees. "Monkshood. Aconite poisoning." She turned to me. "Is that what killed him? Oh, the symptoms were textbook."

I nodded. "Do you ever work with it? I mean, it could have been an accident."

"Never touch the stuff. Oh, I know what it looks like and what it does. And I suppose that makes me a suspect."

My eyes went to the longbow and arrow she still held in her hands. Yeah, asking a suspect leading questions while she held a deadly weapon was probably not my brightest move. I swallowed hard.

She must have seen my apprehension because she released the tension on her bow. "Oh, but I didn't do it."

"I was told you supplied the herbs for the reception dinner."

"The marriage feast." She blanched. "I suppose I did. But I know the difference between culinary herbs and poison . . . or is that the point? You think I did this."

"I didn't say that."

"I would never kill Barry, let alone attempt mass murder."

"There's no chance the herbs could have gotten mixed up?"

She shook her head. "Not even by accident. Monkshood

is very distinctive, and I have no use for it at all, not the leaves or the flowers or the root. I suppose you know the root is the most toxic part. It's not used in any of my tonics. There is no way it got into the pot from anything I supplied. It must have been something else he put in it."

"Who?"

"That baker they hired."

I sighed. Back to Nick. "But Nick had no motive."

"No motive that you know about. Or what if *he* got mixed up?" When I didn't answer right away, she went on, "I see. So he's the local boy who could do no wrong."

"I didn't mean to imply—"

"You didn't have to."

"Before we decide it was just an accident, has anyone recently asked you questions about herbs or flowers? About monkshood in particular? Or just any questions out of the ordinary?"

She placed a fist over her mouth and thought for a moment. "I wish I could supply a name for you," she said, "but I honestly have nothing."

When I left Raylene Quinn, she was still taking out her aggressions on those targets, and I made a mental note to avoid the archery range when carrying out any future interrogations.

But I had put it off long enough. It was time to find my father. Hopefully Bixby hadn't arrested him and carted him back to town. I stopped to leave my rosemary with Nick for safekeeping and ask for directions to the friar's tent.

"I can go with you," Nick offered.

But I waved him off. I needed to do this alone.

I followed Nick's instructions until I found my father's tent, not far from Chandler Hines's blacksmith area, but Hines was apparently on a break because there was no pounding, clanging, or whooshing taking place. Directly across from the friar's tent was a food vendor who was also doing little business and leaned on his counter half asleep.

"Hello?" I called into the tent.

I strained my ears, but didn't hear anything. "Hello?" I tried again.

When no one answered, I peeked my head in the tent flaps and was relieved to discover it was unoccupied.

I scanned the nearby area. Not many people were in this end of the camp, but those who were there didn't seem interested at all in what I was doing. I waited until one woman ambled up to the food vendor and distracted him, then I ducked into the tent.

At first I couldn't see much. What little light was available had diffused through the tent itself, making the inside claustrophobic, musty, and gloomy. I could see why Opie had said he didn't seem to want to be here. He'd always wrinkled his nose at the suggestion of camping for our family vacations. Looking at this space, I had to contend that he was on to something. This was not how I'd want to spend my vacation.

Or was he even here on vacation? He'd said he didn't know I was going to be here, so he didn't come for an overdue family reunion. If he was a bounty hunter . . .

My mind went back to our brief conversation in the woods. *Dangerous things were happening here.*

Was he here on business? A bounty hunter would mean there was a fugitive in the camp, someone who had jumped bail.

But that couldn't be Barry Brooks. He was the president of his own company, not running from the law.

By this time my eyes were beginning to adjust to the darkness.

The tent wasn't a large walk-in model like Nick had. This was more of a camping tent, with a sleeping bag on the floor next to a lantern and a knapsack of sorts. Very Spartan.

I riffled through the knapsack. It held a change of clothing, some modern and clean (hopefully) undergarments, and a bottle of cologne. I unscrewed the top and sniffed. It was the same scent I remembered as a child, when I'd climb onto his lap and he'd tell me a story. I swallowed hard and put it back, then tried to arrange the sack as it was before I touched it.

It was then that I felt more than heard the buzzing sound. I pulled back, thinking I'd managed to trap a bee in the sack, but then I peeked in and saw the rectangular outline of a cell phone screen shining through the fabric. I didn't see a pocket, so I ran my hand around the outside of the sack and then the inside and finally found the cleverly hidden compartment. The buzzing had stopped by the time I got my hands on the phone.

"A forbidden cell phone." I *tsk*ed, even though my own phone was packed into my bag. "It seems like you like to stay in touch with someone." Fortunately, like me, he couldn't be bothered with passwords, so I was able to access his phone just by turning it on.

I flipped through the contents of his cell. A lot of numbers in his contact list, but the names meant nothing to me and didn't seem to contain any of the reenactors. These names could represent clients or friends. They could even be a new family. Wife. Even more children.

But if he had children, surely he'd have pictures. So I went to his camera app.

Bingo.

Only not children. But there were lots of pictures taken at the encampment. Many of the shots were unfocused, the subjects of the photographs were not centered, and no flash was used. Either my father was the worst photographer in the history of man or these shots were taken secretly. And a good number of them involved Barry Brooks and his entourage. Was Father Richard aka Richard Wilson aka Jeffrey Bloom simply catching up on his former employer? Or was he looking for something else?

I sat down on the sleeping bag and continued to go back in time via the cell phone pictures.

There were several provocative shots of Brooks and Raylene. If the nature of their relationship was only theoretical before, it was now proven. QED.

A few other photos showed Brooks with his son. One with Brooks in conversation with his then-future daughter-in-law. And a lot with Brooks apparently flirting with a number of women. I stopped dead when I saw him leering at Melanie, Opie, and Carol. That swine. I pushed back the thought that someone had done the world a favor by killing Brooks. After all, death hadn't been a penalty for infidelity and lechery since . . . maybe medieval times.

As I continued to flip backward in time, the pictures of Brooks stopped abruptly. Perhaps he hadn't arrived yet. Or maybe my father hadn't run into him. Had he known Brooks was going to be there?

But there were a number of shots of Chandler Hines talking with the food vendor I'd seen just outside the tent: a mousy-looking man wearing a stained apron. It looked like Hines was just setting up his forge, so perhaps these were early in the encampment.

Then the pictures changed dramatically. No medieval backdrop. These were unknown people, and not the nicest-looking people at that, set across a Western backdrop or lined up in front of walls that measured their heights.

There were only half a dozen or so of these, and then they also stopped abruptly.

“New phone,” a voice came from behind me.

I didn’t have to turn. I knew that voice.

“Hello, Dad.”

Chapter 11

"You know, the Supreme Court ruled the police can't search a cell phone without a warrant. That is, if you're here in some official capacity. Did you find what you were looking for?" My father crouched as he made his way into the tent, and then he collapsed on the sleeping bag next to me. "Ouch. Either I'm getting older or the ground is getting harder."

I resisted the natural impulse to smile at him. "I'm sure you must find yourself sneaking around in similar circumstances often in your new line of work. Or is it new? Come to think of it, I have no idea how long you've been a bail bondsman slash bounty hunter."

"You got that from my phone? I'm impressed."

"Not from your phone. From Googling a name I knew to be false."

"And you find that suspicious," he said. "I didn't kill Barry Brooks, if that's what you're worried about."

"I find it suspicious that your cell phone is full of pictures of the dead man. And that you're here under some fake name."

"Not fake. Legally changed."

"Was it so bad to be Jeffrey Bloom?" I drew up my legs until I was sitting cross-legged, not an easy task in that cramped tent.

"Not as bad as I thought at the time . . . until it became impossible. There's so much you don't know. Audrey, I'd love to be able to explain what happened back then."

"I'm listening." I leaned forward, resting my forearms on my knees.

His jaw quavered for a moment. "I wouldn't know where to begin."

"Let's work backward, then. Why are you here? I know you used to work for Brooks. Did you come back to settle an old score?"

My father shook his head. "I didn't even know Brooks would be here. If I had, I might have . . ."

"What? Avoided him like you tried to avoid me? You seem good at that. Why would you not want to see your former boss?"

My father looked up, apparently studying an empty corner of the tent. Was he trying to remember past events? Or make up a new version? "He wasn't exactly my boss. Look. Back then I was an accountant for Brooks Pharmaceuticals. Barry was an employee, just like me. Supposedly. He worked in my office. Or whatever it is the boss's son called work."

"Oh, a loafer. And you didn't get along?"

"We didn't *not* get along. I didn't really know him all that well."

I tilted my head.

"Okay, perhaps I was a little jealous. He had just come back from a stint in the military. All kinds of rumors swirled around the office. Some said he was a Navy Seal. Others that he was taken prisoner and released in some hostage exchange. Some of the secretaries had heard that he'd been injured in a clandestine operation that he wasn't allowed to talk about. They acted like he was a mix of John Wayne and Oliver North, with a hint of Batman. His father asked me to take him under my wing, give him light work to help him reacclimate to normal society."

I nodded. That could fit with what Raylene had said about Brooks being in the CIA.

"All the girls swooned around him."

"And that bothered you? Jealous of that, too?" I bit back another accusation and I was immediately ashamed of the contentious tone in my voice. Not only would it not entice my absentee dad to open up to me, but I was beginning to sound like my mother.

Instead of clamming up or shouting back, he actually laughed. "Believe it or not, I wasn't interested in the women. Maybe I was a little jealous about how people looked up to the guy. And the way things were going between your mother and me added to the stress. I supposed it wore on me, because I started finding accounting errors I don't know how I could have made. I made good the difference from my personal account and swept it under the rug as best I could. It wasn't much—a few hundred here. Once a couple of thousand."

"You put your own money into Brooks Pharmaceuticals? Isn't that like reverse embezzlement?"

"It's not quite kosher. I figured it would cost less than losing my job. The old man, Brock's father, was a stickler when it came to money. Well, most people are sticklers when it comes to money."

"Was that why you left?"

He adjusted the folds of his cassock and paused before speaking. "I never intended to leave. At least not permanently."

"Your clothes were all gone. What? Did you take them all to the cleaners and get lost on the way back?" There was my mother again. I mentally slapped myself.

He stopped for a moment and studied the ground. If he were really a friar, I'd have thought I caught him in the middle of prayer. Then he raised his head and looked me squarely in the eye with a gaze so intense I had to resist the urge to look away. "It's hard to see you so bitter. I guess I deserve that. But the truth was that I just needed to get away for a few days." He swallowed. "Your mother and I had just had another row. I'm sure you were old enough to remember them."

I nodded.

"I wanted to scare her a little. So she'd know I was serious. So I packed up all my things, took a few vacation days, and checked into a hotel. I never even left town. I figured she'd calm down and then we could talk it over."

He stopped and fingered a loose thread on his sleeping bag before continuing. "Only I was watching television in the hotel, and my picture flashed on the screen. At first I thought your mother had reported me missing. It turns out I was wanted. Me. Wanted by the police." His eyebrows went up to show he considered this an absurdity.

"So I turned myself in. Apparently I was suspected of embezzlement. More money had gone missing from the company when I did, tens of thousands of dollars this time, so I was their lead suspect. Only I didn't have it in my bank account. I don't think they ever found anything to connect it to me, so they never pressed charges. I asked to see Brooks, to help go over the books to try to figure out what happened, but the old man picked that moment to have a stroke, so it was Barry who came to talk to me."

"And?"

"It was chilling. He said he'd make sure I was never charged, but only if I took off. Just disappeared. It became pretty clear where the money had gone at that point. And probably all the missing funds before that." He shook his head. "In trying to cover those unexplained losses, I was covering for him. I'm sure he replaced me with one of his cronies and probably kept right on bleeding his old man dry."

"And you left, just because he told you to? So he could rip off his father?"

He shook his head. "You don't understand. Brooks boasted about his powerful connections in the government. He didn't say, but strongly implied, that the money was needed for some covert operation . . . like he was still an active agent or something. That the government would replace it in time. And if I got in the way, I was expendable. Pity if something were to happen to me or my family."

"Brooks said he was in the CIA?"

My father shrugged. "Never said it outright, at least not to me. Just all these oblique references. But if he was CIA, he was dirty. Money laundering. Black ops. I was frightened."

"So you ran because you were afraid."

"Afraid for you, peanut. Of the cloud you would grow up under. Frightened for your mother. Frightened of what would happen if I tried to stay to fight him. I guess I convinced myself I was doing the right thing for all of us."

"But you never wondered what had happened after you left?" I swallowed a lump from my throat, but it crept right back.

"Of course I wondered. I wrote you tons of letters."

"I never got any."

"I never sent them. After a while it just seemed better to let you live your life in peace."

"Peace? Is that what you call it?"

He answered with only a pained expression.

Meanwhile Nick's cheerful—and loud—voice filtered in from outside the tent. "Well, hello, Chief Bixby." Nick was clearly giving me a warning that the chief was headed this way. He needn't have bothered. The sneeze that followed would have given him away just as well.

"I've been trying to avoid him," my father said. He grabbed the phone from my hands and stuffed it into his cassock. "He doesn't need to see that. Does he? At least not without a warrant."

By the time Bixby's head poked into the opening of the tent, my father looked every bit the angelic friar.

"Oh, there you are," Bixby said, his gaze fixed on my father. "I've been looking all over for you."

"For me?" He put on his most beatific expression. Gag. I tried not to roll my eyes.

Bixby must have noticed my effort, because he seemed to be studying me more than he was my father. I can't claim the acting skills my father exhibited. But I smiled pleasantly all the same.

"Audrey, it appears you've beaten me to it," Bixby said. "Were you having a nice discussion?"

"She was asking me about this Brooks fellow," my father said. "I'm afraid I really couldn't shed any light on the matter. I have no idea who might have wanted to kill him."

Bixby squinted at me. I sent him what I hoped was my most innocent smile, but my throat was hot and my eyes probably glistened with unshed tears, so I'm sure it looked pretty scary. "Well, I should probably be going and leave you to it," I offered.

"You don't want to stay while we talk?" Bixby asked.

"No. No, I think I've had enough." I pushed my way out of the tent and down the pathway.

"Audrey, wait up!" Nick called.

I slowed but I didn't turn and didn't speak. I'm sure my expression and voice would have betrayed me.

Nick fell into step next to me. "I hope I did the right thing. I saw Bixby headed this way and tried to warn you."

"Thanks." I slowed my pace just a little more.

"So what were you and the friar talking about for so long?"

I stopped and turned to face him. "You were watching me?"

"I was a little worried. The other day you were asking questions about the friar, and today you were alone with him. I just wanted to make sure you were okay."

I stood, looking into Nick's warm brown eyes, unsure whether to be mad that he had followed me, or glad that he was watching out for me. Instead of deciding, I leaned into him for a hug.

"Are you all right?" he asked.

I nodded into his chest. "Just a trying day, is all."

I sighed and he pulled me closer. "Want to talk about it?"

"I think maybe I just want to go home."

The bright blue roof was new. But as I got closer to the cottage, I realized it was just a tarp placed over what little remained of my roof.

Chester bounded up to the door as soon as he heard me

and circled my legs until I relented and gave him the last few tablespoons of wet food I had in the house. No sooner had he taken a bite than the black kitten appeared out of nowhere and nosed him out of the way. Before long the food was gone, and Chester sat there on his haunches, eyeing the empty dish then giving me a reproachful look, before he headed to the larger dish and crunched on a few pieces of the hard food.

"Well, sometimes life's tough that way," I told him, and then slid a frozen pizza into the toaster oven and plopped onto the sofa. I checked my phone, which was jammed up with new messages from Liv and a few from my mother. They could wait. I wasn't sure I wanted to talk with anyone.

I refused to get all maudlin and gloomy about the conversation with my father. Only moping on the sofa encouraged that sort of thinking, so I stepped outside to the front garden and started pulling weeds, loosening the roots with a trowel. This job would be a little harder when all the blooms died back, although I was pretty good at differentiating the flowers from the weeds based on their stems and leaves.

Here I recalled one of Grandma Mae's lessons. Only she wasn't talking about flowers. Not really.

"The soil is where the plant comes from," she'd said. "Everybody comes from somewhere. Some of it's good and some of it's bad. But a plant is so much more than soil. It's water and sunshine and all the promise in the seed." I could almost feel her fingers ruffling my hair.

I closed my eyes to relish the feel of her fingers.

"The same soil can grow weeds or beautiful flowers. It depends on what you plant, what you water and tend to. You are so much more than the soil from which you come."

I swallowed hard. I hadn't understood what she was

getting at then. But I understood it now. She didn't want me limited by anything that happened in my childhood.

I took a deep breath and sat in the garden cherishing those memories until the smoke alarm called me back in to dine on what was salvageable from my burnt pizza, which was basically the charred pepperoni from the top.

I was shuffling around in my fridge to find a cheese stick or something else to go with the pepperoni when the knock on my door made me jump and hit my head. Once I'd extricated myself, I could make out Nick's frame through the wavy glass.

"I thought you'd be over at the encampment," I said as I yanked open the sticky door.

"Just closed up shop and came by." He held up a textbook. *Daily Life in the Middle Ages*. "Carol said you forgot this."

"Ah, yes. For Opie." I set it on the table. "You didn't have to come all the way out here to bring that. Wait, did you sneak through Larry's place?"

"With his permission." Nick pulled out a chair and sat at the table.

"Good. He's getting a little antsy with that shotgun."

"I think he's calmed down a bit. He's now charging five dollars a head." He stopped as he eyed the brown and black disk on my plate. "And I brought you something." He whipped out a loaf of bread.

"Oh, I love you!"

"Kind of what I was going for." He winked.

I went to retrieve a sharp knife and brushed more drywall dust from my cutting board. "Stay to share some with me? I think I still have some butter. Or peanut butter if you're daring to sneak in some New World food."

"I think I can evade the anachronism police for an evening."

I dug out plates, knives, and the peanut butter, and I even managed to find a small jar of jelly. "And wasn't there something you wanted to talk with me about?"

"That can wait." He smeared a bit of peanut butter onto his bread. "The book was just an excuse to see you. I suspect there was something about that last conversation that threw you a little. I know you're trying to keep Liv out of it, so I wondered if you needed someone to bounce ideas off of. But first, I have something more pressing to ask you."

He looked deeply into my eyes. "Would it be terribly impertinent if I asked to use your shower?"

"My shower?"

"I'm afraid I'm a bit rank from all that roughing it at the camp."

"My shower?"

"You do have one, right?"

"In a manner of speaking. There's next to no pressure, though. I've mainly been using the tub. But you're welcome to it." And I hoped I'd remembered to put away my razor.

"Let's take a look." He made his way to the bathroom and turned on the tap, then the shower. A slow trickle made its way out of the shower head and into the old claw foot tub.

"That's a beauty of a tub," he said, ignoring the peeling paint and the chipped mismatched tile. "Should last you for another hundred years or so. Do you have a wrench? And some vinegar?"

"I think so." I ran to collect the tool set that Liv had given me as a housewarming gift and a dusty gallon of vinegar I had seen in the pantry when I moved in. Grandma Mae always did like her homemade pickles. I sat on the edge of the tub and handed him tools for the next twenty minutes while he took my shower apart and soaked several parts in the sink full of vinegar. Eventually the pieces started going together again, and Nick turned on the water. A full spray came this time, instead of the trickle.

I clapped my hands. I still had no roof, but at least I had a working shower. Baby steps.

"May I?" He gestured toward the tub, so I got him a towel and washcloth from the linen closet and then left him to it.

He whistled while he showered. I kind of liked that. I imagined he was enjoying removing the layer of grime from the camp, luxuriating in the warm water and the clean scent of soap bubbles. Then I moved away from the door back into the kitchen, both to give him a little privacy and because my imagination was just a little too vivid. I decided to pop some popcorn, drizzling a little of that new butter on it.

Nick came out wearing a clean tunic that must have been in his bag. "I hand-washed the other clothes and have them hanging up to dry."

"I guess that means you're not going back tonight."

He gestured to the setting sun. "Too late to get back before dark anyway."

And all of a sudden things got quiet between us. Nick had very old-fashioned manners—which I simply adored—and I didn't think he was going to change that now.

"So," he said as he found a spot on the sofa next to me and pulled the popcorn bowl between us. "Tell me about the case. Who are your lead suspects?"

"Well, as far as motive goes, I guess young Melvin Brooks is top on the list. He stands to inherit. And his new wife would get a bit of that since Melvin tore up the prenup."

He winced. "They seem like too nice a couple."

"I'd like to think it's not them, either. But I haven't ruled them out. Kathleen Randolph is on Bixby's radar, but I'm not sure I agree she has motive. Too much time to cool off since the divorce."

"What divorce?"

"Kathleen Randolph was also once married to Barry Brooks."

"But that would make Andrea and Mel . . ."

"Not blood related. Just awkward at the family reunions."

"I daresay. Anyone else?"

"Well, of course the current Mrs. Brooks wasn't here at the time, so she's out of the running—unless she got sick of him and hired someone to get rid of him while she had an alibi. But my money's on Raylene Quinn," I added. "I had a nice chat with her today, too."

He reached for a fistful of popcorn. "Do tell."

"She'd certainly have the knowhow. Besides being a trained biochemist and who knows what else, she's the camp herbalist. She'd also have the opportunity to get close to Brooks anytime she wanted. And she's got motive in spades. I'm pretty sure she was involved with Brooks."

"I honestly don't know how he managed that. I guess I'm not the best judge, but was he really all that attractive? Unless they're after his money."

"He was no Cary Grant or even George Clooney, if that's what you mean. He may have had a little more going for him than just his money. He had an awfully good line."

Nick raised his eyebrows.

"Seems Brooks was telling people he was CIA."

Nick coughed on a mouthful of popcorn. I ran to get him a glass of water. He was rubbing tears out of his eyes when I got back.

He sipped. "CIA? I don't suppose there's any truth to it."

"I haven't a clue," I said. "How can you check if someone was in the CIA? I mean, I don't expect there's a master list on Google somewhere. Maybe Bixby can find out."

"So you think the lure of being involved with some kind of James Bond type was his ticket to getting women?"

"Maybe," I said, "but Brooks might have also used those inferences in other more lucrative ways."

"What do you mean?"

"It's just a half-formed idea," I said. "But think about it. The CIA is intimidating. No one wants to be on their bad side. So all Brooks needed to do was drop a few hints about what might happen if people stood in his way . . ."

"And everyone bends over backwards doing what he wants without asking too many questions." Nick shook his head. "He could have been manipulating employees, competitors. Someone he'd had under his thumb for a lot of years might have wanted out."

I couldn't help the quick inhalation. My father was one of those people feeling the pinch of Brooks's largest digit.

"What?" Nick said. "You think of something?"

I waved it off. "Worth considering."

"And how does the good father fit into all of this?"

"The . . ."

"The friar. Father Richard."

I closed my eyes. There was no way this wasn't going to become public knowledge at some point in the investigation, so it was better if Nick heard it from me. "He's my father."

"The father is . . ."

"My father. Confusing enough yet?"

"Your *father* father? But his name's not . . ." The black kitten hopped into Nick's lap and nosed his water glass. Nick wiped a few spilled drops of water from the front of his tunic, set his glass on the side table, and stroked the kitten behind her ears.

"He had it changed."

"I see." Nick slid a little closer to me and put an arm around my shoulder.

"He's apparently now a bounty hunter. From Texas."

"A bounty hunter. Here on business?"

"He didn't say. He did say that he didn't know I was going to be there, and he didn't know Brooks was going to be there. But I did learn that he used to work for Brooks Pharmaceuticals."

Nick tightened his grip on my shoulder. "That's some coincidence."

"He also admitted that he left town because he was accused of embezzling a large amount of money."

"But he didn't." I wasn't sure if this was a question or a statement.

"I'd like to think he didn't," I said. "He claimed that Brooks fixed it so that nobody would press charges as long as my dad left home. Ambiguous bad and scary things might happen if he didn't. Mentioned that whole CIA business."

"Oh, Audrey. I'm sorry." Nick pulled me even closer and kissed the top of my head. I could feel the tears gathering in my eyes.

"At least now I know why he left."

"But not why he came back. And not whether he could have had anything to do with the murder of Barry Brooks."

I shook my head. "I don't want to believe it, but especially if Brooks framed my dad and ran him out of town, my father has more motive than anybody. And I really don't know him anymore. Just vague memories."

The kitten nosed Nick's chin, then rested against him like a newborn baby. I guess we were having a group hug.

"I should get my camera," I said as the kitten sighed and snuggled against him.

"What? And destroy my macho reputation in Ramble?"

Nick stroked her shiny black coat. "I think now I understand why you haven't named her."

"I just haven't thought of the right one. There's time enough for that."

Nick looked skeptical.

"Okay, Sigmund. Why haven't I named the cat?"

Nick paused, the humor gone out of his face. He pulled me closer. "Just understand: not everyone leaves."

Bang, bang, bang!

I awoke with a start, jumped up, and was chagrinned to find a stream of drool from my mouth to Nick's tunic. I quickly wiped it while he was stirring.

His comment about why I hadn't named the kitten had cut a little too close and had opened the floodgates. I'd practically cried myself to sleep on Nick's shoulder. Okay, there may have been some cuddling and a few passionate kisses involved.

I glanced at the mantel clock over the crumbling not-to-code fireplace. Three a.m. Who was banging on my front door?

While I was frozen in place by a shot of adrenaline not accompanied by coherent thought, Nick went to the door as the banging started up again.

When he pulled it open, Bixby was standing on my doorstep. He looked at Nick in his damp tunic, then at me, then a silly grin crept across his face. "I hope I haven't disturbed anything. I saw the light on."

"No," I said. "We were just . . . no." I raked a hand through my hair. "Come in."

Nick stepped back, allowing Bixby to enter, causing all kinds of racket on the squeaky floorboards. When he found a quiet spot, the chief gave Nick's bare legs a long look.

"Maybe I should see if my pants are dry," Nick said, and headed back to the bathroom, squeaking the floorboards all the way.

"What are you doing here?" I asked, wondering just how bedraggled I looked. "At this time of night." I caught a glimpse in the mirror and discovered the crisscross imprint of Nick's tunic tie embedded into my cheek. There really is no way of carrying on a conversation with your hand draped casually covering half of your face, but I gave it a shot.

"I've been thinking about this case," he said with that silly grin still on his face. "Just driving around. Like I said, I saw your light. Look, I'd appreciate if you don't hide things from me. You should have told me about Richard Wilson."

So he came clean after all. "I'm sorry, Chief. I'm sure you can understand why I . . ." Soon everyone would know.

"I think I do," he said. "And it's partly my fault because I didn't include you in the investigation. I suppose it's only natural for you to go off on your own and try to prove something. That's why I've decided you're probably safer fully briefed."

"Fully briefed."

"We might have saved some time if you'd informed me that Wilson was a bounty hunter." Bixby shook his head. "In all my years on the force, I've never met one—not in real life. He's not like they make them out on television. All the leather, tattoos, and hair." Bixby snorted. "Wilson looks more like an accountant or something. Maybe that helps him. Takes people by surprise. Now, I still don't want him participating in the investigation."

"Of course not . . ."

"But since he's been there from the beginning, and he must have had some training . . . or at least experience in the field . . ."

"I suppose."

"Then we can eliminate him from the suspect pool and maybe even glean some insight of people's behavior just prior to the events in question."

"But I was there, too, remember. Just prior to the . . . events in question."

"Audrey, it's no time to quibble over such things. I meant a trained observer. And I just said that I would make sure to brief you regularly on what we discover. I hope I can count on you to do the same?"

Would that include informing Bixby of Wilson's real identity? And that he once worked for Brooks Pharmaceuticals? And that he had a clear motive for the murder of Barry Brooks?

Come to think of it, I now had a motive for the murder. Should I voluntarily recuse myself? But that was ridiculous. I knew I didn't have anything to do with it, so why should I?

I think my jaw was hanging down, but fortunately Bixby attributed lack of protest to agreement to his arrangement.

"So tomorrow, you come with Lafferty and me to the encampment. We can talk about anything else you learned on the way. Don't get me wrong, Audrey. I still think Foley was an idiot for deputizing you, but I'd rather have you safe where I can see you. Besides, you never know what you might stumble into. You seem to have a talent for that."

"Why, thanks." But inside I was already beginning to seethe. Bixby may have had all the training, but I thought I was doing okay getting people to open up to me. And since Bixby was headed out the door, I had until tomorrow to decide how much of what I learned I would share with the chief.

Chapter 12

I awoke again, this time to bright sunlight and the smell of bacon, which certainly hadn't come from my empty refrigerator. And if Nick had sponged it off my neighbor, I'd be the talk of Ramble for weeks.

"I hope you don't mind"—Nick slid two plates of eggs and bacon onto the table next to already poured glasses of orange juice—"but I borrowed your car to run to the grocery store. You seemed out of a lot of things."

"Mind?" I grabbed a fork. It was like having June Cleaver on call. By the smacking sounds Chester and the kitten were making over dishes of wet food—which hadn't magically appeared from my near-empty cupboards—they enjoyed having Nick around as well. But soon the meal was over and Nick rushed back to the encampment.

As I filled up the sink with soapy water to wash our breakfast dishes—which was when I realized why I don't cook breakfast for myself that often—my cell rang.

I checked the number. Mother.

I slid into the chair and stared at the ringing phone until the call went to voice mail. I guessed I shouldn't have delayed the inevitable, but I was too tired to deal with the dishes and too conflicted to talk with my mother.

Instead, I sipped the rest of my coffee as Chester headed for the water bowl. No sooner had he lapped up a bit than the kitten yet to be named scampered over and nosed Chester out of the way.

He sat on his haunches for a moment, probably shocked by the audacity. He meowed once at me.

"Sorry, bud. Y'all are going to have to learn to get along."

His whiskers twitched, as if he was considering my advice. Then he reached over one gray paw and bopped the kitten on the head.

She swished her tail a few times but backed off until Chester had his fill and moseyed on to the living room. After a couple of sniffs at the water, she lost interest and chased after him.

I headed to work, doubling back only once to get Opie's book—and shoo the kitten off the counter.

Thursdays weren't the busiest days, but I had one small wedding job to do, so I wanted to make sure the flowers had arrived. But when I walked into the back door of the shop, Liv and Opie were already hard at work, processing our latest delivery by deftly cutting off the old ends—at the prescribed angle—and putting the newly cut stems into preservative.

Liv's hands automatically continued as she looked up. "Audrey, what in the world are you doing here?"

"I work here, remember?" I set Opie's borrowed book down on the edge of her worktable before pulling my apron from its peg. "How's the paper coming?"

"It's coming," Opie said. "The book will help a lot,

though. If I weren't such an honest person, I'd offer Carol money to write this paper for me. Come to think of it, she'd probably enjoy it. I could kick myself for getting thrown out of that camp."

"Are we such bad company?" Liv asked.

"No." Opie stopped as she found a rotten spot on the calla lily stem she was cutting. She made her cut just above the mushy area. She held up the flower with a now three-inch stem. "Is it worth keeping?"

"For a boutonniere or corsage maybe," I said. "But you managed to dodge the topic. Are we such bad company?" I winked at her.

Opie held the calla lily where a lapel would be—not that you could really wear a boutonniere with the black studded T-shirt of a skull with a pink bow on the top of its head. Then again, why not? She shrugged and put the lily into the bucket. "Not at all. It's this paper that's lame. And here I thought that camp was lame. I should have listened to Melanie and Carol and tried harder to follow those—"

"Lame rules?" Liv suggested. "But our lovely intern isn't the only one to skirt questions this morning. I seem to recall asking what you were doing here when you could be hunting for clues and interrogating suspects."

"I'm going in later. Believe it or not, with Bixby."

"Then I guess I need to tell you what I learned while digging on the Internet last night," she said.

"About?"

"About everyone I could think of. I couldn't sleep." She patted her belly. "I think these hormones are all messed up."

I gnawed on a dry cuticle. It really wasn't fair to saddle Liv with all the work of running the shop, especially in her condition. "Maybe I should stay here today while you go home and rest."

She shook her head. "Amber Lee's coming in later today, and I have Opie hanging around me like a mother hen. I half suspect Eric of paying her to play nursemaid."

Opie smiled but didn't answer. Apparently Liv was on to something.

"Did you find anything interesting?" I asked. "Online, that is?"

"I learned a little more about the gruff Chandler Hines. He does quite a business online in metal working. Mostly armor and armaments for enthusiasts. He's even done some work for the motion pictures industry. Very pricy stuff, though. And a very limited market. At least for people who want to be truly authentic, and that's what he does."

"He didn't seem to have much tolerance for Brooks and his factory-made armor," I said, "but that hardly seems like a motive for poisoning someone."

"Oh, you don't know these guys," Opie said. "They're nuts about this kind of stuff."

"Hines told me that he'd challenged Brooks to a joust to settle the dispute," I added. "Why would he then go and kill the man?"

"Got tired of waiting?" Opie suggested.

"If he got tired of waiting, you'd think a man obsessed with antique weapons would choose something other than poison." I turned back to Liv. "Does Hines have any education or training in plants or chemistry or anything like that?"

"Not that I could find," Liv said. "He's former military. Went straight from firing modern weapons to crafting medieval ones."

The "former military" part rang a chord.

"Brooks was also former military," I said. "Might they have met? Perhaps even served together?" Or if Brooks were involved in black ops, as my father suggested, would that have put him at odds with the military? I really should have paid more attention to all those spy movies Brad had dragged me to.

"That's going to be harder to find out," Liv said, "but I could try. I mean military records are protected, and I'm no hacker. But perhaps someone posted old pictures on Facebook or something. That's how I found out about Chandler Hines. His old unit is into social networking and quite the raucous reunions. I can try to find a connection between him and Barry Brooks."

And I knew by that determined look that if there was anything to learn, she would find it.

"But if he's former military," she said, "wouldn't that mean he's had some kind of survival training? Do they do that? Or is that just Boy Scouts?"

I shrugged.

"That I can look up," she said. "But if Hines had survival training, learning what you can eat while stranded in the woods could be just as helpful in knowing what you can't eat. Right?"

That made sense in a Liv sort of way.

"Did you come across anything on Raylene Quinn?" I asked.

"She's a very intelligent woman, but she has a very depressing Facebook page. Kind of passive aggressive. The whole world is bad, it seems. And then more about how adversity makes you stronger. And then she rants when people invite her to play games."

"Probably trying to cheer her up."

"That's what I thought," Liv said. "If she'd bothered to take the 'What Winnie the Pooh Character Are You?' quiz, she'd be a definite Eeyore."

"I can see why." I leaned against the table. Apparently

just thinking about her could drain the energy from someone. "She's invested a good part of her life in Brooks Pharmaceuticals and in Barry Brooks personally. And I'm not sure it's done that much for her."

"How do you mean?" Liv asked.

"She took up with Brooks right after college," I said, "apparently trading certain . . . favors . . . for rapid advancement in the company."

"So she slept her way to the top," Opie said. "It happens."

"Yes, but for someone clearly as intelligent as Raylene, it has to be galling," I said, "to know your promotion didn't come from your accomplishments."

"Maybe those advanced degrees were Raylene proving to herself that she was worthy of the promotions Brooks was giving her," Liv said.

"Or proving it to others," I said. "The sad thing is, I wonder how far all her education and experience could have taken her if she'd worked elsewhere."

"Brooks wouldn't have let her go to the competition," Opie said. "Not without a fight."

I nodded. "And I'm sure he had ample ammunition to smear her reputation if he'd wanted to. She was stuck. No way for her to rise any higher at Brooks Pharmaceuticals, and no door open to go anywhere else."

"Far cry from the Hundred Acre Wood. And," Liv said, "if she suddenly came to realize Brooks was using her and holding her back . . ."

I tapped my nails on the table. "She's still my best suspect."

The bell over the door rang, and Opie excused herself to check on the customer.

Liv watched her leave. "Well, did you find out anything?" Liv asked in hushed tones, moving closer to me. "Did you get to talk with *him*?" She leaned in so close I could no longer focus on her face. "Did you talk to your f-a-t-h-e-r?"

"Good heavens, Liv. Even if Opie could hear us, she knows how to spell. But yes, I talked with him. Briefly. Bixby was looking for him and found him right after."

"And?"

"We're taking that long-promised trip to Florida and he's buying me a puppy."

She hit my arm. "Will you be serious?"

"Being serious is depressing. But don't worry. I won't post that on Facebook."

She gave me the glare, so I recounted my visit, starting with snooping on my father's cell phone and ending with Bixby interrupting our discussion to question him. I then filled her in on Bixby showing up at my house at three a.m., but I left out the part about Nick being there in a drool-covered tunic and the imprint of the tie on my cheek.

"But Bixby doesn't know he's your father?" she asked. "Are you going to tell him?"

"I'm not sure. I'm not sure it's relevant."

Liv closed her eyes. Meanwhile the bell up front chimed twice, meaning Opie would be tied up longer with customers.

Liv pushed herself up onto a stool. "Well, I did find your father mentioned in a number of cases. He's a legitimate bail bondsman *and* bounty hunter, and apparently very good at it. Never did a guest appearance on *Dog the Bounty Hunter*, though. Such a pity. Not even any photographs online."

"He would have avoided being seen on TV or posting pictures. Why change your name and then risk being recognized by putting your image out there? Can't imagine Mother watching an episode of *Dog*, though, so if he was hiding from her, that would have been safe."

"I also couldn't find any records of a wife or family, but he pays his taxes, apparently runs a clean, profitable business, albeit in a shady part of town. But I expect most bail services are near the jails."

That made sense.

She winced. "I did call my mother."

I inhaled through my teeth. "That's pretty risky." Liv's mother and mine, like many twins, seemed to have some kind of psychic connection. It was impossible for one of them to keep a secret from the other.

"I know," she said. "But I didn't tell her that he was here. I just said that you were in a relationship and seemed to have trouble committing, and I wondered if it could be because of your father."

My jaw dropped, so I snapped it shut and closed my eyes, then hid my burning face behind my hands.

"Well, it's true in a way," Liv hedged. "And Mom bought it. That's all it took to get her talking. Your mother hasn't been telling you everything about him and why he left."

I peeked out from between my fingers. "Did she know about Brooks?"

Liv shook her head. "Not about those supposed CIA connections, at least as far as Mom told me. But she did say something interesting that plays right into that angle. She said Brooks was far too accommodating after your father left."

"What does that mean, *far too accommodating*?"

"Just the words my mother used. But I gathered that Brooks came on to your mother."

"So Dad left under a manufactured cloud of suspicion, and then Brooks made a play for my mother?" By this time my cheeks were hot and my stomach gurgling. "Good thing," I said. "All I can say is that it's a good thing."

"Audrey, you're frightening me. What's a good thing?" She hopped off her stool and made her way to where I stood clenching my fists.

"Good thing he's dead," I said. "Otherwise I might have killed him myself."

Opie walked in on my last statement. She looked at me, then at Liv, then back at me. Very softly, she said, "Audrey, there's a medieval peasant who looks an awful lot like Chief Bixby waiting for you out front."

I was very grateful that Bixby's allergies had kept him on our front stoop, well away from the door in case any renegade pollen escaped. I'd have a hard time explaining my threat to kill Barry Brooks myself. Although I doubt it's a crime to threaten the life of someone who was no longer breathing. In any case, Bixby had to wait for me to change back into my Joan of Arc costume.

The ride over to Larry's was pretty quiet. Bixby drove. Lafferty claimed the front seat, leaving me in the back with a cage separating us. I tried to ignore the stains and the smell in the carpet and the upholstery. The camp would be worse anyway.

I didn't think I could tell him about my father without falling apart, so I said nothing. And Bixby had apparently thought twice about his promise to brief me, because he said nothing. The only one who spoke was Lafferty, who held up a couple of pictures of what he thought Judith's flowers should look like. When he told me Judith didn't agree, I started ignoring him until he got to his sixth or seventh suggestion that she carry paper roses made from the *Town of Ramble Police Code Book*. At that point Bixby turned on the radio. Loud.

But he turned it off less than a minute later when the police radio crackled out a message. Lafferty translated the codes. "A disturbance out at the campground."

Bixby had the lights and sirens on in a flash, and the rate at which he tore around those country roads left me scrambling for something to hold on to for dear life. Instead of parking at the bottom of Larry's driveway, he tore up it instead, leaving a cloud of dust in our wake.

The car jerked to a stop and he yanked up the hand break. In one fluid motion, he pulled his gun out of his glove box, checked his clip, and said, "Wait here." He jogged toward the path with Lafferty close on his tail.

I waited for a good ten seconds before I climbed out and followed them. I figured if he was truly serious about wanting me to stay in the car, he would have locked me in.

I ran, following the clamor of men's voices, and found the disturbance centered around the area that held Hines's blacksmith operation and my father's tent.

"Dad!" I called out, and then hoped my words had been drowned in the confusion of voices. My father didn't seem to be involved. He stood in front of his tent, his hands folded in front of him, looking innocent and practically beatific, while two other men rolled around on the ground. To my relief, they were also not Shelby and Darnell.

One of them, I could tell by the gruff baritone swearing, was Chandler Hines.

The other, a much smaller man, seemed to be eating a lot of the dust from the ground. When he rolled into a fetal ball, I caught a glimpse of his face and identified him as the mousy food vendor.

Bixby made his way to me. "I thought I told you . . . never mind." He thrust his gun at Lafferty. "Here, hold this. Last thing I want to do is add a gun into that situation."

Bixby broke through the crowd that had gathered to watch and made his way to where the two men were scuffling. He barked out orders, which pretty much went ignored.

Lafferty bounced on his heels, weaving to get a good view of the action. He tensed when Bixby went down. "Here, *Deputy*, hold this. The chief is right. The last thing that situation needs is a gun." His words seemed to carry more bravado than actual bravery.

I took his gun gingerly—I can't say I ever held one before—and Lafferty guided my hand toward the ground. "Please don't shoot anybody." Then he joined the scuffle. Bixby pulled Hines away, and Lafferty attempted to subdue the much small vendor.

I spotted Carol and Melanie a few feet away, so I made my way over to the them. "What's the fight about?"

"Potatoes," said Melanie.

"Potatoes?"

"The vendor was selling them. Hines found out and had a fit."

"Why would Hines care if the vendor was selling potatoes?" I realized while gesturing that I had carelessly lifted the gun, so I inched down my arm until the gun was once again safely pointed toward the ground.

"They're against the rules," Carol said. "No potatoes in the Middle Ages. The Spanish conquistadors didn't introduce them to Europe until the 1500s. They're as strict about potatoes here as they are about cell phones."

I turned back to watch what was left of the scuffle. The vendor had settled down, but Hines broke free from Bixby and made one last lunge toward the little guy.

Until Bixby got a hold of Hines's arm and wrenched it behind his back.

"That's it. You're going in," Bixby told Hines, wrestling him against a nearby tree. "Dang! My cuffs are back in my other pants." He looked to Lafferty.

"Same here," he said with a fierce blush. "Other pants."

"May I?" my father said. He pulled a set of cuffs from the long sleeve of his cassock and tossed them to Bixby.

While Bixby managed to cuff a squirming and swearing Hines, my father headed to Lafferty, removed another set of cuffs, and slid them around the vendor's wrists.

"Thanks, but I wasn't going to take him in," Bixby said. "He stopped fighting as directed, and this guy"—he pointed his head toward Hines—"was clearly the aggressor. This is my prisoner."

"I know, Chief," my father said. He gestured toward the vendor. "And this is my prisoner. He jumped a forty-thousand-dollar bond in Houston, leaving his poor mother homeless, I might add, and has evaded police for almost three years. Just remember, I want credit for bringing him in."

Bixby stopped and studied the crowd for a moment. "How about we all go in?"

Mrs. June's eyes bugged out when we entered the police station. I couldn't blame her really. We must have been quite a sight. I, in my Joan of Arc duds, was first in the door, followed by my father, still dressed as a medieval friar. Behind us were Lafferty and Bixby in their peasant guises with Chandler Hines and the food vendor both sporting shiny, anachronistically modern handcuffs. And all this in Ramble's police station with its historic colonial brick walls, desks from the seventies, and modern computers.

Organized chaos seemed to ensue from that point, with

forms being filled out, fingerprints and photos taken. My father headed to the phones, which he used without asking permission, which oddly didn't seem to bother Bixby.

I leaned against the wall with nothing to do, enough out of the loop that I couldn't help with any of the paperwork or other tasks, but apparently involved enough that I was expected to stay. So while Mrs. June hustled to find the proper forms ("It's a county arrest, dagnabbit," Bixby shouted), I busied myself by clearing the sludge out of their coffeepot and making more. Coffee, that is. Not sludge.

The pot just finished dripping when Bixby summoned me into his office. "Well, Deputy, would you like to listen in on the interrogations? I did promise to keep you in the loop."

I nodded, and carefully handed him back his gun.

When he was done glaring at Lafferty, the chief secured his gun in his desk and took Chandler Hines into the interrogation room. Lafferty and I got to watch and listen through that big one-way mirror, the kind on all those cop shows. Only the line of sight wasn't as good as television would lead you to believe. We had to stand on the far ends of the mirror in order to see Hines's face instead of just the back of Bixby's head. And the audio quality was just a little bit better than the drive-through at Chick-fil-A.

At least Mrs. June took pity and carried in a cup of coffee for each of us. And a doughnut. Coffee and doughnuts while watching an interrogation? I felt like such a cop.

Hines was brooding and had to be drawn out. Bixby started by confirming his name and other details.

"Look, can we just get on with it?" Hines said. "I know what I did."

"You seem to have a pattern of assault," Bixby said,

thumbing through the paperwork "I take it you have quite a temper."

Hines didn't answer.

"So tell me what started the fight with Eli Strickland."

"Who's Eli Strickland?"

"The guy you clobbered in front of a few dozen witnesses."

Hines squinted. "He always went by the name of Joe."

"Joe is an alias. He's a fugitive."

"Well, I'll be." Hines leaned back in his chair. "Do I get a reward?"

"No, you get arrested. So what started the fight?"

Hines took a deep breath through his teeth, then focused his gaze squarely on Bixby. "It sounds silly now."

"You must have had a reason."

Their voices got lower. Lafferty turned up the speaker volume.

Hines looked down and studied his still-cuffed hands. "I guess I take it a little too serious sometimes. But I'm not one of these Johnny-come-latelies that come for the weekend on a lark. I make my livelihood doing these camps. And I spent a lot of hours making everything just so. There are easier ways to work metal than the medieval way. But I stick to the old ways. Have a lot invested in it."

"And Mr. Strickland did what to threaten that exactly?"

"I don't care what the tourists do when they come in wearing polyester and dressed for the wrong century. But the artisans, you see, the artisans should know better."

"I don't see what you're getting at," Bixby said.

"The food vendors are supposed to be artisans as well. They have to do things the way they were done in the Middle Ages. And I guess it is hard on the food vendors, having to keep up with modern food service laws while conforming to medieval society. So I can forgive the occasional food thermometer and cooler. As long as it's disguised, of course."

"But Mr. Strickland went beyond that?"

"He was serving potatoes," Hines said. His voice was even-tempered, but his face flushed and a single vein in his forehead pulsed.

While Hines went on to explain the travesty of potatoes, I glanced out at my father, who seemed to be eavesdropping on the interrogation through the door. We shared a glance, then I turned back to watch Bixby question Hines. Once the assault questions were out of the way, he shifted gears to the murder.

"So talk with me about Barry Brooks. Were you angry with him, too?"

"Now, wait a minute," Hines said, his eyes getting wide. "Just because—"

"Just answer the question. We've established that you have a temper. Were you angry with Barry Brooks? Yes or no?"

"Yes, I was angry with him. No, I didn't kill him." Hines was definitely nervous now, his gaze darting around the room, focusing at last on the mirror where we stood unseen to him. "I know how this works. You need to send someone up, and I'm convenient. I think I want a lawyer now." He then set his jaw tight and stopped talking.

"A lawyer you want, a lawyer you get. You can tell him we're booking you on assault. For now."

Bixby came out of the room, called Lafferty over, gave him some instructions, and soon Lafferty was escorting Hines away, presumably to the county jail.

Bixby whistled when Lafferty was halfway out the door. "Back in uniform first, though."

"Oh, right." Lafferty looked down at his clothes, then

gestured that Hines have a seat on the bench against the wall. He attached Hines's cuffs to a bracket I hadn't seen before.

Next up in the interrogation room was Eli Strickland. This time my father joined me behind the mirror.

"So this is the guy you were after all along," I said to him while Bixby rattled off the preliminary questions. "What did he do?"

"Guy was a pharmacist."

"Hardly illegal," I said. "There must be more."

"Oh, yeah. He was watering down the painkillers and other drugs for his paying customers and selling the good stuff out the back door on the street. A lot of people were in a lot of pain because of it. He's lucky he didn't kill anybody."

"You said his mother lost her house because of him?"

My dad nodded, then scratched at his collar. "Hot in here, isn't it?" He unbuttoned his cassock and removed it, including the paunchy stomach, which appeared to be some kind of prosthetic. The man underneath wore a trim T-shirt and long shorts that wouldn't appear beneath the cassock. He draped the garment on the chair. Now he looked more like the man I remembered, except this man had less hair.

"But yes," he said. "The DEA confiscated the small drugstore he ran, and his mother was foolish enough to cosign for his bond. She put up her house. When he skipped, she was forced into foreclosure."

"What mother wouldn't do that for her son? To take her house seems cruel."

"That's the system."

I nodded and turned to watch the interrogation, which had gone past today's assault. I turned up the volume.

"Were you acquainted with Barry Brooks?" Bixby asked.

"The guy who got himself killed?"

"Got himself killed?" Bixby parroted. "It sounds like

you think he had something to do with his own death. Maybe you think he deserved it?"

"Hey, wait a minute. Don't go putting words in my mouth. I barely knew the guy. Seen him around some."

"Your paths never crossed before?"

"Why would they?" Strickland looked unconcerned.

"Well, it says here that you were a pharmacist."

"So?"

I turned to my father and put a hand on his arm. "A pharmacist would probably know about poisons."

My father patted my hand and turned back to the window.

Bixby went on. "Barry Brooks ran a large pharmaceutical company."

Strickland turned ashen and his Adam's apple bobbed before he answered. "Brooks Pharmaceuticals?"

"Then you have heard of it. We can check the records and see if you've had any dealings with them."

Strickland sighed and let his head rest back against his chair. "Will it help me if I talk?"

"No promises," Bixby said meekly. "But I'll see what I can do."

Oh, brother. Bixby was attempting his Mr. Rogers routine on Strickland.

Strickland paused for a minute. "Then Brooks was a crook, too. Or someone in his organization."

"How's that?" Bixby asked.

"They got me for watering drugs, right?"

Bixby nodded.

"And selling them to kids on the street," my father said under his breath.

"Yeah, well, I'd been doing it for quite some time. Nobody ever noticed. No complaints. Nobody got hurt. I knew exactly how much I could take. It was only when we started filling scripts from Brooks's company that I was caught."

"Meaning?" Bixby asked.

"The drugs were cut before we got them. Before they left the plant. Does that help me at all?"

Bixby said, "I don't see how."

But my father snapped his finger. "Of course," he said. "They'd cover for him, too." He grabbed my shoulders. "Don't you see? Those inferred secretive connections. Brooks could get someone on the floor or in the labs to cut the drugs. Then he was free to sell the extra and the money went straight into his pocket. But that would have been large amounts! Ha, ha!" He pulled me into a hug and practically twirled me around the room. "We got him. That would prove Brooks's connection with organized crime."

"Got who? Brooks is already dead."

That took the wind out of his sails pretty quickly.

"Was that why you were taking pictures of Brooks?" I asked. "You were trying to catch him in the act of doing something unseemly."

He nodded.

"You should show those pictures to Bixby. Might be something to help him in his case."

"How would I explain them without . . " His arms were still around me when Bixby exited the interview room. My father cleared his throat and stepped back. "Well, Chief? Can I take my prisoner?"

"Not yet," Bixby said. "I can hold him on assault in the meantime. But I'd rather you stick around while the murder investigation continues."

"Do you suspect me of something?" There was that beatific smile. He could pull it off without even wearing the garb of a friar.

But I wasn't sure if he was any match for Bixby's Mr. Rogers routine. Bixby sat on the corner of his desk, crossed his arms casually in front of him, and tilted his head. "Should I suspect you of something?"

My father just shrugged and smiled back at him.

After a moment, Bixby turned to me. "So, Audrey, when we first arrived at the scene of the fight, exactly why did you call out, 'Dad'?"

Chapter 13

I ate another chocolate kiss from Mrs. June's desk and looked back at the closed door of the office where Chief Bixby was talking with my father.

"You should go home, child." she said.

Instead I stood up and paced in front of her desk again. "Can Bixby hold him on anything?"

"Hard for me to say," she said. "Could . . . your father . . . have interfered in the investigation in any way?"

Was hiding the fact that you once worked with the victim interfering? I flung myself back into the chair and buried my head in my hands. "He didn't kill Barry Brooks. I know that much."

"Shh." Mrs. June rolled her chair over to mine and waited until I managed to look her in the eyes. "Of course he didn't."

"Audrey?" I hadn't heard the door open. Chief Bixby took two steps out of his office. "Mrs. June, could you give us a couple of minutes?"

Mrs. June patted my hand. "I've been meaning to run to the ladies' room all afternoon. I'll be back in a few."

As she scurried off, Bixby lowered himself into her chair, still facing mine. "This must be difficult for you."

I nodded, not trusting my voice.

"You should have told me. He should have told me."

I nodded again, in danger now of becoming a human bobble-head doll.

"I'm going to keep him."

I opened my mouth to protest, but Bixby held up his hand. "Not that I think he killed Brooks, but I need to get the whole story. Do you trust me?"

Good question. I'd known him to arrest the wrong person before, but not without good evidence. I didn't always think he told me the whole truth, but perhaps that was part of the job. "I think you're good at what you do," I finally managed.

"I'll take that," he said. "But I want you to go home now. There's nothing else that you can do here. If your father is open and honest with me, he could be out later today."

"He didn't kill Barry Brooks."

"I hope you're right." Chief Bixby stood and held open the door for me. "Mrs. June can drive you home."

When I got back to the cottage, I stayed inside only long enough to feed the cats before I grabbed my shovel and headed out to the grassy area by the driveway, where I wanted to plant some shade trees. I attacked the ground with gusto, rehearsing recent events in my head to the cadence of the shovel breaking the dirt. I ignored the mosquitoes, the clouds of gnats, and the burning where my ungloved fingers chafed against the wood shovel handle, and I stopped only when I heard the crunch of tires in my driveway. I looked up to see Liv and Eric hop out of his truck. Well, Eric hopped. Liv half climbed and half slid to the ground.

I rubbed the back of my hand against my sweaty forehead and went to meet them. "What's up?"

"Eric wanted to double-check the tarp on your roof and I rode along," Liv said.

"May be a storm this weekend, they're saying on the Weather Channel." While Eric pulled out his ladder and headed to the roof, Liv joined me where I'd been digging.

"Who are you planning on burying here?" she asked, pointing to the embarrassingly massive pit I'd excavated. "Kane Bixby or your father?"

"I just got carried away." I wagged a finger at her. "But I like the way you think."

I moved over to where I wanted the next tree and started a new hole.

"Who are we planting in this one?" Liv asked.

"It's a good thinking activity," I said. "Digging. I was thinking about the case, but then I started thinking about my dad and what it was like when he left. If it weren't for Grandma Mae, I never would have made it through. Mom hasn't seemed completely happy since, either. It's amazing how much misery one man can cause."

I didn't look up to see Liv's reaction. I just kept digging.

"And then I was thinking about Raylene Quinn. Barry Brooks made her life miserable. What a brilliant woman, and here she was kowtowing to a sleazeball like Brooks." I looked up. "Notice the theme yet? The common thread?"

"I'm not sure I like where you're heading," Liv said.

"And then there's Kathleen Randolph. She seems quite happy running her business as a single woman. Happier than with any of her exes, that's for sure. And when I remember the funk I was in when Brad left—"

"Audrey—"

"Whoever said happily ever after had to involve a man? Here I was thinking I had to decide between Nick and Brad. But guess what? There's another option. I can choose neither. I can decide to live a perfectly happy life without either of them. No more drama. Maybe I've decided to do just that."

"Oh, Audrey. And what? Live here with an increasing horde of cats?"

"I have my work. I have this place to fix up. I have you. Maybe I just have no desire to have my happiness tied to a man. Any man."

Liv spent the next few minutes stammering and sputtering, doing her best to persuade me not to decide anything rashly.

"I tied down that tarp the best I could," Eric said, loading his ladder into the back of his truck. "It should hold up to a decent storm."

"Thanks," I said.

I watched as Eric held open the car door and then helped hoist Liv into her seat. She gave me a worried look as they drove away together. Back to their house that they were fixing up and turning into a cozy home. Eric just finished remodeling the kitchen, turning it into a chef's dream, despite that fact that Liv's most extravagant cooking endeavor to date was mixing together two different kinds of canned soups. Still, their house was the place where family and friends gathered, and the walls echoed with love and laughter, even if Eric eyed a few cracks in them critically, threatening to eventually rip off the plaster to see what was going on behind them.

And now the cute green and yellow nursery with the

hand-painted giraffes and the frilly white curtains stood completed at the end of the hall, awaiting only their baby.

And suddenly my commitment to this new solo-life thing dissolved like sand slipping through my fingers.

I spent the rest of the evening consuming most of a box of stale graham crackers while watching a marathon of *Dog the Bounty Hunter*, wondering what life was like for my dad after he left us. The stress of the day must have tired me out, because I fell asleep on the couch with the little black kitten lying on my chest. When I woke up, moonlight was streaming through the multipaned windows and I somehow caught a whiff of Nick's scent still lingering in the sofa pillows.

The kitten shifted and started purring loudly. Or maybe she was snoring.

I lay there, exhausted but awake, for what seemed like hours, my mind awash in thoughts of the investigation, my relationships with Brad and Nick, and my father's arrival. Sleep wasn't coming anytime soon.

As I stroked the kitten's shiny, soft fur, I knew Nick was right about one thing. She needed a name. I looked up at the moon. "Hello, Luna," I said, trying the name out loud. "Maybe Clair de Lune, Luna for short?" She nuzzled my chin.

And Nick was right about something else. I couldn't live my life waiting for people to leave. And despite my earlier impulsive rationalization that I could be perfectly content embracing a single life—and that was probably true—it wasn't what I wanted. No, I couldn't say I was unhappy being single and working at the shop. It was a good life. But I also wanted a home and family of my own: crying babies, runny noses, soccer games, teenage angst, grandkids someday. And

I wanted a good man to stand beside me. I was also pretty sure I knew who I wanted that to be. And I needed to tell him that.

I settled the kitten onto her favorite throw pillow, slipped back into the bedroom, and changed into my Joan of Arc clothes. My heart beat faster with new resolve. I would not let past disappointments keep me from committing to a relationship. Wouldn't Liv be surprised at the sudden turnaround!

I fed the cats their breakfast early—in my experience, cats are always ready for breakfast—and left the house, driving the CR-V to Larry's place. There was no sign of him guarding the fence, but I hadn't expected to see him at this time of night. There was, however, a lock box near the fence with a cardboard sign that said, "TOLL: FIVE DOLLARS." I wasn't sure it applied to me, but since I hadn't brought five dollars, it wasn't an issue.

The moonlight that had helped me navigate Larry's driveway wasn't as helpful in forging my way along that deer path through the woods. I clutched my arms, as the air seemed chillier than I initially thought. Or maybe I was cold from the blood loss, because the mosquitoes had taken enough to support a whole colony for three years. I managed to find my way more from memory, and was relieved when I stumbled into camp—yes, literally. Stupid tree root.

At least here I was free of the dense canopy of leaves, and the moonlight made the camp navigable. Bats and moths weren't the only things flying around. I had more than a few butterflies in my stomach as I stole through the deserted pathways to Nick's tent.

Only somewhere along the way I lost my nerve again. Which was probably for the best. The last thing I needed was to bounce from one rash decision to another. Whatever happened to levelheaded Audrey? Apparently she was a bit stressed at the moment.

And unfocused. What in the world was I doing running around camp in the middle of the night, thinking of love, when there was a possible murderer still on the loose? Ugh, my father's reappearance seemed to short-circuit my rationality and send me right back to adolescence. I was surprised my face hadn't erupted into acne.

Perhaps the cooler temperatures had frozen some of the giddiness out of me and replaced it with cold, hard facts. If Nick didn't want to commit to a relationship until the bakery was solvent, what would he do if Mel Brooks's lawyers sued him over the poisoning? Even mounting a defense against the litigation could put him under. No, any serious talks about the future of our relationship would have to wait until the killer was identified and behind bars.

I wandered around the camp a little longer, rubbing my hands together to try to generate some warmth. I felt foolish for having come all the way out here, but it didn't make sense to trek back through those woods in the dark. Maybe I could just wait somewhere until the camp woke up.

And then I remembered. Chandler Hines, Eli Strickland, and my father were all in custody, leaving that whole area of the camp unoccupied. I could hang out there and wait for morning to come. After all, my father had a warm, empty sleeping bag in his tent.

Better yet, I could do a little snooping.

I was tempted to search my father's tent again, but as I approached the food vendor's empty stall, I thought about how Barry Brooks had been killed. Someone had put monkshood—probably a cooked root—into his food. But only his food. Which means the killer had some means of cooking it.

Eli Strickland would have had a fire or stove or something. If he'd cooked potatoes with nobody noticing, why not monkshood? And maybe he'd only pretended to be surprised to learn who Barry Brooks was. Strickland had a twisted motive, if he somehow attributed his arrest to Brooks.

I didn't know if Strickland would be stupid enough to leave evidence lying around, but he hadn't been the focus of the investigation. And he couldn't have predicted that he'd be in jail right now. Was it too much to hope that he'd left something incriminating behind?

And searching the food stall wouldn't even be breaking and entering. The booth was open to the elements.

I slid under the counter, finding a cardboard box underneath the draping. Did they have cardboard in the Middle Ages?

I tugged the box onto the counter into the moonlight and started to rummage through it. On top were several printed flyers for various Renaissance fairs—apparently Strickland traveled the circuit. Underneath were all kinds of modern kitchen supplies. Matches. A lighter. A vegetable peeler. MSG. Yeah, Eli Strickland wasn't really with the program. Perhaps the medieval circuit was just his way of staying off the radar and avoiding people like my father.

I had my nose buried in the box. Something in the bottom was wrapped in layer after layer of shiny butcher's paper. Very suspicious. What was the mousy little food vendor hiding in the bottom of this innocent, albeit anachronistic cardboard box?

I removed layers of paper much as one might unwrap a mummy—or perhaps more like trying to get the toilet paper off the trees during spirit week at the middle school. I had just reached the center when I encountered what felt like fingers of dried flesh. I dropped them back into the box. I shined my cell phone into the bottom to see what exactly I had touched. A little bit of wrapping remained. Dried cod. At first I was relieved, until I caught instructions on the side for something called lutefisk. Yeah, sure. Take these dried-up leathery bits of fish and soak them in lye. Yum? I shuddered.

Only then did I catch a glimpse of movement in my peripheral vision, then a sudden blow to the back of my head.

As I fell to the ground, almost in movie slow motion, my subconscious decided to provide a sound track. Perhaps the dried fish reminded me somehow of the sea, because I lost consciousness to the lyrics of "Yellow Submarine."

Chapter 14

My head was throbbing, compounded by crowd noise, as if I were at some raucous college football game. I was upright somehow, but every muscle in my body screamed. I opened my eyes but they refused to focus. I tried to move, but my hands seemed restrained. No, more than my hands.

Finally the world swirled into focus and I saw feet gathered around me in a circle. And when I cautiously lifted my head, something struck me on the cheek.

I must have been dreaming because I suddenly smelled tomatoes, that glorious scent of summer.

I blinked and looked up again, and there was Brad with his camera.

"Hello, Brad," I croaked. Had to be a dream.

"This is great!" he said. "Audrey, you're such a sport!"

A nearby spectator threw another tomato. This time I

saw it coming and tried to duck, but when I jerked away, the sore spot on my head came into contact with a hard object.

"No, not the tomatoes!" someone called. "They're a New World food. Use the cabbage."

By this time I was awake. "What's going on? Where am I?"

"Stop!" Now I was hearing Nick. Soon his face appeared in my field of vision. "Are you okay? How did you end up in here?"

"In where?"

"Audrey, you're in the pillory."

"The what?"

"The . . . the stocks." A mass of rotten cabbage landed nearby. Nick turned to the crowd. "What's wrong with you? Can't you see the lady is barely conscious? Get out of here. Show's over."

Brad set down his camera. "I'm sorry." He looked around. "I had no idea. Everyone was buzzing about someone in the stocks, so I wanted to get some shots. I figured you were doing this for fun."

"Does it look like she's having fun?" Nick asked Brad. "Help me get her out of here."

Together they lifted the top of the stocks and Nick helped me upright. I had trouble standing. My back and my legs were stiff and achy and any sudden motion made my head swim. When I was finally able to straighten, stretch my back, and take in my surroundings, the sun had just cleared the horizon. It couldn't be much past dawn. And the sky was red with color.

Red sky in the morning, sailor take warning.

Or maybe I was seeing the world through tomato-colored glasses.

Nick and Brad helped me hobble to a bench.

Soon Melanie and Carol hustled over. "We're sorry, too," Carol said. "We just figured it was part of the whole experience."

"I saw someone in the stocks," Melanie said. "But I didn't know it was you. Or else I wouldn't have thrown that—"

I held up my hand, then reached back and felt the knob on the back of my head. "Does anybody have ice?"

"We're not supposed to have ice in the camp," Melanie said.

"But I can get some if you don't tell anyone where it came from," Carol added, half running off.

"Mum's the word," I said. I really didn't care about the whole bizarre black market in this place.

Nick slid next to me on the bench. "Here, let me see that." He gently pulled back my hair. "There's no broken skin, although you're getting quite a lump. It looks like you've had a significant encounter with the not-so-proverbial blunt object."

"And here I was just filming it!" Brad raked a hand through his hair. "I can be so dense sometimes."

I opened my mouth but was in no mood to argue with him at the moment.

"Do you remember what happened?" Nick asked.

"I was coming to see you," I started.

"Me?" he asked.

"But you weren't awake yet, so I wandered around the camp a bit. I went to check out the food vendor's stall. And . . ." After that an old Beatles song played in my head, but it hardly seemed relevant, so I didn't mention it. "That's the last I can recall."

"We should call Bixby," Nick said.

"He's the one who cautioned me not to come out here

alone. If he gets wind of this . . ." What could he do? Technically we were both deputies, equal in rank. Unless some deputies were more equal than others. I suspected that was probably the case.

"But you can't let someone get away with assaulting you," Brad said.

"I'm not. Because I'm going to catch whoever did this," I said with mounting resolve. "The more I find out about Barry Brooks, I'll admit, the less I like him. But now my father is in jail, Nick could get sued, and whoever did this"—I pointed to my throbbing goose egg—"well, they've made it personal."

"Audrey." Brad collapsed on his knees in front of me. I sure hoped he hadn't picked this moment to propose. "We have to get you to the doctor. You're not talking sense."

"What did I say?"

"That your father was in jail. He's been gone for years."

"No," Nick said. "The father is her father."

"Huh?" Brad looked up at Nick.

"Father Richard, the friar, is really Audrey's father," Nick said. "He's a bounty hunter."

"Whoa," said Melanie. "Your father is a priest *and* a bounty hunter? That's kind of freaky. In a cool sort of way."

"He's not a real priest," I said.

Carol rushed back with ice bound in what looked like old rags. "They're clean," she said. "Just dyed to look like old rags." She looked around at the faces. "What did I miss?"

"How about we take Audrey back to our cottage and get her cleaned up," Melanie said. "I think there's a story here."

Since the cottage the girls shared was just outside the clearing with the stocks, I agreed. And they even allowed me to walk unaided, with a quick stop at the nearest garderobe, although Nick was close by in case I should take a tumble. Fitting us all in that cramped cottage was tight—Nick, Brad, Melanie, Carol, and me—but I was glad to no longer be a public spectacle. So I told them the whole story while Melanie and Carol tried to blot the tomato juice out of my Joan of Arc outfit.

"Well, Bixby's right about one thing," Nick said. "You shouldn't be wandering around here alone. Apparently you're on someone's radar."

"Liv's been dying to come," I said, "but if I let her, Eric would kill me."

"I don't blame him," Nick said. "But I'd be glad to help."

"So would I," Brad said.

Melanie and Carol nodded.

"I can't keep you from the other things you're supposed to be doing." I looked at Nick. "Your baking." I turned to Brad. "Or your filming." I looked at the girls. "Or your schoolwork."

"But if we take turns, it's not so much," Melanie said.

"But no more wandering around in the dark." Nick tapped the tip of my nose to emphasize his point. "Especially if it was the killer who attacked you."

"Who else would it be?" Brad said. "I can't imagine anyone bonked Audrey over the head for no reason."

"You must have been getting close," Melanie said. "Where exactly were you when someone attacked you?"

"I was in the area by the blacksmith and the food vendor, across from the father's—my father's—tent. But all of them are in jail."

"Not anymore," Nick said. "I saw Chandler Hines this morning. Looks like he made bail."

I bit my bottom lip. "I'll bet my father's out, too, then, considering that's what he does. Strickland may be the only one still locked up. Or Joe, as I guess he's known as in these parts. Which does, oddly enough, eliminate the one clear felon of the group."

"At least as far as the head conking goes," Carol said. "The person who attacked you might not be the killer."

"True," Melanie said. "But who else here would have attacked Audrey?"

"Could it have been some kind of prank?" Brad asked. "Maybe Strickland did kill Brooks and someone else just hit you on the head because . . . okay, I got nothing."

"I can't believe Joe's some arch-criminal," Carol said. "I worked with him last year. He wasn't that friendly, but I would never have thought he was a fugitive."

"Just your common, everyday drug dealer," I said.

"So," Melanie said, "someone bonked you on the head and carried you over to the stocks. We're going to be looking for a fairly strong man. No offense."

"I don't know." I pounded some dust off my clothing. "I'm awfully dirty—and sore. I'm going to lay odds that I was dragged. So the person who conked me could be a man or a woman. I wasn't in a condition to put up a struggle at that point. But this cottage is right near the stocks. Did any of you see or hear anything?"

Melanie shook her head. "I'm a pretty sound sleeper. I think it's all this fresh air."

"I might have." Carol furrowed her eyebrows. "I woke up once, maybe around four. And I heard a woman talking. Would that have been the time?"

"I arrived sometime between three thirty and four, I think. I didn't look at the time. Did you recognize the voice?"

Carol nodded. "I think so. It sounded like Raylene Quinn. But I can't be sure."

"That's interesting," I managed. Again, another clue seemed to point to Raylene. "Carol, you and Melanie work for Brooks's entourage, right? In the stables? Any chance I could tag along? I'd like to get to know everybody a little better."

"Yes," she said, "but I'm off today. Tomorrow might be better anyway. It's tournament day. There'll be plenty of work to share, and everyone will be around."

"Plan on it, then."

"But there's no proof, even if it was Raylene talking," Nick said, "that she attacked you. Or that she killed Brooks."

"No," I said. "But if it was Raylene, we've just learned that she had an accomplice."

When heads snapped toward me, a question on every face, I explained. "Well, she wouldn't be wandering around the camp at four in the morning talking to herself, would she?"

Nick insisted on walking me to my car, driving me back to town, and escorting me directly to my doctor's office—despite my insistence that I was fine. I would have appreciated a change in clothes first. One little girl in the waiting room must have jumped to the conclusion that I was an elf, because she kept dropping hints of what she wanted for Christmas. But the doctor squeezed me in, and I accepted his free sample of painkillers anyway and promised him that I'd be sure to call the office if I experienced any signs of concussion.

When we finally went back to my place so I could change, Nick volunteered to wash out my costume—well, technically it was still his costume. And with all that work that went into hand-stitching it, I figured he had a right to see to its proper maintenance. It was still drip-drying in my bathroom when we headed to the shop.

"I can drop you back at camp, if you'd like," I offered.

"The doctor cleared me for driving. And all I'm going to do this morning is make bouquets for a wedding tomorrow."

"He might have cleared you, but the meds he gave you say you're not to drive. So get used to being chauffeured." He pulled the CR-V into my spot behind the shop and was about to open the back door when I heard Liv yelling.

I tugged open the door. "What's wrong?"

A red-faced Liv was nose-to-nose with my father, giving him a piece of her mind. Well, more like nose-to-chest, but she was still intimidating with her cheeks flushed and her eyes flashing. He was backed into a corner, taking it. Amber Lee stood at her work station trying hard not to look amused.

"Well, hello, Dad," I said. "I see you've found your way out of jail."

He smiled at me. "Your cousin and I were just getting reacquainted. She sure takes after your mother's side of the family."

Liv crossed her arms and glared at him.

"I'm declaring a moratorium on infighting until after the killer is caught," I said, then adopted a casual air. "So when did you get out?"

"About ten last night. The accommodations weren't exactly to my liking. And I'm not fond of orange as a wardrobe choice. I will add that you have several fine choices of bond service here in this part of Virginia."

"That's a relief to know," Amber Lee said, then went back to her work.

"They don't like giving discounts, however," he said. "Even though Chandler Hines and I shared the same bondsman, so we saved him a trip. I was hoping for a two-fer."

"So he got out last night, too?" I asked.

"Yes. They'd rather not hold you if they can help it. But why the curiosity about Chandler Hines?"

"Someone attacked Audrey early this morning," Nick said.

"Are you all right?" Liv was at my side in a shot, poking and probing.

I shooed her away.

Nick offered his hand to my father. "By the way, Nick Maxwell. Nice to meet you, sir."

"Sir?" he said. "Must be a suitor. Audrey? Is this your young man?"

"Dad. Not now."

"Ha! I know that blush." He turned back to Nick. "We'll talk later."

"I'll say it again," Amber Lee said, not even trying to hide the broad smile on her face. "I love my job."

"Well, let's get to it, then." I pulled on my apron and started collecting the white roses we needed to make the bouquets for our latest bride. Since white roses mean *innocence*, they've been a favorite of mine for wedding bouquets. Not all brides get into the whole innocence thing. But this one had.

"I should let you get on with your work," my father said, heading toward the door.

"No, stay, please," I said. "There are a couple of things I'd like to ask you."

He looked at Liv and Nick, and then at Amber Lee. "Are you sure it's the best time?"

I set my knife down on the counter. "Questions about the murder. Remember, there's a moratorium on infighting, so we won't discuss . . . anything else."

He pushed himself up onto a stool. "Whatever you'd like to know."

"Did you go back to the camp last night?" I asked. Then I couldn't resist one last dig. "After you got out of jail?"

"No, it was late. I found a room at a charming inn, just at the edge of town."

"The Ashbury?"

He nodded.

Good. I could check that. "What about Chandler Hines?"

"He got a room, too, but I don't think he was happy about parting with the money. We shared a taxi back to the hotel, but I can't say I saw him after that. I draw the line at sharing rooms with people I don't know, especially when they just got out of jail. I suppose that's a double standard in this case."

"He was seen at the camp just after dawn," I said. "Kathleen Randolph might know when he checked out."

"Want me to call her?" Liv said, halfway to the phone.

"No, I want to stop by and talk with her later anyway, especially since she was once married to the victim."

"Kathleen . . . the mother of the bride?" he asked. "Wait, that was Kathleen Brooks? I thought she looked familiar."

"She's Kathleen Randolph now, and she owns the Ashbury. Did you know her back then?"

"Saw her at company parties. Felt sorry for her at the time. She'd be standing by the wall talking with some geeky chemist and Brooks would be out on the dance floor making a fool of himself with the secretarial staff. They were divorced by the time I moved away. Wait, you don't think she could have . . ."

I sighed. "Not saying she couldn't, but if she had, I think she would have done it years ago. Did you know Raylene Quinn?"

"Not back then. I've seen her with Brooks here, though. I gather they were involved."

"That, and she's the head of Research and Development for Brooks Pharmaceuticals."

"Not when I was there. There was some other woman at

the time. Pretty thing. Come to think of it, she always seemed chummy with Barry, too. Her name was Diane something. Diane Graham."

"Want me to look her up?" Liv asked.

I shrugged. "I'm more curious about the people who are with him now. If Raylene was the killer, and if Raylene was the one who attacked me last night, then she had an accomplice. I'd like to know who we're dealing with." I turned again to my father. "You've had a chance to meet the rest of his entourage?"

"Met, taken names, and"—he pulled out his phone—"taken pictures."

Within half an hour, Liv managed to print out the pictures and tack them onto her growing murder board.

"I see I'm on here," my father said.

"Yes," Liv answered with her perky, dimpled smile.

I left my station and went over to take a look at the new additions to Liv's murder board.

Dean White.

My father tapped the picture of the balding gray-haired man with gray glasses. "I had a nice little chat with him over a decent piece of mutton the other day. He's their CFO. If Brooks was still involved in any crooked financial dealings, this guy would have to be in on it. Otherwise Brooks would have gotten rid of him somehow."

The next picture was of an attractive young woman. Kayla Leonard.

"What does she do?" I asked.

"I haven't a clue," he said. "Tried to have a talk with her. It was like talking to one of those clown heads at the drive-through. You're never quite sure if you're getting the message to a live person, and even if you do, it's kind of freaky.

If she had the brains to kill anyone, then she's a very good actress."

"Which is possible," I said. "And she seems like Brooks's type."

"Female?" Amber Lee asked.

"That's the type." I turned back to my father. "How did Kayla and Raylene get along?"

"Like Clark Kent and Superman. Never seen in the same place at the same time."

"There you go again," I said, "destroying my childhood illusions."

"Uh-uh," he said. "Moratorium, remember. Your idea."

"My bad." I passed to the final photograph. Kenneth Grant. "What's his story?"

"Evasive little guy. As best I could tell he was in distribution. But I don't know the organization anymore. The company has grown so much since I've left it."

"Want me to do a background?" Liv asked.

My dad's head jerked up. "You can do that?"

"She's not the FBI, but it's amazing what she can find sometimes." I turned to Liv. "Sure. Work your magic. By the way, do you know what happened to my copy of Bixby's witness statements?"

Liv shuffled through the files and piles of paper next to the computer and pulled it out. "Here you go."

I handed it to Nick on the way back to my workstation. "Could you read me the statements from Brooks's people? I want to make sure we didn't miss anything. Include Raylene's, of course."

For the next half hour, Nick read and we all listened while Amber Lee and I finished up the remaining bouquets and four boutonnieres.

Raylene had said that she was busy getting dressed and came to the wedding at the last minute. She didn't see anyone by the food. She wasn't sure where the food was, but she hadn't seen Barry since lunchtime. They ate the same thing for lunch, and she suffered no ill effects.

Dean White claimed to have left the camp to handle a business call. He was late to the wedding so he stood in the back and watched, but he had been talking to Brooks when he collapsed.

Kayla Leonard claimed to have taken a long walk with Brooks that afternoon, and he was fine.

"A walk?" my father asked. "Is that what they're calling it these days?"

"Well, some form of cardio, I'm sure," Amber Lee teased.

The statement went on to say that she knew nothing about Brooks's death.

"Doesn't surprise me," my father said.

And Kenneth Grant got to the wedding early and saved seats for the rest of the crew, but they never came. He thought it was a lovely wedding, but didn't see anything happen. He'd returned to his tent to retrieve his forgotten wedding present, and by the time he got back, Brooks was writhing on the ground.

"That doesn't tell us much, does it?" Liv said.

I shook my head. "You already said Kayla avoided Raylene. But did either White or Grant seem especially chummy with her?"

"Not that I saw," he said.

"Well, those are the two most likely accomplices, then." I turned to my father. "Were you planning on heading back to the camp?"

He sighed. "Just to get my tent. I'm not that fond of camping. But I can if you need something."

"I was wondering if you might do some secret surveillance on these four." I pointed at the pictures. "Especially Raylene. And maybe talk to the people at camp. See if anyone knows anything about who locked me in the stocks this morning."

"By now they'll know me as a bounty hunter. It will be harder to get information out of any of them."

"Isn't that what you do?"

He saluted. "You're right. I'll do my best. I did hope I was done with that stupid friar's costume. That thing itches." And he walked out the back door.

I hung my apron on the wall.

"And where are you heading?" Liv asked.

"The Ashbury. To check on his story. Also on Chandler Hines. And hopefully Kathleen Randolph, if she's not as tipsy as she was the other day. I suppose I should see if she could tell me what she and Andrea were doing just before the wedding."

"I thought you didn't suspect them," Liv said.

I stuck my thumbs in my belt in a mock macho gesture. "But I'm a lawman now. Have to get the facts."

She threw a balled-up piece of tissue paper at me, and I was out the door—with my chauffeur in tow.

Chapter 15

Nick and I found Kathleen Randolph behind the front desk of the inn, checking in two customers wearing medieval clothing. As they disappeared up the stairs, she leaned in closer and whispered, "I always get a few deserters this time of the week. They shower. They nap. They get on the Internet to check their Facebook and flip on the TV to see what's happened in the world—or maybe to catch up on their soaps. And they always order the turkey dinner with mashed potatoes before they head back, as if to make sure New World foods haven't disappeared while they've been gone."

"So you haven't been back to the camp since . . ."

"Not since the wedding," she said. "I hadn't planned on it. Even before what happened to Barry. I figured I'd give Andrea and Mel some privacy, without her mother hanging around. Besides, I knew this place would be hopping with refugees." She must have seen my smile. "Yes, refugees from the Middle Ages. That's what they look like anyway. I can't say I'm fond of the practice. If they're here for the immersion experience, why wreck it? But I do appreciate their money. How's the case coming?"

"It's coming. Do you have time for a few questions?"

"Yes, I do. If you two don't mind asking them in the kitchen. I'm a little short-staffed today, and I have to peel potatoes."

It was my first time in the Ashbury kitchen, and I guess I was expecting it to be as quaint and historic as the rest of the inn. But instead I was greeted by a harshly lit sea of stainless steel. One other woman was already amassing a huge pile of potato peelings next to her. A television screen in the corner alternated shots of the lobby and the restaurant.

"I never knew you had cameras," I said.

She returned from the sink, where she'd washed her hands. "I had them installed a couple of months ago, after that *Fix My Wedding* fiasco. They do double duty. This way when I'm in here, I can see if someone comes into the lobby or restaurant. And they give another level of security if something should happen."

Nick went to the sink and washed his hands.

"What did you want to talk about?" Kathleen said.

"First, I need to check if a couple of people who claimed they registered here last night were telling the truth."

"Last night? Did something else happen?"

"The killer attacked Audrey." Nick examined a knife before he picked up a potato and started helping.

"Well, we're thinking it might be the killer. Can't prove a connection yet." Oh, dear. I was starting to sound like Bixby.

"Good heavens!" she said. "Who else would attack you? Are you all right?"

"I'm fine. But the two people I want to check on are Chandler Hines and Richard Wilson. They would have come in later in the evening."

"The blacksmith and the friar. Yes, they did. I was still at the desk, though. Came in together. No luggage. I thought . . . well, you probably don't want to know what I thought. But they took separate rooms."

"Can you tell me when they checked out?"

"They both used the quick checkout, so no. But . . ." She gestured toward the screen. "If they left through the front door . . ."

It turned out that the Ashbury's cameras fed into a normal DVR, so soon I was fast-forwarding through the time-stamped footage.

Just after three, Chandler Hines left through the front door and climbed into a taxi.

"There's an eager beaver," Nick said.

It wasn't until seven thirty that my father entered the lobby, grabbed a paper and a free cup of coffee, and headed out. I let out the breath I'd been holding and glanced up to see Nick's grim smile.

"You had to check," he said. His voice held understanding, but I still felt guilty for needing to be sure.

Kathleen squinted at me.

"Long story," I told her. "Hey, has Raylene Quinn stayed here at all?"

"I'd think this would be the last place she'd come," Kathleen said. "With a former and current Mrs. Brooks both here."

"I don't know. You and Dottie seem to get along."

"Maybe I'm special. Or maybe we get along because we've been through some of the same things. And her relationship with Brooks began long after mine was over. At least I think it did. But the current wife and the current mistress? They'd repel like similar ends of a magnet."

"Like polar opposites," Nick said.

She shook her head. "Polar opposites attract. Those two would keep their distance."

"So if Raylene Quinn and another female member of Brooks's staff were also keeping distance from each other . . ."

"Oh," Kathleen said, setting down her knife. "That sounds promising. Things were such a whirl before the wedding that I didn't see which of his cronies were traveling with him this time. Was it a big group?"

"Just four. Two men and two women." I listed the names for her, but she shook her head until I got to Raylene.

"She's the only one I've met," Kathleen said. "The others may have come to the camp before, but I've been keeping my distance from Barry. But are you thinking Raylene could have done it?"

"Isn't that quite a double standard?" Nick asked. "Could a mistress be motivated to kill because she discovered the man she was having an affair with was having an affair with someone else? Why would she expect him to be faithful to her?"

"Funny how the mind plays tricks on you when you're in the middle of a bad relationship," Kathleen said. "Maintaining a double standard is easy."

Nick worked his jaw, like he was probing for a bad tooth. "So the scenario could be that Raylene Quinn suddenly discovered that her lover was having another affair with whom? That Kayla chick? So the not-so-good Dr. Quinn gets furious and kills him with the first thing she could get her hands on—the monkshood—hoping that it will be written off as natural causes."

"That's pretty much the theory I've been working at the whole time," I said. "But a couple of things still bother me. The accomplice, for one."

"What accomplice?" Kathleen said.

"Just about the same time I was attacked, a witness heard a voice she thought was Raylene's talking with someone. But who would Raylene reach out to for help if she wanted to kill Brooks?"

"She'd look for someone who also had motive," Nick said.

"Only there's an awful lot of those people around," I said.

When I got back to the shop, I gave my chauffeur the afternoon off. Nick didn't need to stay to babysit me, not with Liv, Amber Lee, and Opie around. When I walked in, they were surrounding a workstation covered with red roses, and Liv looked like she was making a bridal bouquet.

"New order?" I asked.

"Don't worry," Liv told me. "We can handle this."

"Handle what?" I said.

"You mean she didn't call you?" Amber Lee asked.

"Who?"

"Your Saturday bride," Liv said. "It seems she now wants red roses instead of white, and could we please change it. She seemed furious at you, but I think I got her calmed down."

"At me? Why? We didn't have any problems in the consultation. She said she was glad I worked with the language of flowers."

"Yes, and you told her white roses meant what exactly?"

"Innocence. Purity. She's a preacher's daughter, and she said it was exactly what she was going for."

Amber Lee chuckled. "Yes, well, it seems she came across

a magazine while she was getting her hair and makeup trial that said that the white rose symbolized 'a heart unacquainted with love' or something like that. The whole bridal party was teasing her about being frigid and she was mortified."

"Oh, dear. I did warn her that the language of flowers can vary from dictionary to dictionary."

"Yes, but she wasn't buying it," Liv said. "So she now wants red roses to symbolize love. I think we have enough here to fill the order."

I pulled on my apron and picked up one of the deep red roses. "I sure hope nobody tells her that the red rose suggests passion and the crimson rose is also a symbol of mourning."

"Really?" Opie eyed one of the darker blooms. "Wicked."

Amber Lee bit her lip.

"What?" I asked.

"Just thinking. Passion and mourning. A better analogy for marriage I never did hear."

Liv playfully swatted her arm and we got working.

"So, Opie," I said. "I'm supposed to work with Melanie and Carol tomorrow, I guess, in the stables for the tournament. Any pointers?"

"Yes," she said. "Try not to laugh too hard."

"Why would that be a temptation?" I asked.

"Don't expect it to look like the equestrian events at the Olympics," she said. "Or some old Errol Flynn movie. It's more a bunch of middle-aged guys who've never been on a horse in their lives trying to perform stunts they can't do. Monty Python was never so funny."

"I'm surprised you know who Errol Flynn is," Amber Lee said. "I'm impressed."

"I always liked movies with horses in them. I rode quite a bit growing up. Did some jumping. Took either first or second in all the local competitions."

"And you gave it up?" Liv asked.

Opie focused on the flowers in her hand, but I could see her throat working to swallow. Without lifting her eyes, she said, "Horse had to be put down. I guess I took it pretty hard. Dad said he'd get me a new one, but only if my grades got better. Back then he still had hopes I'd go to law school."

"And you weren't interested in another horse?" Amber Lee asked.

"Wouldn't be the same. You can't replace a horse like you can a car when it wears out. I told him exactly what he could do with his bribe, and that afternoon I went out and got my first tattoo. Here." She lifted up the sleeve of her shirt to expose the rearing horse on her shoulder.

When we'd ooh'd and aah'd over the workmanship, she went on, "I do miss horses, though. That's why I thought it would be fun to work in the stables."

"Do Melanie and Carol like horses, too?"

"Carol, not so much. I mean, she can ride, but she's not nuts for them. I think she might just want to work in a different place every year to learn the ropes."

"I guess that makes sense," Liv said.

"But what you should watch out for is the men," Opie said.

"Even with Brooks dead?" I asked.

She laughed. "I didn't mean that, but yes, when he was alive, the stable girls—that's what we ended up being called—had to watch out for his advances. The other men aren't nearly so forward. But what I meant is this: these guys go out there dressed up like fierce knights of the realm, trying to look like they know what they're doing, and of course they fall, get banged up, and look like idiots. And then they go looking for someone to blame. Usually it's the horse. But it's often the stable girls."

"Any of the stable girls Brooks was overly friendly with?"

"He was coming on to Carol pretty hard. But I guess Carol had a talk with him and he totally backed off."

"What did she say to him?"

"No idea, but I wish I knew. Then he started asking me or Melanie to take care of his horse. We mostly avoided him, though."

Opie then went into detail about how to treat the horse after an exertion, letting it cool down and withholding food until it was rested. "Melanie knows all that, though. She can step you through it."

"Melanie's good with horses, too?"

"You remember when I said I took first or second in all the local competitions? Well, if I was second, guess who was first."

We listened to Opie chat on about horses while we finished up the rest of the wedding flowers. Before an hour had passed, we were almost done, so Liv hit the computer and sent Opie out on a delivery while Amber Lee and I finished up.

Amber Lee had just stuck a large pin in her last red rose boutonniere when the bell over the door chimed and she excused herself to check on the customer. Moments later she ushered Brad back into the room. He was showered and changed and wearing street clothes instead of his Peter Pan outfit.

"What brings you to the current millennium?" I asked.

"Well, I just got good news and bad news," he said.

"Could use some good news," I said.

"Here goes. The National Guard got partial control of the fire and opened the road, meaning my crew is no longer trapped at that farmhouse. Good thing, because that gouger expects me to pay him rent."

I couldn't help a smile. "I guess that is good news. They'll be here in time for the tournament, at least."

His face fell.

"Is that the bad news?"

He nodded. "They cleared the road leading *away* from town first, and since we missed so much of this one, I made the executive decision to send the crew home."

"Oh, Brad. Does that mean your pilot is canceled?"

"Not at all. It just means we have to wait for the next camp, and I'm kind of excited. Now that I think about it, I'm convinced it will be an even better location."

"Where is it held?"

"Florida," he said. "Bordering some swampland." We must not have looked as excited as he wanted us to, because he put his arm around me, pointed at the blank door of the cooler, and said, "Think about it. Knights in armor, shining in the Florida sun. Damsels in tall hats. And get this, gators. Knights *and* gators."

"I don't—"

"Oh, it's a glorious concept, don't you think? The network is excited. Said they had a sponsor who loved the idea of *Tropical Knights*. This could go viral. Like *Sharknado*."

"How do they justify gators in the Middle Ages?" Opie asked.

"I think they call them dragons," Brad said, almost giddily. He rubbed his hands together. "There be dragons in yon bog!"

I wasn't so sure, but Brad looked excited.

"But that also means that I'm available to escort you this afternoon," he said, "if you want to go back to the camp and poke around."

I looked at Liv.

"You might as well." Liv palmed the rest of the stems and leaves from the table and threw them in the trash. "Your wedding work is done, and we don't have that much work ahead."

But then the bell rang again.

"After I take care of this customer," I said. "I think I'm getting out of practice."

But when I walked to the front of the shop, nobody was there. I paced through the shop to make sure no customer was in the consulting nook or behind the large autumn display. I shrugged, chalking it up to buyer's remorse. Moments later, however, Opie opened the door, squinting as she came in from the bright sunlight.

"Did you just open the door?" I asked.

"No, just got here. Hey, did you find that yellow cloak of yours? The urine one?"

"No, I haven't." I went to the door and peeked out, but couldn't see anybody who might have tried the door.

When I turned to look back, I noticed an envelope on the floor. I picked it up and pulled a folded sheet of paper from it.

"That's funny," Opie went on. "Because I just saw someone wearing it, walking down Main Street."

"Did he open the door of the shop?"

"She, from the looks of it. I don't know. She had already passed the shop when I rounded the corner."

I caught a chill as I opened the paper. On it, all in caps, were the words "*Check the Dumpster at the Ashbury.*"

"All I can say," Brad said as he tossed another green bag out of the Ashbury Dumpster, "is that as far as secret messages and amateur sleuthing go, this one lacks a certain romance. I'll bet Magnum never had to search a Dumpster."

Liv pulled the bag onto the plastic table that Kathleen

had let us borrow, and which we'd covered with a shower curtain liner from the dollar store, where we'd also bought thick gloves to wear while sorting through the trash. We were on our twelfth bag, with about four left to go. With any luck, we'd finish just before the sun went down.

"Viewers didn't tune in to watch Magnum go Dumpster diving," Liv said. "They tuned in to watch him take off his shirt."

Brad rolled his eyes at Liv. "What I'm saying is what self-respecting detective would be searching through a Dumpster? You'd never catch Sherlock Holmes knee-deep in garbage."

"He'd send Watson," I said.

"Nero Wolfe?" Brad suggested.

"He wouldn't fit," Liv said.

"He'd send Archie," I said.

"Nancy would send Ned, I bet," Liv said.

"And I'll wager Miss Marple or Jessica Fletcher would probably find a nephew or niece to do it," Brad said. "See, always the dirty jobs went to the plucky but not-too-bright sidekick."

I looked at Liv, who winked at me and turned back to her work.

I turned away to hide the smile that was tickling my lips.

"What?" Brad said.

The laugh at Brad's expense was short-lived, however. A few minutes later, Liv, a clear look of disgust on her face, used her gloved fingertips to move a dirty diaper into the new trash bag that awaited the sorted garbage.

"You'd better get used to that," I said.

"What, diapers covered in used coffee grounds? I don't think so. I swear, if I discover Chief Bixby wrote that note to keep you busy and out of his way during the investigation, well, there'll be more diapers showing up soon. On his doorstep. In his desk drawer. In his squad car. Oooh," she said with a wicked gleam in her eye. "In his lunch box."

"I don't think he'd stoop to that. He's more direct. Besides, Opie saw someone walking away from the shop wearing that yellow cloak." I tossed a handful of banana peels swarming with fruit flies into the can. "Someone sure liked bananas."

"I can't believe someone stole your cloak," Liv said.

"I can't believe someone stole *that* cloak," I said. More than that, he or she was using it to disguise their features. And I had a sick feeling that my subconscious rendition of "Yellow Submarine," just as I had lost consciousness, had come just as much from a flash of yellow I'd seen in my peripheral vision as it had from the dried cod in the bottom of the box.

"Still, don't you find it odd that Bixby didn't want to come to search the Dumpster himself after we showed him the note?" Brad said. "He looked awfully amused when he said you should check it out."

"I was going to anyway," I said.

"I want to go home," Liv whined.

"Nobody's keeping you," I said. "You're the one who insisted on coming."

"I'm staying," she said. "It just felt good to complain about it." She tossed another handful of trash into the can. "Wait, what's this?" She pulled out a wad of crumpled newspapers and opened them up. "Apparently someone likes turnips, too. Or didn't like them."

"Wait!" I stopped her just before she was going to toss them into the can. "Let me see."

The objects in the newspaper did look like turnips, cooked and rather limp looking.

"This might be what we're looking for," I said.

"Does that mean I can come out now?" Brad called from inside the Dumpster.

"Yes," I said, looking past what I strongly suspected were cooked monkshood roots, and focused on the newspaper behind it, which in its masthead showed that it came from Richmond. I tapped it with my gloved hand.

"Richmond!" Liv squealed. "That's where Raylene lives."

"And where Barry Brooks lived with his son," I said, "and presumably where the rest of the Brooks people come from."

"But that links them to the killing," Liv said. "One of them anyhow."

I scrunched up my nose. Something stank, and it wasn't just the dirty diapers and rotting produce in the Dumpster. "No, it only proves that someone wanted us to find this, and wanted us to associate the monkshood with Raylene or someone else from Richmond."

"Look." Liv pulled a long hair out of the paper. She held it up to the light. "Platinum blonde," she said. "Except at the root."

"Could be Raylene's," I said. "But what we have here is not evidence. I think it's a plant."

"Well, if that's monkshood, then it would be a plant, right?" Liv said. "It's not animal or mineral."

"No. The note. The monkshood. The paper. All pointing to Raylene, but nothing that really ties her to the crime at all. Now I know why Bixby wasn't all fired up about Dumpster diving with us."

Liv squinted at me.

"This is a diversion."

Early the next morning Bixby and I were seated at an outdoor table at the Brew-Ha-Ha. The local eatery was doing a thriving business, and about half the patrons stocking up on their specialty coffees, lattes, and cappuccinos were dressed in medieval garb.

The sky looked dark, but I couldn't tell if that was Eric's promised storm beginning to materialize or the smoke from the distant wildfires.

I detailed the results of our search and presented our findings to Bixby in a large sealed baggie. He tried to hide his smirk behind a cup of coffee.

"So, Deputy," he said, "what do you think this evidence means to the investigation?"

"Absolutely nothing."

"Good girl." He took the bag and poked at the cooked roots inside. "I wonder if having these analyzed makes any sense."

"We can't prove anything by the evidence, but we can infer a few things."

He laid the bag on the table. "And what can you infer from this?"

"I suppose one might conjecture that since the killer is trying to frame Raylene that Raylene is not the killer." I hated to admit it. She was my best suspect.

"That's assuming that the killer was the one who sent you the note. It could be someone who just doesn't like Raylene and wants to get her into trouble."

"And Opie said she saw a woman leaving the shop." I nibbled on a dry cuticle. "But we can't be sure that was the person who left the note."

"I suppose I can have Lafferty check if there's any security footage of the Dumpster, to see if your mystery woman threw this evidence in there herself, but it's not likely they have cameras focused back there. Unless that Randolph woman was trying to catch a band of scavenging raccoons."

His smile disappeared and he set his coffee cup down hard. "But you must admit, she could have motive for trying to frame Raylene."

"Kathleen Randolph? No way. Raylene wasn't even in the picture when . . . oh, but Dottie Brooks was also staying at the Ashbury. She'd probably like to see Raylene sent up for killing her husband. Dottie Brooks and Kathleen Randolph. And Kayla Leonard, I think." I counted them off on my hand.

"Yeah?"

"Were involved with Brooks and might have reason to kill him. And frame Raylene."

"Assuming the killer is a woman, which is a pretty big assumption based on what your intern thought she saw."

I bit my lip. "What if I were to tell you that I have another reason to believe the killer is a woman?"

"Then I'd say you should tell me that reason."

"I kind of went to the camp alone early yesterday morning."

"After I told you . . ." He stopped and glared at me. "Okay."

"Very early. Before dawn. And I was looking around Eli Strickland's booth."

"Apparently we need to talk about warrants and evidence."

"It's an open-air booth," I said.

"What did you find? Or dare I ask?"

"It's not what I found so much, but rather who found me. I was attacked."

"By a woman?"

"I don't know. I was hit from behind."

He crumpled his empty coffee cup in his hand. "Which is why I told you not to go out there alone. But you never saw who hit you?"

"No, but when I woke up in the stocks—"

"The stocks? This just keeps getting better."

"You might have enjoyed it. I was being pelted by rotten vegetables."

"I'm sorry I missed my chance," he said. "But if you never saw who hit you—who also may or may not be our killer—why do you think it was a woman?"

"Because Carol thought she heard a woman talking outside, around the time I must have been put in the stocks."

"So you've eliminated half of our suspect pool based on what one young woman thought she saw and what another young woman thought she heard."

"I know it's not much," I said.

"Look, I'll talk with this Carol about what she thought she heard, because we can't have you getting attacked. And I'm really sorry that happened to you. But, Audrey, there's no real evidence here." He leaned forward, his elbows on the table. "But there's another inference you can make from all this. Another woman who could be implicated by this all, who would know how to find monkshood and cook it, and who would benefit by framing Raylene."

"Who's that?"

"You."

"Me? Why would I frame Raylene?"

"Because you know that your father is now a suspect. He knew the victim before and had a motive. He'd been interested in Brooks. I know about his cell phone pictures. If you wanted to sway the investigation, you could easily plant the phony note yourself, toss the monkshood into the Dumpster where you'd find it, all to exonerate your own father."

"But I would never—"

He smiled. "I knew that for sure when you said your evidence meant absolutely nothing. Which is why I won't tell you not to go back to that camp. Just not alone."

I raised my hand. "Scouts honor. I'm working in the Brooks' stables with Carol and Melanie today, so there'll be people around at all times."

Bixby rose to leave, looking almost sad. "Just do me a favor."

"What's that?"

"Don't quit your day job."

Chapter 16

Larry's place was hopping when Brad and I arrived. Cars were parked on both sides of the narrow street, with happy lords and ladies marching up the hill with their gourmet coffees and takeout bags.

When we got to the top, however, Larry was in a discussion with a very red-faced King Arthur, who was surrounded by his trumpeters.

"You can't do this," the king said. "We will not permit it."

"Well, 'we' don't really have a say about what I do on my own property, do we?" Larry said with a bit of uncharacteristic petulance. "*We* were not keeping our *animals* on our side of the fence. We were not keeping our *people* on our side of the fence. So *I*—since I'm only one dad-blamed American—decided to give free enterprise a chance and make the best out of a bad situation." He reached into his strongbox and made change for the jester who ran up the hill with a six-pack of beer and a bag of ice.

The king let out an exasperated grunt, turned, and marched off with his merry men looking discomfited as they ran to catch up with him. One of them stayed behind and, as soon as the king was out of view, fist-bumped Larry.

My friend's pique may have been exaggerated, because he smiled instantly when he turned around to see Brad and me.

"Good morning, Audrey," he said. "Brad."

"I see business is booming." I pointed at his strongbox.

"I should just about break even for the damage those animals caused. But I did seem to irritate that little guy."

"King Arthur? Yes, I daresay you did."

"He'll get over it," Brad said.

"Audrey, I . . ." Larry scrubbed the back of his neck with his hand. "I hope you don't mind me butting in, but are you all right?"

"I'm fine," I said. "The doctor gave me a clean bill of health."

"That's always nice, but that wasn't what I meant. See, these people talk—some of them are really quite nice—and someone told me that, well, that your father is back. I remember things weren't always good between the two of you, and I just wanted to make sure you were all right."

"Yeah, right now we're fine."

"Well, if you ever need to talk about it . . . I may not be Dr. Phil, but I know how to listen."

"You're sweet." I kissed his cheek.

Brad reached into his pocket for the ten dollars that would let us cross, and Larry waved him off. But he did reach out a palm for the troubadour who tried to squeeze in with us.

"Oh, Larry?" I turned back. "You haven't by any chance seen anyone coming or going wearing a yellow cape, have you?"

"I can't say as I have, but some of these getups are so crazy I might not even notice."

"Keep an eye open, okay?"

"For you I'll keep both open."

One place I hadn't been yet was the stables, but fortunately Brad knew the way, not that the camp was so large that I wouldn't have found them eventually.

They really weren't stables in the sense of a permanent structure, rather more like a large army or circus tent, with straw on the floor and "stalls" created from rough wood rails or by stacking provender between the animals. These makeshift stalls contained at least five horses. One of them neighed a welcome, and I startled. Just unexpected.

There were only a few cows, making me wonder where all that butter and cheese for sale actually came from. Come to think of it, the sign "BUTTER CHURNED FRESH DAILY" that stood prominently in the dairy maid's stall didn't actually mean that *all* the butter was churned fresh daily, just that they churned something.

I found Melanie just outside one of the first stalls, explaining to two rather disappointed children that no, they could not feed carrots to the horses now.

"Not so close to when they're going to be working out," she said, "or else they'll get sick."

The kids walked away with their heads down and lower lips protruding about half a foot.

After they were out of earshot, Melanie giggled. "I let them feed a carrot to one of the horses the other day, and ever since they've been trying to do it nonstop. Those poor horses are going to turn orange at this rate." She blew out a deep breath. "Oh, I'm so glad you're here. This is going to be a crazy day."

"We're here to help," I said. "Put us to work."

"We?" Brad said, and when I gave him a sideways glance, he winked. "Just kidding. What can we do?"

"Do you know horses?" Melanie asked.

"I had a couple of riding lessons when I was a kid," Brad said.

I shook my head. "Not unless you count merry-go-rounds." And that had been an unmitigated disaster. But surely now that I was an adult, horses wouldn't seem so big and ferocious and terrifying. Liv had once teased me about having equinophobia, but calling it a phobia would mean admitting that my fear was irrational, and I wasn't quite sure that was the case. But surely I'd outgrown that fear. I mean, I could even watch *Bonanza* without getting queasy.

"Carol and I have to work on the barding, that is, get the horses saddled and dressed and out to the tournament grounds, and there's really not time to teach you how to do that. I hate to do this to you, but perhaps for now you could muck out the empty stalls."

"Muck out?"

"Clean them. Take out any manure or wet bedding and replace it with fresh."

"Kind of like a cat's litter box," I said. "I'm familiar with that concept."

Carol peeked her head around one of the stalls and came out with a beautifully attired horse. It wore what looked like a mask with eyeholes cut into it, and something rather similar to the surcoats the knights were wearing, in a pattern of yellow and red.

"That's gorgeous," I said. It took my breath away. Literally. And my heart was pounding a mile a minute. I smiled, trying not to show my unease, and forced myself to breathe regularly. What was that technique they teach in Psych 101 for overcoming phobias? Systematic desensitization. Working around the horses was my chance not only to snoop and learn more about Brooks's employees, but if I played my cards right, score some free therapy as well.

"Isn't it a beautiful caparison?" Carol said. "That's what this getup is called, and it's probably one of the main reasons why I wanted to work the stables this year. It's not everywhere that you can play dress-up with live horses."

"Here," Melanie said, "let's just tighten these up." She reached out to tighten the bit of the costume that resembled a mask; it had slipped over the horse's eye. Once the mask was back in place, the horse seemed to stare at me, sizing me up. Fresh meat?

"Not that I'm any good at it," Carol said ruefully.

"You're learning fine," Melanie said. "The rest looks good. Why don't you walk her out to the grounds."

Carol saluted and led the horse out by the reins. I could feel my pulse go back to normal. That wasn't too bad.

Meanwhile Melanie had scavenged two pitchforks and a rustic-looking wheelbarrow, and Brad and I soon began mucking out the stall the gorgeously attired horse had come from.

"Have you pimped my ride yet?" a male voice called from the doorway. I left Brad in the stall and I peeked up to see one of the faces I recognized from my father's photographs. Dean White, Brooks's CFO. He was attired as a knight, but not with a lot of exposed armor. Just a little chainmail for his head, a bit of metal at his shoulders and covering his hands. Somewhere the word "gauntlet" flashed into my mind. He wore tall leather riding boots and a long, colorful surcoat in blue and gold. The accoutrements of warfare had certainly devolved a long way from the ostentatious fashion plates of the Middle Ages to the drab camouflage of today's military.

Melanie's clear laughter rang from a nearby stall. "Just finished." She led a spirited bronze-colored horse, attired in a coat of blue and gold that matched White's surcoat. It amazed me that horses could be so beautiful and scary at the same time. Perhaps if I focused on the beauty aspect . . .

"That's a photo-op," I said. "May I?" I reached into my bag and then remembered where I was.

White laughed. "Don't worry. I won't tell on you." He removed his glasses and I snapped a couple of photos with my cell phone camera.

"I'm going to miss this." He tucked his gauntlet under his arm and pulled the glove off, then used his free bare hand to stroke the horse.

"The horse?" I asked.

"The horse and everything about this place. The end of an era, so to speak. I expect Dottie is going to want to sell the animals. Can't blame her really. She's not into this sort of thing."

"I take it you like it here. Why not come back?"

"This camp has been a sort of retreat for a few select members of the company. Camping with Barry, working together—that whole medieval mystique. Codes of honor and chivalry. Better than those silly teamwork exercises where you fall back and some nitwit from Purchasing is supposed to catch you. Still, it wouldn't be the same without Barry." White's expression became grim. Genuine sadness? Or just what he'd decided was a suitable response. Still, it opened the door to ask more about Barry Brooks.

"He was the dark knight, I hear."

"When you say it, it sounds silly. But there was a certain

air to that man. In any gathering, he'd draw a crowd, and they'd fall over themselves to get his attention."

"Women?"

"Women, sure. But colleagues as well. Successful businessmen often do have this magnetism. That inexplicable charisma. I wish I did."

"I've certainly heard some interesting things about the man," I said tentatively. "About his service to his country, for instance. What branch of the service was he in exactly?"

White shrugged. "I'm afraid I can't share that with you. Not everyone who served our country fits into those narrow boxes."

I must have looked confused, because he went on. "I did see that sheriff deputize you, so I'm not trying to be unhelpful. But with someone like Barry, there's just certain things I cannot divulge."

"Maybe a little more recent, then. The day he died. Did anything unusual happen?"

"Unusual, how?"

"Any conflicts or arguments?" I asked. "Did he seem uneasy in any way?"

"Come to think of it, he did seem a bit tired."

"Tired?"

"Yes, kept asking me to run errands that he used to take care of himself. The day before the wedding he sent me to town for hair dye. Said he felt old. I figured he wanted to look his best for the cameras."

"Just that he felt old? What other errands did he have you run?"

"Just the other day we'd taken the horses out for some tilting practice. He was supposed to have that joust with the blacksmith. You probably heard about that?"

I nodded.

"After a little while he just dismounted. Said he was worn out and asked if I'd take his horse back to the stable for him. Things like that."

"Any problems with Raylene . . . or any of the other female staff members?"

"If you mean were there any blowouts, no. Just business as usual." White put his foot in the stirrup and swung himself up into the saddle. "But the tournament awaits. I hear some damsels need rescuing, so I must be off."

"Thanks," I said, thinking he underestimated his own magnetism. He was quite a polished and distinguished figure, especially dressed as a knight.

Carol returned a moment later and went straight to helping Melanie dress the horses, so Brad and I resumed mucking out the stall that White's horse had come from.

"Audrey?" Melanie called a moment later. "Could you walk this horse down to the tournament grounds? She's pretty tame." This horse was smaller and a lovely dappled gray. It wore a coat of lighter blue with shields appliquéd on it, and even had a bit of armor for its face. I was about to decline when she came closer to me and whispered, "You probably want to be where the suspects are. This one goes to Kenneth Grant."

Ah, Brooks's other male employee. I wanted to meet him and talk with him, so I needed to buck up. Melanie stepped me through how to lead the horse by the reins, which fortunately did not necessarily involve touching the animal. "Feel free to stay at the tournament, if you'd like."

But when Brad started to go with me, Melanie stopped him short. "Not you, stable boy. Someone has to finish the mucking."

"But I swore I would stay with Audrey," he said.

"I'll be there," Carol said, leading yet another dressed horse out of a stall.

Soon Carol led her horse down the path to the tournament grounds while I managed to keep up. Partway there I decided walking with this gorgeously attired horse wasn't that scary after all, and I stood up straighter and walked taller. And I could have sworn a flash or two went off on the way, although when I turned around, there was no camera in sight.

Shortly before we reached the tournament corral, my father called out and fell into step next to me. He was wearing his cassock again, his hands folded above his prosthetic belly, looking every bit the meek medieval friar.

"Good morning, Audrey. Liv told me you would be here today. She told me a few other things, but let's not get into that now."

"She's got my back."

"Maybe you should give her a refresher on your moratorium against infighting. But I've been keeping an eye on Raylene Quinn for you."

"Anything to report?"

"Yes. When you pay too much attention to one woman, she starts to get the wrong idea. I think I'd better keep an eye on the other three today."

"Then we'll bump into each other again. That's what I'm working on."

"Audrey . . . this stuff is dangerous. I don't trust any of those people. Brooks was a magnet for trouble. Does your mother know you're messing with this murder business?"

I stopped in my tracks and the horse did as well. I bit back the obvious retort, that neither my mother or me were any of his business. Meanwhile the horse plopped a load of manure into the pathway.

You got that, sister. "I need to get this horse to the tournament," I managed to say, and left the good friar standing next to the fragrant lump.

Carol led the way to the small corral where the horses were waiting for their riders. Meanwhile, out of harm's way, archers were competing on the longbow. I wondered if Raylene was in the thick of it.

Carol leaned against the fence. "So that was your father back there, huh?"

"I guess so," I said.

"You didn't look too happy to see him."

"It's complicated. He's been out of my life so long that I don't know what our relationship is supposed to be."

"Be careful. You know what they say. The one who stays cares the most. My mother raised me singlehandedly, and I don't suppose I appreciate her enough."

And my unreturned calls to my mother burned my conscience. "But my father came back. That has to count for something. I guess I owe him—"

"I doubt that you really owe him anything. But I hope it works out for you."

"Thanks." Come to think of it, he hadn't really come back since our encounter was an accident.

I picked up a tall blade of grass and put it in the corner of my mouth, like the cool cowboys always did in the old Westerns. But it tasted terrible, so I spit it out. "So what's the agenda today?"

"All messed up, as usual," she said. "They're starting with the archers. Longbow first, then crossbow. After lunch, they're having the melee, and then the jousts. Of course, in the Middle Ages, the joust would have been first, the night before the melee."

I nodded, even though I only could follow about half of what she was saying. "The melee being?"

"The battle itself. It includes the archers, the warriors, and the horses."

"Sounds dangerous."

"Maybe a little," she said. "That's why they make everyone sign a release. Still, there are rules. The weapons are dull, and a strike counts as a kill. Think of it as an ancient version of paintball."

I watched as the crossbow participants took their stances at the line and made their first shots. Many went wild of the target area.

"My horse ready?" Kenneth Grant, the other male member of Brooks's team, stood just outside the corral.

"You bet," Carol said.

"I'd better warm her up before the melee." He climbed the fence and walked to the horse whose coat matched his own surcoat. Like medieval Garanimals. After one aborted try, he mounted and rode to the gate, which Carol opened and then closed behind him.

"The horses don't get hurt in all the fighting?" I asked.

"Never seen it happen," Grant said. "Although this is only my third year here. Everyone's really careful about the horses. Barry made sure of that." He shook his head. "The games won't be the same without him." Grant looked over the crowded tournament stands. "It wouldn't surprise me if this was the last year."

"Surely they can get horses from somewhere else," Carol said. "I'd hate to see them close down this place."

"Not everybody liked Barry Brooks, but in a lot of ways, he was a lifeline for the Guardians of Chivalry." Grant shrugged. "Gotta take the bad with the good."

"Was that how it was to work for him?" I asked. "Did you have to take the bad with the good?"

"Like anybody, I imagine."

"Well, one hears rumors," I said. I'd once seen Amber Lee use this line on a woman, who then unloaded about half a dozen items of gossip. Amber Lee confessed to me later that she hadn't heard anything, that she was just fishing.

But Grant didn't look as anxious to take the bait. He pursed his lips and squinted at me. "What are you asking?"

I took one step backward, grateful that Carol was nearby and I wasn't alone with the man. But what could she do to help if Grant turned violent? At least there was a crowd of people nearby who could hear me scream if he got out of hand. Including my father, whom I spotted still mingling in the crowd, his neck craned in my direction.

Grant leaned a little closer. "Yes, there were some irregularities in the business, but I was trying to do something about it."

I took another unconscious step back. In the corner of my eye I saw Carol move closer. "Brooks couldn't have been happy about that. Perhaps you fought?"

Grant's jaw tightened. "I'm pretty sure Brooks didn't have an inkling of what I was doing. If he had . . ."

"What exactly were you doing?"

Grant looked around him. He dismounted his horse before continuing. "I have the number of a guy in Washington. Look, if you check with him, you'll discover that I was working with law enforcement."

"With law enforcement? Were you some kind of informant?"

He shushed me. "Not so loud. Right now with Barry dead, I have no idea if they're going to follow through on the investigation. The FDA was about to bring in the DEA and the FBI, but now? I don't want to be without a job if they drop the whole thing. After all, there's not much call for FDA informants these days."

"FDA? So the business irregularities you're talking about was the diluting of the drugs."

"Which is why it fell under the FDA," he said, "but when I got wind that they were selling the extra . . ."

"Selling where?" I asked.

"That I never figured out. Brooks has that whole organization so divided, and the people so intimidated, that I never get a decent lead."

"What did you learn?" I asked.

"The company ran just one shift. I'd leave at night, and there'd be boxes stacked up on the dock, ready to ship the next morning. When I came in the next day, they'd be moved around. At first I thought it was my imagination because nothing was missing. Kind of like that old Steven Wright joke about everything you have being stolen and replaced with an exact duplicate." He paused.

I shrugged.

He sighed. "I guess you have to be Steven Wright to pull that one off. Anyway, when I paid more attention, I could tell they weren't just moved around. The labels would be different. Sometimes you could see where the packing tape had been removed and put back on. There was never anything missing, so I don't know how long it went on before I noticed."

The horse grew a little antsy, but Grant removed his gauntlet and stroked the animal and it settled down, like a cat might. Maybe that was the secret to overcoming my unease with horses: to think of them as just very large cats. But then a panther sprang to mind as an example of a large cat, so I decided I'd better squelch that thought.

"Brooks was doing it," he said. "I stayed late one day, hid in the men's room until I heard someone coming, and caught him lifting one of the boxes. I asked him what he was doing, and he told me Quality Control needed to inspect the outgoing shipments."

"But you didn't believe him."

"As if the CEO would be spending his time running errands for Quality Control, rolling boxes around on a dolly. No. Something about that guy was oily. For a couple of weeks I checked the labels of the boxes that"—he made air quotes with his fingers—"Quality Control had checked against the shipping manifests, and they were always drugs that could be sold on the streets—opioids, stimulants like Ritalin. But it's when those weeks went by and nothing happened that Brooks must have figured I was playing his game. There was a twenty percent raise in my paycheck. I started getting free sports tickets and invites to things like this place. So I called my cousin in the FDA."

Carol shook her head. "Lowlife." While Grant was talking, she must have crept closer.

When Grant blanched, she clarified it. "I mean Brooks, taking drugs from people who needed them and selling them on the streets."

"That was the theory," Grant said, "but we were never able to prove it. Only that he took the drugs—and that they lacked potency on delivery. The FDA intercepted several shipments and found the drugs were cut with inert fillers."

"So the drugs arriving at the drugstores were already compromised," I said. "Strickland was telling the truth."

"Who?"

"Your contact in the FDA didn't mention him?"

"To be honest, they seemed more interested in getting information than giving it out."

"So you have no idea who else in the company was involved?" I asked.

"That place is a fortress with security cameras. We know Brooks must have had at least one accomplice—someone willing to look the other way—in Security. And there's only so many places in that building that wouldn't be captured on film."

"What about Raylene Quinn?"

"I wish I could say I knew she was involved. She was close to Brooks. She might have had her hand in it. And she'd definitely be able to handle the lab work part of it."

"What about Kayla Leonard? What does she do in the company?"

"Now that's interesting," he said. "She's actually in Quality Control. But like I said, we have no proof."

"Did you tell any of this to Bixby?" I asked.

"No. Didn't think it was connected. And I didn't want to say anything until I talk to my contact in the FDA. I'm not sure they even know Brooks is dead. Unless it's been on the news. I don't have a phone."

"Call them." And I palmed him my cell phone.

"Gotcha." And he awkwardly climbed back into the saddle and cantered off toward the woods.

A much perturbed Brad showed up at the tournament right around lunchtime and found me sitting on the wooden bleachers. He was carrying a trencher containing a whole roasted chicken but no utensils. "I guess you're supposed to tear it with your hands," he said.

I'd washed my hands under the pump near the horse trough, but I was glad I thought to carry my hand sanitizer in my little bag. I shared it with a grateful Brad.

"I washed my hands three times," he said, "and I still couldn't seem to get the stink of that barn off them. Thanks for leaving the grunt work to me."

"You did say you wanted to help. Besides, I got to talk with two of the three people I wanted to, so it was all good."

"All good for you, that is." He nudged me in the arm. "Don't look now, but your dad is staring at us."

"He's been doing that all day. I've started to get used to it."

Brad ripped off a chicken leg for himself. It seemed like the most accessible part. "So who's the third person you wanted to talk with?"

"Kayla Leonard." I shared with him all I'd learned from Kenneth Grant, who had promised to hunt down Bixby right after the jousts that night, after getting the green light from the FDA.

"Wow, you have been busy. So how does this Kayla Leonard fit in?"

I considered the chicken and managed to tear off a wing. "Only that Brooks said the boxes were going to the Quality Control Department, and she's quality control. She's also a pretty girl, and I suspect a man like Brooks noticed that."

"Ah."

Moments later Nick slid in next to us. He had grapes and some cheese to share. They were a little easier to handle than the chicken.

Brad also had some grapes and offered the chicken, now void of its accessible pieces, to Nick.

"Don't mind if I do," Nick said, and took out his knife and managed to carve the rest of the chicken for us.

"So that's how you do it," Brad said.

Nick laughed. "Remember, I've been here before."

A man in plain medieval dress walked into the empty tournament area with a falcon perched on his gloved arm. Soon the hawk was airborne.

Brad leaned over and whispered, "I hope he doesn't mind that we're eating his cousin."

I watched the hawk as it rose higher into the sky then effortlessly glided in concentric circles. It was hard to think of murder at a time like that, or even of modern times, just the soaring of the bird as it and its ancestors had for centuries before.

And then the falcon swooped and caught another plump bird right out of the air and, grasping it in its talons, took it to the ground and started plucking and disemboweling it. He really needed to learn some new tricks.

The audience applauded.

I set down my piece of chicken. "Okay, lunch is over. For me at any rate."

I had been scanning the crowd for Kayla Leonard all morning, and I thought I saw her seated in a special box with King Arthur's crew. Mel and Andrea Brooks were also there. I recalled Andrea telling me that the newlyweds had been chosen as prince and princess, so I guess this was one of their perks.

Kayla was dressed royally in a rather warm-looking scarlet brocade dress complete with a matching hat. I wondered what she had done to rate being a part of the court, and then I decided that I didn't want to know.

I pointed out her location to Brad and Nick. "Enjoy your lunch," I said. "I'm going in."

Nick put his knife away. "I'm going with you."

"Me, too," Brad said, licking his fingers.

I shook my head. "I appreciate the offer, but I'll learn more if I go alone, woman to woman. You can keep an eye on me from here."

But when I approached the box, several of Arthur's men, now armed with crude but pointy-looking medieval weapons—I really should have paid more attention to that chapter in high school history— barred the entryway.

I found a seat in the bleachers nearby and watched as Kayla fanned herself in that heavy dress and guzzled quite a bit of wine from the goblet in front of her. Then I knew that it was only a matter of time. Probably about fifteen minutes elapsed before she excused herself to head to the woods.

I stopped her before she got there. "Aren't you Kayla Leonard?"

"Sorry. Do I know you?"

"Audrey Bloom," I said. "Deputy Audrey Bloom, actually."

"Oh, right. I already talked to that fellow Bixby, so if you could excuse me . . . " She was eyeing me with the same anxious expression women eye long restroom lines at public events, just before they band together and take over the men's room.

"It will only take a minute," I said.

"Fine, but come with me."

"Come *with* you?"

But she was already darting between the trees, so I followed her and turned my head as she spread her skirt and did her business.

"This is something the medieval women got right," she said. "Long dresses. No underwear. What could be more private?"

That was too much information, but not the kind I was looking for. "I wanted to ask you a couple of questions about Barry Brooks and what it was like to work for him."

"Okay, shoot."

"I hope you don't mind, but I have to ask this. Did you have a personal relationship with Barry Brooks?"

She came from behind the tree rubbing her hands on her skirt. I offered her my hand sanitizer.

"Ooh, contraband," she said. "But I'll take it." She squeezed the sanitizer onto her hands and rubbed them together. "Now, about me and Barry. I guess you could say what he and I had was strictly business."

"Are you saying you didn't have a personal relationship?"

"If you mean did we have sex, the answer is yes, but it wasn't personal."

I could feel my jaw dropping, and with the number of flies in the woods, probably collecting around the human droppings, that probably wasn't a good idea. I closed it.

She laughed. "So old-fashioned. I can see it in your face. Look, Barry wanted sex. I wanted to get ahead. We had an arrangement. But if you think I was personally involved, like passionately in love or jealous or any such thing, you're mistaken."

"You do realize you're not the only one."

Kayla looked at me like I'd transported in from Mars. "Well, yeah. I can name several off the top of my head. Including that Raylene Quinn. And if you're looking for someone who might have had a personal motive, I'd check her out."

"Believe me, I have been. But do you think she killed Barry?"

"She had reason to. Look, she didn't play it smart. She fell for the boss. And he used her. She could have gone on to any number of companies and advanced much farther than she did. But in that way"—Kayla tapped her forehead—"she was dumb as a rock. And Barry wasn't about to reward her faithfulness, either." She rolled her eyes. "She was getting a bit . . ."

"Long in the tooth?" I asked. I must have still had horses on my brain.

"She wasn't a vampire, for Pete's sake. Just old. There were younger fish in the sea."

"And you were one of those younger fish."

"Yeah, like those little fish that swim with the sharks, and the sharks protect them."

"Pilot fish," I said.

"That's the name, but she didn't remember that the shark doesn't give a fig about the pilot fish. He just lets them stay around because they help him."

"That's rather Machiavellian, isn't it?"

"I don't know who that is," she said. "But in case it's an insult, let me just say that it's gotten me where I want to be, so I really don't care. Look, nobody's getting hurt. And marriages were probably saved in the process."

"Marriages saved?"

"Yes, from what I heard, before there were more women in the workplace to choose from, Barry used to go for his employees' wives."

I didn't want to go there, considering my father was once one of those employees.

We walked back to the tournament grounds, and just before she climbed back up into the box, I said, "But about nobody getting hurt . . . remember Barry Brooks is dead."

Chapter 17

When I returned to the place in the stands where Nick and Brad had been eating lunch, I noticed they were talking to a woman. A woman wearing my long skirt and shirt.

"Liv! Please tell me Eric knows you're here."

Her nonchalant shrug and failure to meet my eyes told me all I needed to know.

"You're going back right now. Nick, could you walk her back to Larry's?"

"I'm *not* going back. I just got here. I wanted to see the tournament, learn how the investigation was going, and make sure your father wasn't giving you trouble. Besides, I got some of that computer research done and you haven't been answering your phone."

"I turned the ringer off. Mom's been calling me."

"Audrey, you can't just turn off life because you're not ready to deal with it."

"I'm not . . ." I gave a quick shake to my head, as if I were trying to shake her words out of my ears. "Just . . . what did you find on the computer?" I slid into the seat next to her.

"Right. I searched for your Brooks employees."

"And?"

"First off, I followed the money. And Dean White is way richer than he should be."

"He is an executive."

"But not this kind of rich. I mean, the car he drives and his house, at least on the outside, are in line with what he should make. But I think they're just for show, so nobody gets suspicious. When I dug deeper, I found pictures of exotic vacation homes, sports cars, boats. And yes, those are all plural."

"You think he'd be too smart to post that on the Internet," I said.

"He is." Liv smiled. "But his teenage daughter isn't averse to showing off, and she's on Instagram."

"Any chance he could have inherited money? Or married into it? Or won the lottery?" I bit a broken fingernail. That didn't make sense. "He wouldn't have needed to hide any of those."

Liv shook her head.

"So chances are good that he was involved up to his ears in whatever illegal activity Brooks was."

"Does that help?" Liv asked.

"It suggests he's dirty, but why would he then kill Brooks, especially if Brooks was sustaining his lifestyle? It would be like taking the goose that laid the golden egg and making pâté de foie gras out of it."

Liv shivered. "Can we leave the goose livers out of this discussion? Oh, and I have proof that Brooks and Kayla were involved, you know, sexually. Well, pretty near proof."

"Old news," I said. "She admitted as much."

"She did?"

"Pretty uninhibited, our Miss Leonard. Said she was sleeping with him, but didn't really care about him. She was using him to get what she wanted, which was advancement in the company."

"And you believe her?"

"Yes, actually I do."

"And Kenneth Grant," she said. "Do you know about him?"

"I'm more curious about what you learned," I said.

"It seems Kenneth Grant has a bit of a record. I found some old newspaper articles. He and a buddy looted a bunch of empty homes after they dropped out of high school. Only once a home they broke into wasn't empty, and they roughed up an old man who lived there."

"That I didn't know. Did he do time?"

"Apparently Grant testified against his friend and was released for time already served. Said his friend did most of the beating."

"So he was a snitch back then, too." I said.

"Snitch?" Liv said.

I waved her on.

"But he's been a model citizen since. He completed his GED, went to and graduated community college, and has a clean record with Brooks Pharmaceuticals."

"Okay, that helps. But you're still going back." I started to get up.

"But wait. I saved the best for last."

I sat back down. "And what else did your magic fingers come up with this time?"

"More on Brooks," she teased. "But if you really want me to go back . . ."

"Spill it. What did you find?"

"More of what I didn't find. I was trying to figure out when Brooks might have done his supposed military service.

Your father told me that Brooks had come back to the business suddenly in 1990."

"When did you talk to my father?"

"This morning, when he came by to ask where you were. I wouldn't tell him until he answered my questions."

"You're ruthless." I couldn't help the smile.

"But here's where it gets interesting. If we assume that Brooks's secret missions happened in the late eighties . . ."

"You'd have to. If you went back any farther, he'd be too young."

"Right," she said, whipping out a printed page detailing military operations in the 1980s under Reagan and the senior Bush. I scanned the page.

"Most were part of the drug war in South and Central America," Liv said, "but a few were in the Middle East, precursors of Desert Shield to follow."

I nodded. I had only vague memories of much of this, too recent to be included in the outdated history books when I was in school—and it if was, I hadn't been paying attention that day—but I'd been too young to recall much of it from the news.

"Where did you get this?" I asked. "Please tell me you didn't hack the Pentagon." All we needed were government agents surveiling our little flower shop.

"It's all on Wikipedia now. But get this: most of these operations have blogs or websites so people can keep track of those they served with. You know, 'What ever happened to Charlie who fell off the boat in Panama and got bit by a poisonous snake?' So while there are no official records available to people like me, you can track some of these veterans unofficially."

"Which is where you found Brooks."

"Which is where I didn't find Brooks," she said. "Not really."

I rubbed my eyes, trying to ward off a headache that I knew was about to come.

"What do you know about IP addresses?" she asked.

"Nothing. Just summarize." I had to speak louder, because the tournament field was filling up with men in armor, archers, and the knights on their horses. They weren't actually doing anything yet. Probably planning who was going to kill whom.

"Okay, I found a site someone set up about an operation in the Philippines. Involved fewer than a hundred guys. Hardly anyone ever responded. I think the poor guy who ran the site was talking to himself. But there was one post that got more traffic than the others. Someone wrote in, asking if anyone knew what had happened to a young officer named Barry Brooks. Said Brooks was rendered unconscious in a skirmish while saving three other men and the poster wondered if he ever had gotten the medal he deserved."

"So Brooks *was* military. Some kind of war hero."

"No, that's where the IP address becomes important."

"Summarize, remember."

"I'm pretty sure Brooks wrote it himself," she said. "Or someone who has access to his computer. There was one other comment on that post, also from the same IP address. It basically said, 'Yeah, I remember him. Great man.'"

"Why would he . . ." Although before Liv could answer, I said, "Maybe because he was never in the military in the first place and was trying to manufacture proof."

"Possibly," Liv said. "But then I thought, if he wasn't in the military, where was he for those missing years?"

I squinted at her. "You know, don't you."

She squirmed in her seat, completely unable to conceal her excitement. "I think so. I was able to find court records"—she pulled out a mug shot from her bag—"from the same time period. Can't be two places at once."

"Barry *Brocks*?"

"Could have been a clerical error, but the picture doesn't lie. That's definitely him. And that little slipup in names was enough to keep Bixby from finding it. I e-mailed him a copy, by the way. I hope you don't mind."

I shook my head and read the court report Liv had attached to the mug shot. "Fraud, racketeering, embezzlement. Sounds like he was learning his trade. So we can probably wipe foreign enemies completely off our suspect list."

"Unless Brooks ripped them off. He seemed to have been carrying on some international swindles."

I rubbed my temple. Trying to think above the growing crowd noise was giving me a headache. Or maybe it was that knock on the head. "So Brooks ripped people off, probably by implying some secretive government involvement, no doubt. Why, carrying on an illegal drug trade using Daddy's pharmaceutical business must have been cake for him. He was practically slacking off."

"So I did good?" Liv asked. I suspected she already knew the answer.

"You did great," I said. "But I still wish you hadn't come out here."

"But since I'm here now . . ." She turned to the tournament grounds, where the opposing armies had taken their starting positions on opposite ends of the field.

Liv found and pointed to Shelby and Darnell, who somehow managed to swear their allegiances to opposing sides. They were glaring at each other across the narrow no-man's land that separated the two armies. Flags flapped in a growing breeze. Armor glistened and clinked. And the spectators in the stands sat on the edges of their seats.

"Hark, who goes there?" a deep baritone called out. And soon the melee began.

Arrows flew, hopefully away from the spectators. Horses galloped safely apart from the fray. I guess they didn't want PETA coming down on them. Most of the action was from two armies, one in bright blue and gray, the other in yellow and red, advancing on each other. The men wore an eclectic collection of whatever armor they had amassed and carried an assortment of medieval-style weapons. Men with large drums marched in the rear, beating a lively cadence. But the only other sounds were the grunts of what appeared to be mostly middle-aged men whose wooden shields barely covered their beer guts.

They slashed at each other with swords and took exaggerated dives to the ground as they "died." Minutes later the battlefield was full of the injured and dying. Several limped off the field with looks of genuine pain on their faces. And the victors danced on the field, waving their flags and shouting, "To God, the king, and Saint George!"

"That was it?" Liv said.

"'Fraid so," Nick answered.

Carol ran up the bleachers. "Audrey, come help. We need to get the horses back."

I walked with her back to the corral, where all the horses were waiting in their brightly colored costumes. "What about the jousts?"

"Too dangerous," she said. "There's a storm coming in, and you really don't want to be high up on a horse, wearing metal armor, and carrying what amounts to a lightning rod in an electrical storm."

I looked up. The dark clouds were gathering, only this time it wasn't just the smoke from the nearby fires. Carol and I took two trips to get the horses back safely in the stable while Melanie rushed to get all their metal armor off and neatly stowed away.

"I don't know how these horses do in lightning," Melanie

said. Just as she finished speaking, a low rumble sounded in the distance. A stiff breeze had picked up, rustling the tent. The horses already appeared to be getting a little antsy. She talked softly to the horse, stroked his nose, and then stripped him of his fancy dress. She turned to me. "Make sure all the horse stalls have food and water. And let's try to confine those chickens." She looked around, hands on her hips. "That's all we really can do for them."

When I left the barn, a few droplets of rain were beginning to fall and residents were scurrying to their tents. Even more were snaking down the path toward Larry's. I couldn't blame them. I was debating doing that or trying to wait it out in one of the more permanent structures, like the little cottage Carol and Melanie shared. Only there was no guarantee that the storm would let up before nightfall, meaning I could be stuck overnight in a century without running water, working toilets, or microwave popcorn.

I scanned the crowd and spotted Nick's tall head above many of the others. I called to him, and he came over, squinting in the growing raindrops. When he got closer, I could see that Liv was with him.

"Audrey," he said. "We have a problem."

"We sure do. What are you still doing here?" I asked, ready to give my cousin a piece of my mind. "Now we have to walk back in the rain. What's Eric going to say when he sees you?"

"Audrey, that's not exactly the most pressing problem." Nick pointed at Liv's belly.

Liv looked up at me, wide-eyed and contrite. "Sorry, Audrey, but I think my water just broke."

Chapter 18

"It's Murphy's Law," Liv ranted. "Has to be. I've done everything by the book for almost nine months. I found the best obstetrician and birthing center in the whole county. I took those monster prenatal horse pills. I aced all my Lamaze classes, was poked and pricked and prodded through all those tests, and I even ate all my veggies, including broccoli. And you know what I feel about broccoli."

"I do," I said.

"I even gave up coffee. And then that one time I sneak off, color a little outside of the lines, and this happens. What am I going to tell Eric?"

"Any contractions?" I asked.

She shook her head.

"Then let's get you back to town."

The path wasn't wide enough for more than two to walk together at a time, so I walked with Liv. Ahead of us were Nick and my father, acting a little chummier than I cared for and talking just a little too softly for me to understand. Brad took up the rear.

"Wait a second," Liv said. "I need to catch my breath. You're all too tall. You have a much longer stride than I do." She leaned against a tree and several men in armor pushed past us.

"You might not want to do that," my father said. "Lightning could hit the tree."

She moved away as the sky flashed and the rain grew in intensity. "Audrey, I swear, next time . . ."

"I hope there's not a next time. Not like this. We have to keep going," I said. "We'll go slower for you."

She nodded and brushed rain out of her eyes.

The path was beginning to grow muddy, making the going more difficult. Occasionally the wind would blow sheets of cold rain, slapping them into our faces. And the tree branches were waving wildly, as if saying, "Get out of here, you idiots."

"Oh, thank heavens," Liv said, gripping the fence when we got to Larry's.

The man wasn't in sight and people exiting were, for the most part, ignoring the honor box with a slot in the top.

"Do you think Larry would mind if we step out of the rain into the greenhouses for a bit?" Liv said. "I need a breather."

I was considering this—surely Larry wouldn't mind—when the sky lit up again, and several spots on the ground around the greenhouse reflected its glow. Several panes of glass had already blown out and shattered on the ground.

"Not safe. It's not far to the car now."

We struggled down the long, steep driveway. I tried to keep a slower pace for Liv, but every time the sky lit up or the thunder crashed—and the gap between the two was growing shorter—it was like something inside me stepped on the accelerator. I fumbled in my bag for the keys before we even reached the road. Fortunately, Brad and I had arrived at the camp early enough to grab a good parking spot. And soon Liv was in the passenger seat of the CR-V. Nick snatched my keys, so Brad, my father, and I climbed in the back.

Liv panted. "I guess it's as good a time as any to tell you. You know those contractions you were asking me about earlier?" And she continued that heavy breathing that I'd mistaken for exertion, but appeared to be her attempt at Lamaze.

"Just relax and buckle up." If Liv's contractions were just starting, we'd have plenty of time to get her to the birthing center where she'd decided to have her baby.

Nick started up the engine, turned on the headlights and defogger, and flipped the windshield wipers on high speed. It would be a slow drive, but we were moving. For a little while.

We passed my cottage and had gone maybe half a mile farther when red brake lights shone ahead of us through the eerie blackness of the storm. Then traffic came to a halt altogether.

I pulled out my cell phone and wiped it off on my car upholstery. Fortunately it lit up, and I dialed the one person who would know exactly what was happening with the road: Mrs. June.

"Oh, honey! That's the worst place to—" Her sentence was interrupted by a series of crackles and pops. I'd have to remember to put my phone in a bag of rice overnight, to help dry it out. "—road is completely closed due to a downed tree."

"But traffic is coming the other way," I said as I squinted into the headlights of an oncoming car.

"Probably people just turning around," she said, followed by more crackles.

"How long until it's cleared?" I asked.

"No . . . of the tree is resting on the power lines, and the highway crews won't even touch the tree until the power company . . . to tell them it's safe."

"So we need to turn around," I said. "That means we'd have to pick up county route—"

"Closed because of the wildfires. And according to the weather service, there's still lots of this storm left to come. We're now under a tornado watch. Nope, just upgraded to a warning. Get to shelter."

"We can make it back to my cottage, I think."

Nick waited for another car to pass and did a three-point turn.

"Can you get an ambulance to us?" I shouted into the phone while the rain beat down against the top of the CR-V.

But the phone crackled and went dead.

"I'm sorry. I'm sorry. I'm sorry," Liv wailed as we helped her up the front walkway.

Most of the plants were matted down in the yard, and the blue tarp on my roof bubbled and slapped and tugged on the ropes that held it in place. That it was still there was a testament to Eric's attention to detail.

The door had swelled with the humidity, but Nick managed to force it open and he hustled Liv inside.

Before I could join them, I noticed that more headlights had followed ours as two other vehicles pulled into the driveway. I ducked into the shelter of the doorway and watched as the doors open and people climbed out. The first vehicle, a van, held a family. The two children were the same ones who'd visited the stables wanting to feed the horses. They ran to the house and I flung open the door to let them in out of the rain. Yes, I'm a softy.

They were followed by the occupants of the second

vehicle, and I did a double take to see Mel and Andrea Brooks, along with the two men who had been guarding the box at the tournament.

"More's the merrier," I said, which was one of Grandma Mae's favorite expressions. If the floorboards would hold them, they'd be welcomed in this house.

"Audrey, I need to lie down," Liv said. She started heading toward the bedroom.

"Sorry, Liv. Tornado warning. Everybody in the basement."

She gave me one incredulous look. "Audrey, I can't have my baby down there."

But then hail began to pelt the windows and the power flickered. Liv swallowed hard, then grabbed the railing and started making her way slowly down the crude wood steps that led to the basement.

The whole group crept down after her into the musty cellar. Nick and Brad managed to carry my mattress downstairs, where we set it up in a corner. After I got Liv settled, I sent them back up for blankets, pillows, and towels, and then, when they were halfway up the stairs, I asked them to also bring my new toolbox. Brad looked at me funny when I'd asked for the toolbox, but Nick went straight up to get it.

"Audrey," Liv wailed, "why do you need the toolbox? Please, tell me you're not going to cut me open with a saw."

"Shh. It's just to keep them busy," I said.

They were still upstairs when the lights flickered again, and then went out.

In the dark, conversation suddenly hushed. The only sounds were the creaking of the floorboards from the men upstairs and the louder, more irregular creaking of the house as it flexed and groaned in the wind.

I pulled out my cell phone. It was useless for making

calls, but I could still use the light from it to look into Liv's face. "It's okay." I also noticed that my mother had called three more times. Ugh. Then that light died, too.

"Cell phones!" I called. "Give 'em up. Flashlight app, if you have one."

No one moved, so I said, "It's my house, and that's the price of admission. You can't call for help anyway, and Angry Birds can wait. You want to stay, I need your cell phones. I need the light." I'd had one flashlight in the house, but I hadn't seen it since the move.

One by one, even the staunchest medievalist coughed up his contraband cell phone. I placed them around the room to give light where I needed it, then I used one to scan the motley crew now inhabiting my basement. The family was huddled in the corner, the little girl sitting on her mother's lap. Mel and Andrea stood nearby. He was giving her a consoling hug. Or vice versa. And my father stood by Liv's head.

The two guards took up residence sitting on the stairs. And the light from the cell just caught the reflection from the eyes of both cats, who were resting on the tops of the cement walls, just out of sight. They must have instinctively sought shelter down here when the wind started blowing.

The old guards had to get up when Nick and Brad came back downstairs with mounds of linens and my toolbox. But they weren't alone. Bixby and Lafferty followed them.

"I got a call that you needed help—" Bixby started.

Liv took that moment to start her panting again. Or maybe she was hyperventilating. Either way I could hardly blame her. I clicked the stopwatch on my cell to time the contraction.

Bixby stopped in his tracks. "Good grief. She's not doing what I think she's doing, is she?"

"If you mean is she in labor," I said, "the answer is yes."

"She can't have a baby down here," Bixby said.

"You heard the man. I'm not having my baby down here," Liv echoed.

"I'm open to suggestions," I said.

Bixby raked his hand through his hair.

Liv whimpered. "Please, Audrey. Not down here. Not in front of all these people."

"We can fix that," Nick said. "I think there was a box of tacks in this kit." He grabbed one of the cell phones and used the light from it to rummage through the tool kit and pulled out a small box and a hammer. Then he started hammering my new blanket to the rafters to make a curtain for her.

My father took the pillows from a frozen Brad and propped them up behind Liv.

I squeezed her hand. "Better?"

"Not much. Audrey, I'm so sorry. You were right. You were right. You were right." When the pressure on my hand increased and she kept repeating her sentence like a mantra, I clicked the stopwatch again.

"It won't be long," I said.

"But first babies are supposed to take forever. Hours or days, they told me."

"Not all of them. And not this one."

"But we never even decided on names yet," she whined. "I need to talk to Eric."

"Okay, fine." I picked up the driest of all the cell phones and dialed Liv's husband. "If this phone works, you can talk with him, but I need to check you."

She nodded.

"Hey, Audrey," Eric said when he picked up. "I hope you're safe in this storm."

"We're safe. Liv wants to talk to you." I handed her the phone and shooed everyone else out of Liv's curtained area. I picked up the stack of towels and took one last look over the castaways in my basement.

The two guards were keeping their vigil on the stairs. I caught a snippet of their conversation. ". . . a lot stronger in the Middle Ages. No big deal."

"Plop," the other said, "and then back to work. None of this namby-pamby coddling."

I gave him a dirty look, but I doubted he could see me in the dark.

Meanwhile, the young boy had overheard him. "Plop," he said, obviously enjoying the sound of the word, because he then repeated it about twenty-seven more times, giggling each time he said it.

The mother was singing a lullaby to her daughter. Mel and Andrea were caught frozen in that same embrace. And Lafferty was in a wide-eyed panic. Not knowing where he should put his hands or feet, he fidgeted and paced. Bixby was standing, calmly searching on his cell phone.

"I got it," he said. "How to deliver a baby. It's on Wikipedia. Want me to read it to you?"

"Sure," I said. "Nice and loud." And then I closed the curtain leaving Liv and me alone.

Liv had been farther along than even I had imagined. So an hour later, accompanied by a lot of yelling on both their parts, Baby Girl Meyer was wrapped in a clean towel and lying in her mother's arms.

I picked up the phone that Liv had let drop onto the mattress so she could concentrate on her daughter. "Eric? Did you hear that? It's a girl. Not only healthy but beautiful, like her mom. I'll send you a picture."

Okay, I might have been stretching the truth a little there. Her eyes were swollen, her head was lopsided, and she was completely bald.

No, I was right the first time. She was beautiful.

Chapter 19

The power remained off in the morning, but I managed to pull Mrs. June's propane grill into my yard and boil the tea kettle on the side burner to make a cup of instant coffee. I left a few mugs, spoons, powdered creamer, sugar, and the coffee jar there for anyone else as they woke up.

We'd moved upstairs when the storm abated, all exhausted from the sleepless night, but I couldn't say we'd become a chummy group. It became obvious that Mel and Andrea were clinging to each other not only out of love or fear of the storm, but also as a way to avoid Nick, probably mindful of future litigation. I managed to put my cell into a bag of rice, hoping it would dry out and function again, but I was too tired to worry about it. Eventually I found an empty corner and caught a couple hours of sleep.

The old house was now filled with the various sounds of sleep: sniffing, snoring, and rustling of blankets as someone turned to find a more comfortable sleeping position.

Only baby Violet—as Liv had named her last night—had her blue eyes open as she lay next to her mother. In the wee hours of the morning Liv had grown nostalgic in the basement, a place where we'd often escaped to on some of the hottest afternoons of the summer. There'd been an old table down there, and we'd color or do jigsaw puzzles. Once we'd convinced Grandma Mae that we could paint a mural, and we'd started painting a garden on the concrete wall, using only old, leftover house paint from her shed.

Last night, in the dim light of the cell phones, Liv had run her finger along the outline of one of the flowers she had painted. "I do understand why you wanted this place," she said. "I hope my little one can be just as happy as I remember us being here with Grandma Mae. Is there a flower for remembering?"

"Violets can stand for *remembrance*. Or *you occupy my thoughts*."

Liv immediately tried the name "Violet" out on the baby. I hoped she wouldn't change her mind before the official birth certificate could be filed, because I was already thinking about her as Violet.

I picked up the baby as I headed out to the porch, avoiding the squeaky floorboards, to allow the new mother a little more sleep.

I swaddled Violet more tightly in her towel and laid her in my lap with her head cradled near my knees. In the light of dawn her eyes were even bluer than I could see in the dim basement. And I did her discredit when I'd said she was bald, because very fine blond hair crowned her head.

"Well, good morning, Violet. Yes, *you occupy my thoughts*, but that's only purple violets."

She made a noise.

"That's right. Now, blue violets stand for *faithfulness*,

but you don't need to worry about that quite yet. Sweet violets stand for *modesty*. I don't know whether they meant no short skirts or the absence of pride, but I'm sure your mommy will work on both of those with you. White violets stand for *innocence*. When you get married someday—a long time from now—I'd love to make you a bouquet of white violets to match your pretty white dress. And yellow violets mean *rural happiness*, so you're going to have to spend lots of time out here with your . . . I guess we would be cousins of some sort." I wasn't sure if Violet would be my first cousin once removed or my second cousin. "But that's too confusing. So you can call me Aunt Audrey."

She made another little sound.

"It's like she's talking back to you." Bixby swung open the screen door. "Oh, where'd you get the coffee?"

I pointed to the grill and moments later he came back with a cup and sat next to me on the porch steps. "You did an amazing job," he said. "Not the coffee, by the way." He grimaced. "You must have learned how to do that in nursing school."

I shook my head. "Maternity and Pediatrics is a senior course. I never quite made it that far. Besides, Liv did most of the work."

He took another sip of his coffee and winced. "Still, if the Ramble Police Department ever has to deliver a baby, I might deputize you myself."

I smiled at him and we sat there in companionable, or perhaps just undercaffeinated, silence for a few minutes.

"We're down to the wire in this case again," he said. "Tomorrow everybody packs up and goes home."

"Any guesses?" I asked.

"Lots of guesses. But I can't go arresting someone on guesses. What about you, Deputy? By the way, good job getting that Grant kid to open up about that FDA investigation."

"Not sure that it helps us much."

"If Brooks got wind of it, there might have been a confrontation."

I shook my head. "It doesn't work with the method. If there was a confrontation, then you'd expect to see evidence of a fight. A more violent cause of death."

"Then someone was planning this for some time." He set his coffee down on the porch.

I shook my head. "Then why the monkshood? The killer was working with what he could find. I think whatever inspired him or her to kill Brooks had to have happened at the camp."

Violet made a noise.

"See?" I said. "She agrees." I put my hand over her ears. "But this conversation is not for little ears."

"What about Chandler Hines?" Bixby said.

"His only motive that I can come up with would be that Brooks ticked him off by playing the big shot. And by undermining his craft by purchasing imported armor. I suppose he'd have some way of cooking the monkshood in that forge of his, but does it really seem like a method he'd choose? And since he doesn't seem like the kind who would stop and smell the flowers, does he even know what monkshood looks like?"

"Eli Strickland."

I exhaled. "He has motive, but claimed he didn't know that Barry Brooks was the same one who'd been diluting the drugs he'd purchased—which he then diluted again."

"Or so he claimed," Bixby said.

"And since he runs a food stall, he'd have plenty of opportunity to cook up the roots right there and then slip them onto Brooks's plate. Or trencher. Or whatever they used. And I suppose as a former druggist, he might know poisonous plants.

And I was attacked when I was poking around his stall. If he wasn't in jail at the time, my money would be on him."

"He might have an accomplice we don't know about. I sent his pots, knives, and cutting board to the state lab just in case. I almost hope it's him. If it is, at least he's locked up—thanks to your father— although if the lab doesn't turn up anything, I don't know if we could find enough evidence to charge him for the murder."

"And since he kept cooking and selling food using the same equipment, it's highly unlikely they'll find anything. But speaking of my father . . ."

"Audrey, I wasn't going to bring him up."

"And I appreciate that. But I know he's got to be pretty high on the list. He had motive."

"But think about your other criteria."

"I know he's not much of a camper, so I wouldn't expect he knows much about the local flora."

"And?"

"And he didn't really have any way of cooking."

"Feel better?" he asked with a smile.

I exhaled. "Yeah. I don't want to think it was him, but I don't want to eliminate him, either."

"There might be hope for you yet, Deputy. What about Raylene Quinn?"

"If we're going to talk about her," I said, "we might as well talk about Kathleen Randolph, Dottie Brooks, and Kayla Leonard at the same time."

Bixby raised a toast with his coffee mug. "To his wives and lovers, may they never meet? Brooks sure gave a lot of women really good motives."

"Raylene probably had the best motive," I said. "And as to means, she's got all kinds of degrees, and she's the camp herbalist, meaning she has a knowledge of plants. I'll bet she could have cooked the monkshood, too. She has an area where she makes up her tonics. She'd have some kind of equipment."

"She did. She voluntarily surrendered those to be tested. I should hear back from our friendly state lab any month now."

"If she just gave them to you, she's pretty sure they're clean," I said. "Other than that, she's the perfect suspect."

"On paper," Bixby said. "Although I think there's something to your supposition that she might have chosen another time or method."

"Unless something happened at the camp. Something we don't know about, and she decided to do it here."

Bixby nodded. "Now, Dottie Brooks wasn't in town at the time, and her alibi checks out."

"But, and I hate to suggest this, she and Kathleen Randolph were awfully chummy awfully fast. What if they knew each other before? What if they teamed up? Dottie had a greater motive, so she stayed away. Meanwhile Kathleen would be there for her daughter's wedding." I scrunched up my face. "Who would do that at their own daughter's wedding?"

Bixby shrugged. "So Kayla Leonard, then."

"I don't know. She seemed happy with her little arrangement. It's not like she wanted Brooks to leave his wife—or even his other lover—for her. I'm not sure she has motive at all."

"And the male employees," Bixby said.

"Dean White was living high off the hog as Brooks's CFO. I can't see him wanting to mess with that. And Kenneth Grant—"

"The FDA verified his story, by the way. Thanks again for sending him my way. But somehow I think we're missing something."

"An unsub?" I asked, thinking of the empty card Liv had pinned to her murder wall.

Bixby shuddered. "Just say unknown subject. 'Unsub' makes my skin crawl. But yes, there's always the possibility that the killer is someone not on our radar."

"Thanks for not including Nick on your suspect list."

"Can't see what his motive would be," Bixby said, "unless Brooks had come on to you."

I shook my head. "Nope, just Opie, Melanie, and Carol. And that dairy maid. And probably every other woman in this place."

Bixby drained the rest of his coffee. "There's something we're missing. Are you going back today?"

I nodded.

"Then keep your eyes peeled, Deputy."

A car pulled in the driveway next door.

"The road must be open," Bixby said, standing up. "About time."

I watched as Mrs. June and Amber Lee climbed out of Mrs. June's car, then they both stepped around the puddles on their way across the lawn.

"Aw, it's worth wet socks," Amber Lee said and jogged the rest of the way.

Soon Violet was meeting a couple of women who would probably prove to be pretty important in her life.

Finding my lap free, I stood up.

Amber Lee bounced Baby Vi against her shoulder and was rewarded with a burp. "Isn't she precious!"

"I'm next," Mrs. June said, holding out her arms to receive the baby.

"Shouldn't you be getting ready to head to the office?" Bixby said.

"Not on your life," Mrs. June said. "In case you missed it, I was holding down the fort at the office all night. And I expect double time. I came to see this baby and my bed."

"Oh," Amber Lee said, "Opie sent back the book she borrowed. Said she wanted to get it back to Carol before she went home. She wanted you to check out a page. She—"

Eric's truck gunned down the street, coming to a stop in front of the cottage. He bounded out, leaving the door open. "Where is she?"

He was halfway up the steps when he stopped, turned around, and went to Mrs. June, who was still holding baby Vi.

"Is that?" He stopped and stared, then wiped his eyes before Mrs. June placed the baby in his arms against his clean flannel shirt.

Eric stared down at his daughter, and her bright blues seemed to stare right back at him. He blinked back more tears. "Where's . . ." He stopped when his voice grew hoarse. "Where's Liv?"

"Asleep. In the bedroom."

Without breaking eye contact with Vi, he climbed the steps and went into the house.

I couldn't hold back a tear.

Even Bixby sounded choked up. "Trust me, that's the way it is with fathers and daughters," he said, looking after them almost wistfully.

Suddenly the lump in my throat felt like a volleyball. "So," I told Bixby, "how about we head back to camp?"

When we got to Larry's, the ground was speckled with glass fragments, and a goat was happily grazing in his flower beds.

Larry was aiming his shotgun at the goat.

"No, wait!" I cried.

"Don't you dare shoot that goat," Bixby said.

"Look, that critter won't budge. I've tried warning shots.

I've tried dragging it by the collar. I have a right to protect my property."

Bixby took two steps toward the goat, and the goat stared him down. "Lafferty," he finally said, waving the younger officer over. "Get that goat out of here."

"Yes, sir," Lafferty said, and started to approach the goat. He paused after each step, with a grimace on his face that somehow reminded me of Matt Dillon approaching a bank robber or horse rustler for a showdown.

"Let me go get Melanie or Carol," I said. "They'll know what to do." I took off toward the stables.

The chickens were all over the path, and I think I heard a moo coming from the woods.

When I got to the stables, I could see the devastation the storm had left. Frightened animals had apparently jumped or pushed through the makeshift stalls, and the tent itself was compromised, with one side of it drooping oddly. Carol was pushing up a stake that had gotten loose, sending the rainwater that had collected in a pocket cascading to the ground near her feet.

"Melanie's not here," Carol said. "She's tracking down the last two horses and a missing cow. Everything got out in the storm."

"Do you know how to lead a goat?" I asked.

"Are we still missing a goat?" Carol glanced at the pen. "I guess we are. They weren't the highest priority."

"Yes, well, if someone doesn't get it out of Larry's flower beds, he's going to do it bodily harm." I wasn't sure that Larry would actually shoot the goat. I suspected that he just threatened to do so to get someone to move it up the priority list.

"Will do." She went to a large wooden box, pulled out a harness, and was gone.

I looked around to see if there was something I could do

to help. Since my one skill was mucking out the stalls and the horses apparently spent very little time in them, I wandered around checking out the rest of the animals. There were only about three chickens still in the structure, but I spied an egg in the straw on the floor of one of the pens, so I let myself inside and picked it up, feeling all rural and whatnot.

"Audrey, should you be in there?" The voice was my father's.

I turned to face him, holding my prize egg like a trophy, when I heard, rather than saw, the pig. If what happened next sounds odd, keep in mind that my only experience with pigs was Wilbur from *Charlotte's Web*, the ever-lovable *Babe*, and the dapper, bow-tie-wearing Porky from the old cartoons. Pigs are nice, right?

Not this one.

The pig advanced toward me, making grunting and squealing sounds, bumping its nose into the back of my leg.

The bump was all it took to lose my footing on the slick hay, and I tumbled down on top of the pig. The prized egg flew against the wall, dripping yellow yolk down the wood.

I can't say if this particular pig was overly aggressive or not, since I had no standard or previous experience to go by, but he didn't take my intrusion well. More angry grunts and frightened squeals followed, only some of which came from the pig, who kept coming at me. I used my elbows to shield my face.

"Audrey, here!"

My father reached his hand over the top of the enclosure and somehow managed to pull me up to the top of the wall.

In that span, memories flashed before my eyes. Not my whole life, but the life I recalled with my father, being swung in circles in his strong arms. Of his holding my hand when we crossed the streets as we walked to the park or to the library.

Then the pig climbed the wall until it was practically

standing (I thought only cartoon pigs could stand). So I swung myself off the top of the wall, back outside the pen, intending to land on my feet, but I managed to tangle my foot on the way. I fell awkwardly at my father's feet.

I pushed my face out of the straw and struggled to catch my breath.

"Breathe, Audrey," he said, and helped me to my feet.

Bent over, I struggled until the breath finally came. I can't say if anyone has ever died by having the wind knocked out of him, but it sure does make for scary moments until that first gulp of air fills your lungs.

I must have stood there for a full minute, just breathing and relishing the feeling of air going in and out.

I looked down and saw that my ankle was still tangled in the handle of some satchel that must have been left on the top of the makeshift wall. Its contents were dumped in the hay.

I extricated myself to start collecting the items I'd knocked over. There was a pair of leather gloves, some makeup, a bottle of nail polish, a toothbrush, and dental floss, all with bits of hay clinging to them.

My dad looked sheepish when he handed me a tampon. "Here's your . . ."

I took it from him and shoved it back into the bag. "Not mine," I said. "Must belong to one of the girls."

"I'd say the odds of that are pretty good."

I shoved the loose objects into the bag, including a college ID card. Carol Graham. She looked shell-shocked as she stared into the camera while standing in front of a brick wall. School IDs haven't improved much.

I draped the satchel on top of the wall like it must have originally been placed, and I turned to face my father. He was again wearing the cassock. I decided to go for business-like. "Is there something I can do for you?"

"Audrey, I thought we should talk."

"I'm a little busy at the moment." Bixby's reminder that the clock was ticking on the investigation had hit home. Barry Brooks may not have been a gem, but that didn't mean it was acceptable to let his killer get off free. Nor was it acceptable for Nick to suffer through a lawsuit over something he didn't do.

"I've got a flight out at midday tomorrow," he said, "so there's not much time left."

I nodded. I didn't agree or disagree. My emotions were jumbled, compacting the darkness of murder and the joy of new birth all within a short week, and in a week in which I'd had very little sleep. I had no great desire to spend more time with this man, but neither was I as angry and bitter, so I supposed it wouldn't hurt much to talk with him.

Melanie came back in, riding a horse bareback. "Oh, Audrey. So glad you're here. You did come to work, right?"

"I guess I can help for a little while," I said. When Bixby had said that today was the last full day to observe the goings-on at the camp, he really didn't give me any hints on how to spend that day. "What do you need done?"

She pulled her hair back in a ponytail. "I don't care if they didn't wear their hair like this in the Middle Ages, I need to keep it out of my face. Where's Carol?"

"Off to collect a goat. What can I help you with?"

"The horses have to be dressed for the tilting and the joust."

"Tilting? Like at windmills?"

"Exactly. Both the tilting tournament and the joust use lances, except in tilting the knight uses the lance to hit the target and not another rider."

"Sounds safer than jousting."

"You'd think, but it depends. See, the lances are different.

In tilting they're allowed to use a regular lance. But in a joust these days, they have a special one, made of a lightweight wood like balsa. The idea is that you can only use so much pressure before it snaps. Really, the biggest danger with these guys seems to be falling off a horse. Especially if they've had a tankard of ale before the competition." The expression that fell across Melanie's face was the closest that came to a sneer that I'd ever seen on this normally good-natured young woman. "It's like drinking and driving. It ought not to be allowed. In a way I wish I didn't sign up for the stables. I like horses too much."

"I hear you." Then again, I hadn't signed up for any of this.

"And there's another job I've not been looking forward to, either." She looked at my dad. "Maybe you can help."

"I'd be glad to," he said. "What is it?

"We've got to get Barnaby to the tournament grounds."

"Barnaby?" I asked. "Which one is he?" I thought I'd learned all the names of the horses and most of the cows—not that they'd likely name a cow Barnaby, since I knew just enough to know that cows are all the females of the species—but that name was unfamiliar.

"Barnaby is the hog," she said. "Poor thing."

"But why would they need a hog at the tournament grounds?" I looked at the pig, which had gone to eat the egg I'd broken in my unceremonious fall. He was much less foreboding from outside the pen, with his rather complex pattern of black, brown, and milky pink patches. "What kind of sport uses a pig instead of a horse . . ." And then it dawned on me. "Oh."

Life seemed so much harder in the Middle Ages, when dinner might have included an animal you had cared for and tended and become attached to. Then again, was it much worse than raising animals in tightly packed cages? Still, the thought was enough to put "consider vegetarianism" on my mental to-do list.

In the end, my father was the one elected to escort poor Barnaby to his final resting place. To my relief, my father didn't reappear anytime soon. He was too much of a distraction.

Meanwhile Carol managed to wrestle the goat back into his stall, saving him, at least, from the threat of an untimely death. She then went out again to wrangle more of the missing animals while Melanie stepped me through how to dress each of the horses. It was a little before noon when I was ready to lead the first one to the corral near the tournament grounds.

"Wait," Melanie said. "I think it's fair time you learned how to ride."

Over my objections, she rattled off some brief instructions. Perhaps my body was too tired to produce adrenaline, because before long she was helping me up into the saddle. Melanie was a natural instructor. On the first trip, the only thing I had to worry about was staying on while she led the horse to the corral, but for each successive trip, she took off more training wheels, so that on the final trip, I held the reins, and oddly enough, not only did I stay on, but the horse went where I'd wanted it to go and stopped when I wanted to stop. My hands were red and itchy, probably because I wasn't used to handling the reins. I can't say I felt like a natural in the saddle, but I could see why Melanie and Opie loved these animals.

Before long all the horses were corralled.

"You should take a break and enjoy the rest of the tournament," Melanie said.

Enjoy? I doubted that was going to happen. My stomach was already gurgling. Still, I promised to do just that as soon as I retrieved my bag from the stables.

When I arrived back at the stables, however, Carol was in a shouting match with a man I recognized as another of the food vendors. Bixby was trying to referee the discussion, while my father was standing on the sidelines looking uncomfortable.

"What is this?" I said, perhaps taking my deputy status a little too seriously.

"I'll sue," the man shouted. "That pig should have been delivered no later than ten a.m."

"Look," said Carol, "I'm just a student. We had a lot of problems with animals getting out last night in the storm. If I go out and find your pig now—"

"It's too late now," he said. "There's no time to butcher it and cook it properly, and there's no way I'm going to risk getting sued for spreading trichinosis."

I fought hard to hide the growing smile as I glanced at my father, who was looking off into the woods.

I stepped forward. "How much is the pig worth?" I asked.

"On a good day, I could have earned over a thousand dollars selling the meat," he said.

I shook my head. "Not the meat. The pig itself. Of that weight?"

"Four hundred? Five hundred?"

"If someone paid you five hundred for the pig, would that satisfy you?" I asked.

"But, Audrey, where am I going to get five hundred dollars?" Carol whined.

I looked at my father and didn't relax my gaze. "Free Barnaby?"

Finally he sighed, reached under his cassock to retrieve his wallet, and pulled out a number of bills. As he pressed the stack into the other man's palm, I leaned in. "You better get Barnaby back into his pen."

He nodded.

"And since you now own a pig, you'd better figure out what to do with it. I expect that's going to delay your departure tomorrow, since I'm pretty sure the airlines don't allow animals that large to travel in the baggage compartment."

Carol ran up and hugged me. "Audrey, that was fabulous!"

Even Bixby managed a, "Not too shabby, deputy."

As my father skulked into the woods to wherever he'd secreted Barnaby, and Bixby marched off in the direction of the tournament grounds, Carol and I headed back into the stables.

"Now might be a good time to apologize," I said. "I accidentally dumped your bag earlier. I think I got everything back inside. But in case you find a little straw in there . . ."

"Oh?" Carol went immediately to the bag in question and rummaged through it.

"And Opie sent back your book." I pulled the book out of the bag that I had brought, and a piece of paper fell out of it. What had Amber Lee said about a message from Opie?

Audrey, check out page 61. This is very interesting. Not sure what to make of it.

I inhaled a breath through my teeth. Why were history enthusiasts always thinking their discoveries were interesting? And then they recount them, in excruciating detail, to anyone polite enough not to feign a sudden spastic colon. But since Opie was a good kid and my colon was only spazzing intermittently, while Carol continued the inventory of her bag, I flipped to page 61.

I found myself looking at a small section on poisons of medieval times. Featured was a full-color picture of monkshood.

Chapter 20

Monkshood—or at least a picture of it—in Carol's book. What did it mean? Or did it mean anything? Just because you own a book doesn't mean you know what's on page 61. For example, I think I still have a copy of the *Canterbury Tales*, but I couldn't tell you what's on page 61, especially since I quit reading when it got a little too bawdy for my taste. I'm not sure I even made it to page 61—even though I skipped the prologue.

But this was a book that Opie had said that Carol knew by heart. And right there on page 61 was a big glossy picture of monkshood with a caption detailing its use as a poison. I could see what Opie had meant by her note. What did this mean?

Obviously it meant that Carol didn't know the book as well as Opie had first thought. After all, in our little hunt in the woods for the murder weapon, Carol had no idea what monkshood looked like. She'd been the one foolish enough to touch it.

But was Carol foolish?

I wished I could believe that she was. But looking at the worn textbook with neon highlighting striping the text surrounding the photo, I knew she never could have missed it.

But why then would she pretend not to recognize it, especially when just touching it put her in potential danger? It just didn't make sense, so I tried to push the thought from my mind, but it came rushing back in with more.

What motive would Carol have to kill Barry Brooks? By all accounts, she barely knew the man. Yeah, sure, Brooks had made a pass at her, but she was a pretty young woman, intelligent and personable, so I suspected she'd experienced unwanted advances before—and that she had better techniques for dealing with that sort of thing than murder.

And if I asked Carol about the picture in her book, no doubt she'd hit herself on the forehead and exclaim how foolish she was to forget.

But Carol wasn't foolish.

Still, I stuck Opie's note into my bag before handing the book back to Carol.

She tossed it into her bag. "Walk with you to the tournament grounds? I'd love to see the final events."

I nodded. This would be a good time for me to do that observing that Bixby said I ought to be doing.

"That was a great thing you got your father to do for Barnaby, by the way," she said. "Very kind. I'm going to suggest that they make it a tradition—that is, if they don't cancel next year. But freeing the pig could be popular like the presidential pardoning of the Thanksgiving turkey." She laughed. "But I won't mention the turkey part of it; that's a sour subject here."

"Good idea. But I'm afraid I had nothing to do with the 'free Barnaby' campaign. That was all my dad's idea." And it struck me that I was now calling him "my dad" instead of "my father." I wasn't sure what I felt about that, although it no longer gave me that sick feeling in the pit of my stomach. "Although what he's going to do with a pig, I have no idea."

"Does he own a farm or something?"

I shrugged and rubbed my itchy hands on my rough tunic. I looked at them in the sunlight. They were fiery red, with little blisters beginning to appear. Surely the reins couldn't have done that.

I swallowed hard, trying to disguise my increased heart rate. I needed to think this out like a proper investigator, not jump from conclusion to conclusion. Still, I had to admit the rash on my hands was beginning to look eerily similar to the one I'd treated on Carol's hands the night she accidentally touched monkshood in the woods.

Accidentally? There was that assumption again. I tried to recall what I had seen in that quick glance at the article in the textbook. It had briefly mentioned poisoning by ingesting monkshood root. It made no mention of possible contact reactions, which are not as uncommon in the plant world as people might think. Even in the shop there are certain flowers we tend to wear gloves while arranging. Amber Lee has a bad reaction to lily sap, for instance.

But what if the killer had used this very book as their primer on poisons? He or she would have known about the deadly effects of ingesting the roots but have been unaware of the effects of touching it until it was too late.

But that didn't explain the rash I had on my hand. I hadn't touched monkshood. But had I touched something that had been in contact with monkshood?

I tried to think of everything that I had touched since arriving back at the camp. The horses' reins and all their finery. The egg I found? I certainly hoped not, because that wouldn't fare well for Barnaby. And then the contents of Carol's bag, including her gloves.

Come to think of it, with all the rough work she was doing in the stables, why wasn't she wearing the gloves to protect her hands? And why would there be monkshood sap on the gloves anyway?

This was where my slipshod theory failed to develop. Even if I assumed that Carol was some sociopath who responded to unwanted advances by killing unworthy suitors, I couldn't have it both ways. If she knew about the possible contact reaction, she wouldn't have touched it. And if she touched it, it would imply that she didn't know about the possibly dangerous contact reaction, and therefore wouldn't have thought it necessary to wear gloves.

But monkshood hadn't appeared just once. There'd been those roots put in the Ashbury Dumpster with clues pointing toward Raylene Quinn. But why should Carol want to implicate Raylene?

"Although maybe he is worth giving another chance," Carol said.

I struggled to recall what we had been discussing. "The pig?" I felt I missed part of the conversation, or at least the intent. And suddenly every word out of Carol's mouth grew in importance.

"No," she laughed. "Your father. Trust me. I know it's hard to grow up without a father. You know, when I was in kindergarten, we had to draw a picture of our family. I drew a picture of me and my mother and my grandparents and my uncle. The teacher leaned over the table and said, 'Just the people who live in your house.' And I said, 'These people all do live in my house.' Then she pointed to a picture of my uncle and asked, 'Is that your father?' I looked her in the eye and told her that I didn't have a father, that I never had a father."

That was a blow to my heart, maybe an intentional one. I knew that feeling. The loneliness or embarrassment at father-daughter dances. The flat-out jealousy when your friends complained about their strict fathers and you envied every moment they had to suffer because of it. Nothing makes you appreciate the importance of a father more than growing up without one.

But this wasn't about me. Was Carol playing the empathy card to distract me? I could feel my heart rate boost into overdrive. No, Carol wasn't foolish, but there was more here under the surface. Could she be that wily and manipulative?

And what would be her motive? An insane hatred of men perhaps? She resented her father's leaving, and maybe he was a philanderer. So she kills the first philanderer who comes on to her. Or maybe his age was a factor. After all, Brooks was old enough to be her father . . .

Old enough . . . to be her father.

"Did you say you never met your father?" I asked. And I had a sinking feeling . . . *Oh, Carol, what have you done?*

She didn't answer my question, just kept walking toward the tournament grounds, which suited my purposes quite well, since that was where Bixby and Lafferty were. And although I was technically a deputy, they had certain refinements that I lacked. Like a weapon and handcuffs. And a working knowledge of Miranda rights. Already we were within sight and hearing of the grounds, where brightly dressed horses raced and their riders used a lance to attack the targets. This was the tilting competition, then.

A shout went up as a rider fell from his horse.

Carol shook her head. "You know what the whole idea of chivalry was supposed to be, right? We think it's supposed to stand for courage, honor, and virtue, of defending the defenseless and slaying the cruel dragons. But I looked up the word, and you know what? It originally just meant horsemanship. Just a bunch of dumb jocks playing around on horses. All the rest, the knight in shining armor jazz, was probably added to make it seem more romantic."

She stopped in her tracks. "And the knight-errant? I'm beginning to think they were nothing but a bunch of traveling marauders, raping and pillaging as they went." She stared off at the tournament field. "Sometimes a girl's got to slay her own dragons."

"Is that what you did, Carol?"

She kicked a clod of dirt with the toe of her boot. "If anybody figured it out, I knew it would be you. You know what it's like, to want to know your father, to want him in your life, but to fear what he is or might have become. You must know exactly how I feel."

"But to come all this way to kill him?"

"I didn't come to kill him. He and I were both here last year; did you know that? I knew who he was then, but I kept my distance and watched him. I heard the stories. He was supposed to be some hotshot spy."

"I've heard that, too."

"I went home and kicked myself for being too shy to meet him, and then I signed up to TA the course so I could come again this year. This year, I told myself, would be different. So I requested to work in the stables, where I knew I'd run into him. I even took a few riding lessons so I would be more qualified to do that."

"What exactly did you expect?"

"I wanted . . . a chance to talk. That was all, really. I wanted a chance to look him in the eye, tell him who I was, and then . . . take it from there. In my daydreams he'd say how glad he was to meet me and give me a hug. That's all I wanted. I was so excited when he agreed to meet privately to talk with me."

"Carol." And suddenly I felt heartsick for her. The photo that my father had taken of Brooks leering at Carol. "Brooks came on to you."

"He somehow assumed that I asked to meet him for some kind of tryst. And I told Melanie and Opie that he'd made a pass at me, like he had the other girls, but it was more than that. He touched me. I reminded him that I'd only come to talk. Next thing I knew he had me cornered against a tree and he was kissing me. His hands were all over—"

"Carol." I took her hand. "I'm so sorry."

"I felt so sick at that moment. I no longer wanted to tell him who I was. I didn't want anything to do with the man. But he was strong and wouldn't let go. He had me pinned against that tree and wouldn't take no for an answer."

And a shrewd lawyer would have focused on the fact that she willingly met him in the woods.

"It was then I told him," she said. "I had to. It was the only thing that stopped him. At first he laughed. But then I shouted out my mother's name and he stopped. Audrey"—tears were streaming down her red face unchecked—"I would have been okay with an apology. Even then. Call me desperate or foolish. All he needed to say was, 'I'm sorry.'"

Somehow I knew the story just got worse from here. I leaned in and gave her a hug, and she collapsed in a fit of sobbing in my arms. I just hoped no one was around with a camera. I'd hate for that picture to end up in the paper or shown on television as "Deputy hugs murderer. Details at eleven."

When her tears quieted, I asked, "How did he respond?"

"He was angry. He was actually angry at me. Said I

wouldn't get a penny from him. I never mentioned money at all. Honest."

That figured. Since Barry Brooks was the master of the prenup, he probably was not too thrilled about the idea of another mouth to feed—or in his eyes, a possible extortionist or leech.

"And then he started asking how old I was. I told him I was nineteen. Then he started ranting about how old he felt. But that's all he wanted to know, how old I was. Not, 'Did you have a nice life?' or 'How is your mother?' "

And then I recalled the ID card that had fallen out of her satchel. Her last name was the same as the biochemist Brooks had replaced with Raylene. "Your mother worked for Brooks."

"Yup. Dumped and fired on the same day, just before she found out she was prego. And replaced with that bimbo Raylene."

"From all accounts, Raylene is pretty smart."

"Yeah, well, my mother is the most brilliant person I know. She never should have been let go. Do you know how hard it is to get back into the workforce when you've been canned? He couldn't even be bothered to give her a good recommendation."

"Is that why you sent the note and put the monkshood in the Dumpster? To get back at Raylene?"

"I didn't think that would stick," she said. "Not as evidence. I just wanted to make sure the police hadn't missed what kind of relationship they had and what kind of man he really was. I mean, for a day or two after our confrontation, he avoided me. But I followed him. It's like I had to know who he was. To see what happened after the shock wore off."

"But there was no change?"

She clutched her arms in front of her chest as if she were cold, or if the memory were. "He couldn't even keep his pants zipped up." She snorted. "And I mean that figuratively, since there are no zippers allowed here, of course."

"Of course," I simply echoed. One does not argue priorities with the certifiable.

"At the beginning I was jealous of his son, that poor Melvin kid. I figured Brooks had nothing for me because he was already doting on his son. So when I first thought of the monkshood, I was considering dosing the whole wedding party. But then I saw how he treated his son, as if he were an idiot. And his daughter-in-law even worse. I couldn't be jealous of them if I tried. Even that elaborate wedding he planned for them was really all about him. They deserved some happiness."

"That's when you decided to kill just Brooks?"

"I remembered seeing the monkshood in the book, and then a clump of it growing in the forest. Only I messed up and didn't know you needed gloves."

"Which is why you made a point of touching it while helping me search for it in the woods—or at least pretending to touch it. To explain the rash already on your hand."

"I couldn't believe how quickly you figured out it was monkshood. And here I was hoping that his death would be ruled as natural causes, or at least an accident. I knew I needed to help in the search, to keep track of what you were finding out. You're pretty good."

Normally I'm a sucker for flattery, but I determined not to let it sway my opinion of Carol, which had already been swayed from nice girl to diabolical murderer, and then back again to poor, unfortunate soul. "So you needed to cook the monkshood first."

"Not hard. Last year I'd worked for one of the food vendors."

"Strickland? Was he your accomplice?"

"Him? Oh, please." She started to laugh, but then sobered back up. "Yeah, who figured him for a fugitive? I thought he was just a quirky little fellow, but . . . Anyway, I sneaked into his place the night before the wedding and cooked a little of it up. I almost chickened out, but when I saw Brooks prancing around in the dark knight getup . . ."

"I still don't understand how you managed to get the poison only in Brooks's food and not anyone else's."

"That turned out to be the easiest part of it, almost. I figured I could slip it to him during the feast, but I was still watching him before the wedding when he demanded to sample the stew. Sorry about that, by the way. I didn't know the cook was your boyfriend at the time, and I'd just met you. But I watched as Nick spooned him out a bit onto a trencher and handed it to him. And then I called, 'Mr. Brooks! Mr. Brooks!' all nice and sweet." She laughed. "Well, he'd been avoiding me like the Black Death, so when he heard me, he set his sample back on the counter and ducked behind the side of Nick's stall. I just strolled past, still calling for him, but making sure I was always looking in the other direction. When I passed the booth, I palmed the monkshood off into his stew. Then, when he thought the coast was clear, he came back and ate it."

"You watched him?"

"From a safe distance, but yes."

"You weren't worried he'd share it with somebody?"

"What? Him? Share?"

"Oh, right."

"Look, Audrey. I've been honest with you for a reason.

The only thing I regret at all is conking you over the head and locking you up in those stocks. But when I saw you snooping around the place where I'd cooked the monkshood, I was worried you were getting too close. I was trying to scare you off, I guess."

I squinted at her. "And you were the one who told me you'd heard people talking, specifically Raylene."

"Not one of my finest moments," she said.

"Murder isn't a fine moment, either, you know."

"What are you going to do?" she asked.

"What do you mean?"

"I came to you because, of anyone else here, you would know how I feel, why I did what I did."

"And I do."

"Then help me."

"I will, Carol. I'll go with you to Bixby. It will help if you turn yourself in. And I know Opie's father is a really good lawyer—"

"That's not what I meant. Look, it's not like I'm asking you to help me kill someone. I just want you to be quiet about what you know." She took one step toward me. "Can you do that? Will you?"

I intuitively took one step back. I wish I could say I wasn't tempted by Carol's argument, but I did all too well know the sting of loneliness and the pain of rejection. And Brooks had caused a good deal of my pain as well, really. He was the one who had sent my father packing. With all the suffering that Brooks had caused, was it really that important that his killer be behind bars? Especially when it meant that this girl's painful childhood would be rewarded by spending much of her adult life in prison. "Carol," I said at last. "I can't. It wouldn't be right."

She shook her head. "In a world of moral ambiguities, I bare my soul to an idealist."

"Come with me and turn yourself in."

"Fine!" She stormed over to the corral gate, but instead of opening it, she grabbed a lance that had been sitting next to it. She whirled around and pointed it at me.

"Help!" I called. And then did my best horror-movie-impression scream. Only the cheers and the jeers of the crowd overwhelmed the sound I'd made and the attention of the audience was focused on the joust.

She pressed the tip of the lance closer. "Quiet! I don't want to hurt you."

I quieted down, but put my hands up. Perhaps someone would turn our way and see what was happening.

Carol took a couple of fake jabs at me. Not that this lance was fake. This was the real deal, not one of the balsa models the knights had taken into the tournament.

"What are you doing?" I asked as she took one last fake jab.

"These idiots have been staging fake fights all week. What's one more?"

Brilliant. Anybody glancing over here would figure we were playacting. "You can't get away."

"Yes, I can. And here's why. Unless you let me go, I'm going to name you as my accomplice."

"What?"

Before I could even process that, she was across the corral, had swung herself up onto a horse, and was riding off into the sunset.

I cast a glance toward the tournament ground. Even if Bixby was there, with his allergies, I doubt he could chase her on a horse, either. I pulled the cell phone out of my bag, but it wouldn't turn on. The rice had dried it, but the battery had run down, and with the storm and power failure, I'd had no chance to recharge it. Isn't technology wonderful?

"I'm such an idiot," I told myself, and swung up on another of the saddled and dressed horses and headed down the path after her. Only she was a better horseman and had such a head start she was nowhere in sight. After all, she had multiple lessons compared to my one.

The camp was almost deserted. Many of the tents were gone, probably people who packed up after the storm, or had the insight (or weather alert) to leave ahead of it. Those residents who had remained were at the tournament.

But finally I saw the back of her horse stopped at the edge of camp.

I dismounted quickly, well as quickly as I could get my foot untangled from the stirrup. I figured I could be quieter approaching on foot than the horse could. I tied the reins to a post, just like I'd seen on old *Gunsmoke* episodes, and inched forward. She could be lying in wait just around that corner. Then again, she could have deserted her horse and taken off running through the woods.

But when I did see her, she was digging up more monkshood roots using the blade of the lance, pulling the roots out of the ground with her bare hands again. Her cheeks were smeared with dirt and tears.

"What are you doing?" I said. "Who are you killing now?"

She looked up, shook her head, and chomped down on one of the roots like she was eating a carrot.

"Please," she said. "My mother doesn't deserve this. We had a good life together. I should have been satisfied with that, instead of dreaming about my father. Let her think I ate the wrong plant in the woods, or even some big scary bogeyman got me. It will kill her to know the truth."

She took another bite. I inched closer.

"Stop!" she said, picking up the lance and pointing it at me again. "Won't you help me at all?"

"I'm trying to help you." One more step closer. "Do you think your mother would honestly want you dead, rather than find out what you did? Because it's going to come out anyway."

"How will she know?"

"She'll know if I have to tell her myself."

"Why? What good would it do? Have you no pity at all?"

I had plenty of pity. What I didn't have was time.

Already the roots she had eaten were on the way down her esophagus. When they hit her stomach, the acid would start breaking them down, releasing the aconite into her intestines, where it would enter the bloodstream.

I inched closer. "I'm going to tell her all about you, about how you killed your own father and then were afraid to own up to it. She'll have to come to identify and claim your body anyway. I'll speak slowly. She must be an idiot, too, to take up with Brooks in the first place."

Okay, I was laying it on pretty thick, but I didn't have a lot of time to work.

"You wouldn't dare. My mother is a brilliant woman." Confusion was coursing across Carol's face. She couldn't figure out my motives or where I was coming from, and the lack of context was making her scramble to think rather than act. She'd made no more moves with the monkshood or with the lance.

Now, if I could just get closer while she was discombobulated . . .

I took one more step. "I'll tell her that she must have been an awful mother to bring up someone like you. I'll bet she never loved you."

Only I'd gone too far, because Carol's face went from wounded puppy to charging tigress in the matter of milliseconds. She began racing toward me with the lance poised like a javelin.

I was able to duck, just enough. The lance pierced my tunic, but missed me and jammed in the tree behind me. I ripped the tunic to extricate myself.

Carol tugged at the lance, but it was stuck fast in the tree. Her grunts showed her anger and frustration and her tears fell in huge drops onto the dust.

She either didn't notice me circle around and come up behind her, or she didn't care, but I was able to get my arms around her abdomen, just under her rib cage. I tugged hard, swinging her away from the jammed lance with as much force as I could muster. Yes, I guess you could call it a modified Heimlich maneuver.

Carol dropped to her knees, her eyes bulging. Then came the coughing and the choking. And soon the monkshood root came up in a puddle of saliva and landed in the dust.

"I hate you," she said in heaves of gagging and sobbing and struggling to catch her breath. "You did that on purpose. I hate you, Audrey Bloom."

I kneeled next to her and pulled her hair back from her face while she vomited up a bit of her lunch as well. "That's the problem. You really don't."

Carol was still sobbing with her face in my lap when Bixby came charging down the path.

"What's going on?" he said. "Your father said you needed help."

My father, back in that ridiculous friar's costume, came rushing up right after him. "What happened?"

I looked at Bixby. "Carol here killed Barry Brooks. She . . . uh . . . gave herself up voluntarily."

Carol glared at me, then shook her head. "Whatever."

"But we need to get her to medical attention quickly. She might have aconite still in her system."

My father took a sideways glance at the lance still stuck in the tree. "Just how voluntary was it?"

I shrugged. "Enough to suit my purposes. But how did you know I was in trouble?"

"Are you kidding? I saw you ride off on a horse."

Chapter 21

Monday was a series of meetings with men. Since Amber Lee had called me, right after I got my cell charged, both for a recap of what happened and to assure me that she had the shop covered for Monday, I was free. But before she could hang up the phone, I could hear Opie and Melanie nearby, asking to talk with me.

"That's okay," I told her, "put them on."

"Audrey," Opie said, "I don't know what to say. I feel like it's all my fault for sending you that note in the book. But I really didn't know what it meant at that time. Now, I guess it's crystal, but—"

"You couldn't have had any idea. I mean, I saw the note and didn't put it together, either. Maybe it's because we didn't want to."

"Carol seemed so nice," Melanie said.

"I should have known," Opie said. "It's always the good girls you have to watch out for."

"Hey, wait a minute," Melanie said. "Just because she was a total nutjob—"

"Now listen," I interrupted. "There will be no blaming. And let's leave Carol's mental evaluation to the professionals. I'd like to think that she somehow wasn't responsible for her actions, but I'm not sure. There's not really that much difference between hatred and insanity. But it will be up to the doctors and the courts to decide that."

But there was no answer to my comment. "Hello?"

Some kind of kerfuffle was taking place in the background at the shop. I heard the sound of breaking glass, and then could make out Amber Lee's schoolteacher voice, "Hand them over. Now!"

"What's going on?" I asked.

"Sorry," Opie said. "Darnell and Shelby came in to work today, too, since you're off and Liv is on maternity leave."

"Only they brought their swords with them," Melanie said.

I rubbed my temple. "Do I need to come in?"

But then one of the girls handed the phone to Amber Lee. "You stay where you are, boss," she said. "All under control here." And then a little more muffled. "You'll get your swords back at the end of the day, and not ever again in the shop, do you hear. And that vase is coming out of your pay, mind you."

"That wasn't—"

"Yep," she said, "the new red one from that glass blower fellow. The most expensive one in the shop. Murphy's Law."

I could just make out the muffled apologies as Amber Lee said, "Trust me. I got this. You deserve the day off. I'll take care of everything."

And I did trust her. I wasn't leaving my cottage for the day. Chester and Luna needed some attention, my front yard was still littered with shingles and other debris from the storm, and I needed a break as well.

Eric was the first to arrive. He brought a box of Nick's scones and then proceeded to roll over himself thanking me for taking care of Liv, without even a hint of recrimination for her being at the camp in the first place. I guess he'd come to realize that trying to keep Liv from doing something she was determined to do was not only impossible, but sometimes the surest way of impelling her to do it.

But after Eric showed me a dozen or more baby pictures from his cell phone camera, it became evident he also had another mission.

"I also have to apologize for the tarp. I really had that sucker on there tight."

"What do you mean apologize?" I asked. "It held up for the entire storm." It was true. Not one shingle in the yard had been mine.

"That's just it. I was just checking out Mrs. June's roof, and she lost so much that it's a total redo."

"Ouch," I said. Since Eric had been quoting me prices for a roof redo, I could feel her pain.

"But that's my point. Her insurance company is covering everything. Even the new gutters she's been needing for a while. Oh, Audrey, if I hadn't tied that stupid tarp down quite as tightly . . ."

"You were trying to protect me," I told Eric. "Protect us. And considering what was happening in this place at the time, that's a good thing."

"But if you're not particular about the color, I'll do your roof for you." I tried to wave him off, but he wouldn't be persuaded. "After all, you saved me some dough, too. Do you have any idea what the copay was on that fancy birthing center Liv wanted? Huh?" He winked and was out the door.

Brad was the next to arrive—I'd scheduled them at two-hour intervals. This was one I'd wanted to get over. Brad had wanted to talk to me during the encampment, and I certainly hoped that he wasn't intending to propose, because I'd decided that I needed to end things with him. Not our friendship—that I hoped I could keep for some time, maybe the rest of my life. But trying to rekindle any hopes of a long-term relationship with him was bad for both of us. It was time to make a clean break of the flirtatious conversations and move on as friends. This time with no Brad-the-Cad dartboards.

Of course, he arrived with flowers. But potted ones. Two whole flats of perennials. "I thought you might like something cheery to put in your garden."

I busied myself looking at the labels to see what I was getting into. The fall was a good time to plant perennials, and Brad had probably gotten a deal on these.

"I hope they're all right."

I nodded and kept reading labels. There were a few ivy plants in there. Perhaps I could plant those along the ugly side wall. They'd certainly cover the dingy siding, and might even help hold the house together. And ivy represented *friendship.* It was almost a tangible message that I was headed in the right direction to keep Brad as a friend. Maybe it was a sign. I only hoped Brad got the message.

"There was something I needed to ask you, to talk about," he said. "I've been putting it off because it's important, and I didn't want to spring it on you over the phone."

Or maybe he didn't get the message. The next thing I knew his hand was in his jacket pocket fumbling with a bulge that looked suspiciously like a ring box.

"Wait," I said. "Look, I've been wanting to talk with you, too. Sit down." I'd have a lot of difficulty breaking up with him if he were kneeling on my floor trying to jam a ring on my finger.

I reached across the kitchen table and grasped his hand. His palms were sweaty and I could feel his pulse race. Poor boy. "We've been through a lot, together, you and I. Breaking up. Trying out a long-distance relationship. And we've made a lot of changes over the years, too. You're getting out there, chasing that thing you want to do. And I think you have a great future ahead of you."

"Audrey, I . . ." He swallowed, and his Adam's apple bobbed a few times.

"But I don't think that future is going to involve me, at least not as anything more than a friend. Being out in the world, working on reality shows and pilots and those exciting things, is making you happy. Well, maybe not this trip, because it must have been a waste for you. But in general, you seem so jazzed about the travel and your career. And I'm happy for you.

"But my life is here," I continued, looking at our hands clasped against the old Formica-topped table. "I love this small town, the shop, working with Liv. Even this cottage. Being here makes me happy. And that means there's really no future in us."

When I gathered the courage to look up at him, his shoulders sagged, then he let out a sigh of . . . relief? "Oh, Audrey. You don't know how glad I am to hear you say that. I knew we needed to have this talk, and I remember how badly it went last time."

"Oh, don't remind me. I think I called you a big-city show-biz tycoon."

He chuckled and reached out to grasp my other hand. "What was I thinking? I shouldn't have tried to break up with you at the Ashbury. Such a public place. Idiot move on my part. Nevena told me—"

"Nevena?"

He smiled, and perhaps blushed a little. Or was that a glow? "Yes, Nevena. She still does some work for me, and I see her from time to time. And more often lately, in fact. She made that outfit of mine by the way."

"The Peter Pan one?"

"She was thinking Robin Hood, so don't tell her. But she and I, we click somehow. And she likes the work and the travel. We've become quite close."

At another time I would have felt betrayed, but now I only felt happy for Brad. "That's so nice!" I said, realizing I meant every word. "She didn't come with you this time?"

"Well, not to the camp. She knew that you and I were having this conversation. But she's staying with my mom. I thought it was time for them to become acquainted."

"How's your mom taking it?" I asked. Brad's mom had been a major cheerleader for our relationship. And if cheerleading didn't work, I wouldn't have put it past her to rely on force.

"Nevena is so sweet, I'm sure she'll win Mom over in time. Mom will eventually get used to the idea. She's going to have to."

He reached into his pocket and pulled out the lump I'd seen earlier. I was right. It had been a ring box. He opened it to show me the diamond solitaire. "I'm going to ask her to marry me."

Bixby arrived around lunchtime, also carrying in a box of scones.

"Mrs. June typed and spell-checked your witness statement," he said. "I'd like you to sign it."

I got a plate for Bixby and poured him a cup of black coffee before I sat down and started reading through the statement.

"Do you need to read it over?" he asked.

"Just checking. If I'm going to put my official signature to it."

"I see." He opened the box and put a scone on his plate.

"So any new developments?" I asked. When he looked shocked that I'd dared to ask him a question, I added, "You did promise to keep me apprised."

"Which reminds me. I need to call Foley and get him to rescind that stupid appointment."

"Oh, I don't know." For calling it a stupid appointment, he was going to pay. "I think I did a pretty good job as deputy. Catching the killer and all. Maybe I should stay on."

He grunted. "Catching them is one thing. Gathering the evidence they need to convict is another." He sat for a minute, arms folded guardedly across his chest, then he relaxed and took a bite of his scone, chewed, and said, "Still, you did all right. But don't tell me you want to leave the flower business to become a cop. After the morning I had, I might even be willing to trade you." Considering Bixby's almost legendary allergies, he must have had a truly dreadful morning.

"Heavens no," I said. "You're welcome to it. I was just curious if Carol's mother had been notified."

He nodded. "Carol didn't want to give the contact info up, but we found her through the college. She came to see me this morning. Mother's worst nightmare, I can tell you that. She's taking it hard." And by the way Bixby tried to rub away a migraine, apparently it was one of a cop's worst nightmares as well.

"She had no idea?"

Bixby shook his head, the heels of his hands still rubbing his temples.

I went to the cupboard by the sink, retrieved a bottle of painkillers, and tossed it to him.

He shook out more than were necessary into his palm and stared at them. "I'm tempted." He picked up two and swallowed them down with his coffee. "They're still trying to arrange a visit at the county jail. She'll probably get in to see her daughter tomorrow. Meanwhile we're sending Carol for a complete psychological exam."

"Do you think they'll say she's mentally incompetent? Or temporarily insane or something?"

Bixby opened his mouth to answer, then exhaled. "I almost wish . . . but I expect she just hated his guts."

I nodded, feeling suddenly heavy-hearted for Carol. "I know I shouldn't have gone after her alone. I tried to call on my cell, but no battery. And I didn't want her to get away."

"There's more than one way to try to escape. If you hadn't followed her, she'd have been dead by now. I'm glad you saved her."

"But her life will never be the same. She had so much potential."

"That's where the cop shows get it wrong, you know. Law enforcement isn't dealing with criminal masterminds or complete sleazeballs. Ninety percent of the time it's just people making bad choices. That's the heartbreaking part of this job."

"I think I'll keep my bridezillas instead." I scrawled my signature at the bottom of my written statement.

He took the pages from me and stuffed them back into the large office envelope. "By the way, we'll be releasing Strickland into your father's custody tomorrow."

"I thought my father was leaving today."

"No, he said he had some last-minute business to take care of. Something about seeing a man about a pig." Bixby winked at me. "Said he was coming to see you today, too. Seems like an okay guy."

I shrugged. "Better than Barry Brooks. But I still don't know quite how to deal with him or what to expect."

"Can I give you some advice?"

"Not killing him? Yeah, Chief, I think I got that much."

"Well, since you have a habit of intruding on my investigations, I'm going to intrude on your personal life for a minute. All right?" And somehow he managed that Mr. Rogers look. I half expected him to belt out a chorus of, "It's Such a Good Feeling."

I nodded. "Sure. Why not?"

"Not all fathers are as bad as Barry Brooks, but none of us are perfect. You're getting to know a man you barely remember. He's a stranger to you. Treat him like a stranger."

"Keep my distance?"

"I was thinking more of trying to avoid expectations. Don't expect the best. Don't expect the worst. Don't expect anything. Let him show who he is to you, and then decide if that is something you want in your life. You're a grown woman. If you don't want him around, all you have to do is tell him. And if he doesn't respect that, well, you've got my number."

My father was due to arrive in ten minutes. I was thinking about changing out of my jeans and T-shirt and into a dress. Only I couldn't figure out why. Was it some subliminal memory from childhood, of me spinning in a dress in my father's arms? Or did I want to try to impress him? Or just mark an important occasion?

I couldn't figure out the motive, but when the knock came ten minutes early, the choice was made for me. Jeans and tee it was going to be.

Only when I swung open the door . . .

"Mother?" I knew I should have returned those phone calls.

"No, Audrey," she said. "But I'll take that to mean you approve of my new hairstyle. Your mother was always so much better at that kind of thing than I was."

"Aunt Ruth! What are you doing here?"

But I pulled the door open wider and she walked in. "I came to see the baby, of course. And she is simply too precious. I'm spending at least the week with Olivia, and your mother begged me to come check on you. She thought you must be on your deathbed or something, too sick to return a phone call."

"Just tied up with other things. And then our power was out for quite some time."

"It appears to be on now," she said, looking around. She stepped on a particularly loud floorboard, and smiled pleasantly, as if nothing had happened, much like when you encounter the odor of flatulence at a social gathering. Don't ask; don't tell.

"You're absolutely right," I said. "I should have called her. I'll do that this evening."

"Best see that you do. We'll both be in trouble if she doesn't hear from you." Aunt Ruth walked over and touched the cracked mortar in the old brick fireplace. Pieces of it fell to the floor. "Mom sure left you with a lot of work with this old place, didn't she? We tried to help her with repairs, you know, while she was living here, but toward the end, I'm afraid she just got a bit stubborn about doing things herself. Still, it's good the old place is back in the family. You are thinking about bringing the family reunions back, aren't you?"

"Well, I . . ." I hadn't given it much thought. A lot of yard work would be needed to turn the weed and briar-filled backyard into a court worthy to host one of those marathon volleyball tournaments the family was known for. And the only reason I found the old fire pit where we made s'mores by the dozens was because my old lawnmower ran over one of the bricks—which was why the backyard still contained all those weeds and briars. I needed a new mower. Or maybe a goat.

Before I could complete my thought or my answer, another figure walked into the still open door.

"Evelyn . . ." My father stopped in his tracks. He'd made the same mistake I did—not uncommon when your mother has an identical twin. While some twins take on more distinctive characteristics with age, my mother and Aunt Ruth were almost exact duplicates. Only if you look very carefully, Aunt Ruth has a tiny mole on her chin, with one dark black hair in it. But don't tell her I told anybody that.

Aunt Ruth twirled around. "Jeffrey? No, it's Ruth. Jeffrey, what on earth are you doing here?" She started wringing her hands. "This is bad." She turned to me. "Your mother can't know he's here."

"I'm not staying, Ruth," he said. "I'm only here on business and just happened to run into Audrey. I go back to Texas tomorrow."

Aunt Ruth put her hands over her ears. "No, please don't tell me where you're living. I don't want to know. Oh, how am I not going to tell her I saw you?"

"Just tell her about the baby instead," I suggested.

"Sounds like a plan," Dad said.

Ruth walked halfway to the door, looking like she was ready to hightail it out of there, when she turned back to face him. "You're not on the lam or anything, Jeffrey, are you?"

"No, Ruth." He held up his hands, as if to show they were clean. "No trouble with the law."

"Well, that's a blessing, I suppose. Oh, what am I supposed to tell Evelyn?" Her face scrunched up in a near panic.

"Tell her nothing. Except that I'll call her," I said.

She sniffed once and nodded her head, and then skedaddled out the door without saying good-bye.

"I see my sudden reappearance is going to have ramifications," my father said. "I didn't mean for you to get caught in the middle of anything."

"I know that. After all, you had no idea I'd be at that camp; otherwise I wouldn't have seen you at all." I ushered him toward to couch. "Or so you told me. But now that we have seen each other, it's time to decide what we're going to do about that."

In the end, we decided to try corresponding and phone calls. And I promised to give my brother a call and warn him to expect contact by our long-missing father. When we got around to the topic of Mother, I said, "She's married. I'm not sure if you knew."

He nodded. "We do have Google in Texas. Every now and then I'd look you all up to see what was happening."

"You did?"

"It's like peeking in the windows, but yes. I wanted to know what you guys looked like as you grew up. If you were happy. If you were nice." He seemed to study the floor for a minute. "I know I can't claim any credit for it, but I'm proud of the woman you've become."

We chatted for the remainder of the time. I took Bixby's advice and reined in my expectations. In the end, I doubted I'd ever be completely satisfied by his reasons for leaving, nor would that make up for all the missing years. But I did want to keep contact with this man and get to know him better.

We were still talking when headlights swept the room as a vehicle turned in my driveway.

"Expecting someone?" he asked.

"That would be Nick."

"Your young man. I had a nice conversation with him at the camp. It made me feel like a real father, checking up on the boys my daughter's dating."

"I hope you approve."

"I do."

As Nick made his way to the door, my father stood up. "I guess that's my cue to go."

"Don't go on my account, sir," Nick said as he stepped in, and then shook my father's hand.

My father held Nick's hand, for perhaps a little longer than necessary. "It was a pleasure to meet you." Then Dad turned to me. "If it's all right with you, I'd very much like to hug you good-bye."

As he tentatively put his arms around me, I could smell that same combined scent of his deodorant and aftershave. I leaned against his shoulder, feeling as if a missing piece of me had been filled. Not that my father filled a void in my life, but my forgiveness of my father had. It was as if the only emptiness I had been feeling wasn't caused by his absence, but rather by my own bitterness. I squeezed him tighter.

After we pulled apart, he said, "Thank you, Audrey." He turned to shake Nick's hand again and stepped out the door, but then he turned back. "I don't suppose either of you has room for a pig, do you?"

"No, I . . . I did hear that Nathaniel Bacon University is looking for a new mascot."

As my father drove off into the sunset—literally, well, not that he piloted a vehicle into a massive ball of hydrogen and helium, but the sun was sinking below the horizon and he was heading in that direction—in his rental car with a livestock trailer hitched to the back, I couldn't help shedding a tear.

Nick pulled me into his arms and I rested against his chest. "You've had a hard day. We can postpone our little talk for another time, if you'd rather."

"No. Let's get it over with." I led him over to the couch. Nick was a great guy, and I needed to face the music. Our relationship was in trouble. I'd pushed him away by focusing too much attention on Brad. What kind of girlfriend keeps up a constant communication with her ex and then shoves it in her boyfriend's face? I'd been busy with work and the cottage and then the investigation, so much that I'd been ignoring him. He was kind to help me, but I'd taken his kindness too far and used the man. And now, albeit deservedly, he was going to break up with me.

I determined to accept it with grace. I've had enough bitterness tainting my life. No derogatory nicknames. No dartboards. We would be friends.

"I thought we might take a ride, but if you're tired, I guess here works."

He sat down next to me and took my hand.

"Look, Audrey. You know I'm a bit of a lunkhead. I've been saying that I couldn't dream of advancing our relationship to the next level until I could take care of you. Support you."

"It is a bit old-fashioned," I said, "but . . ." I stopped when he shook his head.

"It's never going to happen," he said. "Every little bit I earn ends up going back into the business. It won't be years; it will be decades before I'm earning enough to do the whole nice house and two-car American dream thing, if ever."

"Starting a business is hard."

"And then I see you struggling with this house. Don't get me wrong, I think this little place has good bones and plenty of potential, but it's a lot of work."

There it was. I had been ignoring him.

"I can't just stand by," he said, "and watch you burn yourself out."

So that was it. He was giving me a choice between Grandma Mae's cottage and him. The tears started coming. But I could fix up this place all by myself. How did that saying go? Sometimes a girl's gotta slay her own dragons. Wait, that was Carol's advice. Never mind. I was too stunned to talk.

He used his thumb to wipe a tear from under my eye. "So that's when I decided to stop being so stubborn. Between your business and my business, there's no time for casual dating."

I steeled myself for the next words.

"I think I could help you much more if I moved in."

"Excuse me?"

"Share the expenses. Help with the work. At least we'd be able to see each other more often."

"You want to live here."

He nodded.

"With me?"

He started nodding again, then stopped as his cheeks flushed red. "No, oh, Audrey, this is coming out so badly. What I meant, I mean, what I wanted . . ." He sent me a sheepish smile, then slid off the sofa and onto one knee, sending the floorboard into convulsions of agony. He pulled a ring box out of his pocket and fumbled to open it. "It's not elaborate," he said. "It's kind of been in the family." Inside the box was a simple solitaire.

"Audrey Bloom, I love you. Would you marry me?"

"Nick, I . . ." My brain flooded with emotions. Leave it

to me, who once misinterpreted a breakup date for a proposal, to be unprepared for a proposal while expecting a breakup date.

But here was this nervous guy on one knee before me, ring in hand, ready to brave life with me. And scarier, live in this place.

"I . . . yes. Yes, Nick, I will marry you."